A Summer of Surprises

Judith Keim

D0814193

BOOKS BY JUDITH KEIM

THE HARTWELL WOMEN SERIES:
The Talking Tree – 1
Sweet Talk – 2
Straight Talk – 3
Baby Talk – 4
The Hartwell Women – Boxed Set

THE BEACH HOUSE HOTEL SERIES:
Breakfast at The Beach House Hotel – 1
Lunch at The Beach House Hotel – 2
Dinner at The Beach House Hotel – 3
Christmas at The Beach House Hotel – 4
Margaritas at The Beach House Hotel – 5 (2021)
Dessert at The Beach House Hotel – 6 (2022)

THE FAT FRIDAYS GROUP:
Fat Fridays – 1
Sassy Saturdays – 2
Secret Sundays – 3

SALTY KEY INN BOOKS:
Finding Me – 1
Finding My Way – 2
Finding Love – 3
Finding Family – 4

CHANDLER HILL INN BOOKS:
Going Home – 1
Coming Home – 2
Home at Last – 3

PRAISE FOR JUDITH KEIM'S NOVELS

THE BEACH HOUSE HOTEL SERIES
"Love the characters in this series. This series was my first introduction to Judith Keim. She is now one of my favorites. Looking forward to reading more of her books."

BREAKFAST AT THE BEACH HOUSE HOTEL is an easy, delightful read that offers romance, family relationships, and strong women learning to be stronger. Real life situations filter through the pages. Enjoy!"

LUNCH AT THE BEACH HOUSE HOTEL – "This series is such a joy to read. You feel you are actually living with them. Can't wait to read the latest one."

DINNER AT THE BEACH HOUSE HOTEL – "A Terrific Read! As usual, Judith Keim did it again. Enjoyed immensely. Continue writing such pleasantly reading books for all of us readers."

CHRISTMAS AT THE BEACH HOUSE HOTEL – "Not Just Another Christmas Novel. This is book number four in the series and my introduction to Judith Keim's writing. I wasn't disappointed. The characters are dimensional and engaging. The plot is well crafted and advances at a pleasing pace. The Florida location is interesting and warming. It was a delight to read a romance novel with mature female protagonists. Ann and Rhoda have life experiences that enrich the story. It's a clever book about friends and extended family. Buy copies for your book group pals and enjoy this seasonal read."

THE HARTWELL WOMEN SERIES – Books 1 – 4

"This was an EXCELLENT series. When I discovered Judith Keim, I read all of her books back to back. I thoroughly enjoyed the women Keim has written about. They are believable and you want to just jump into their lives and be their friends! I can't wait for any upcoming books!"

"I fell into Judith Keim's Hartwell Women series and have read & enjoyed all of her books in every series. Each centers around a strong & interesting woman character and their family interaction. Good reads that leave you wanting more."

THE FAT FRIDAYS GROUP – Books 1 – 3

"Excellent story line for each character, and an insightful representation of situations which deal with some of the contemporary issues women are faced with today."

"I love this author's books. Her characters and their lives are realistic. The power of women's friendships is a common and beautiful theme that is threaded throughout this story."

THE SALTY KEY INN SERIES

<u>FINDING ME</u> – *"I thoroughly enjoyed the first book in this series and cannot wait for the others! The characters are endearing with the same struggles we all encounter. The setting makes me feel like I am a guest at The Salty Key Inn...relaxed, happy & light-hearted! The men are yummy and the women strong. You can't get better than that! Happy Reading!"*

<u>FINDING MY WAY</u>- *"Loved the family dynamics as well as uncertain emotions of dating and falling in love.*

Appreciated the morals and strength of parenting throughout. Just couldn't put this book down."

FINDING LOVE – "I waited for this book because the first two was such good reads. This one didn't disappoint.... Judith Keim always puts substance into her books. This book was no different, I learned about PTSD, accepting oneself, there is always going to be problems but stick it out and make it work. Just the way life is. In some ways a lot like my life. Judith is right, it needs another book and I will definitely be reading it. Hope you choose to read this series, you will get so much out of it."

FINDING FAMILY – "Completing this series is like eating the last chip. Love Judith's writing, and her female characters are always smart, strong, vulnerable to life and love experiences."

"This was a refreshing book. Bringing the heart and soul of the family to us."

CHANDLER HILL INN SERIES
GOING HOME – "I absolutely could not put this book down. Started at night and read late into the middle of the night. As a child of the '60s, the Vietnam war was front and center so this resonated with me. All the characters in the book were so well developed that the reader felt like they were friends of the family."

"I was completely immersed in this book, with the beautiful descriptive writing, and the authors' way of bringing her characters to life. I felt like I was right inside her story."

<u>COMING HOME</u> – *"Coming Home is a winner. The characters are well-developed, nuanced and likable. Enjoyed the vineyard setting, learning about wine growing and seeing the challenges Cami faces in running and growing a business. I look forward to the next book in this series!"*

"Coming Home was such a wonderful story. The author has a gift for getting the reader right to the heart of things."

<u>HOME AT LAST</u> – *"In this wonderful conclusion, to a heartfelt and emotional trilogy set in Oregon's stunning wine country, Judith Keim has tied up the Chandler Hill series with the perfect bow."*

"Overall, this is truly a wonderful addition to the Chandler Hill Inn series. Judith Keim definitely knows how to perfectly weave together a beautiful and heartfelt story."

"The storyline has some beautiful scenes along with family drama. Judith Keim has created characters with interactions that are believable and some of the subjects the story deals with are poignant."

SEASHELL COTTAGE BOOKS

<u>A CHRISTMAS STAR</u> – *"Love, laughter, sadness, great food, and hope for the future, all in one book. It doesn't get any better than this stunning read."*

"A Christmas Star is a heartwarming Christmas story featuring endearing characters. So many Christmas books are set in snowbound places...it was a nice change to read a Christmas story that takes place on a warm sandy beach!" Susan Peterson

CHANGE OF HEART – *"CHANGE OF HEART is the summer read we've all been waiting for. Judith Keim is a master at creating fascinating characters that are simply irresistible. Her stories leave you with a big smile on your face and a heart bursting with love."*
~Kellie Coates Gilbert, author of the popular Sun Valley Series

A SUMMER OF SURPRISES – *"The story is filled with a roller coaster of emotions and self-discovery. Finding love again and rebuilding family relationships."*

"Ms. Keim uses this book as an amazing platform to show that with hard emotional work, belief in yourself and love, the scars of abuse can be conquered. It in no way preaches, it's a lovely story with a happy ending."

"The character development was excellent. I felt I knew these people my whole life. The story development was very well thought out I was drawn [in] from the beginning."

DESERT SAGE INN BOOKS
THE DESERT FLOWERS – ROSE – *"The Desert Flowers - Rose, is the first book in the new series by Judith Keim. I always look forward to new books by Judith Keim, and this one is definitely a wonderful way to begin The Desert Sage Inn Series!"*

"In this first of a series, we see each woman come into her own and view new beginnings even as they must take this tearful journey as they slowly lose a dear friend. This is a very well written book with well-developed and likable main characters. It was interesting and enlightening as the first

portion of this saga unfolded. I very much enjoyed this book and I do recommend it"

"Judith Keim is one of those authors that you can always depend on to give you a great story with fantastic characters. I'm excited to know that she is writing a new series and after reading book 1 in the series, I can't wait to read the rest of the books."!

A Summer of Surprises

A Seashell Cottage Book

Judith Keim

Wild Quail Publishing

A Summer of Surprises is a work of fiction. Names, characters, places, public or private institutions, corporations, towns, and incidents are the product of the author's imagination or are used fictitiously. Any resemblance to actual events, locales, or persons, living or dead, is coincidental.

No part of this book may be reproduced or transmitted in any form or by any electronic or mechanical means, including information storage and retrieval systems, without permission in writing from the author, except by a reviewer who may quote brief passages in a review. This book may not be resold or uploaded for distribution to others. For permissions contact the author directly via electronic mail:

wildquail.pub@gmail.com

www.judithkeim.com,

Published in the United States by:

Wild Quail Publishing
P.O. Box 171332
Boise, ID 83717-1332

Dedication

Families are complicated, no matter the size.
I'm so glad for mine. Love you all!

CHAPTER ONE

Jillian Conroy listened to her sister, Cristal's, voice on her cellphone and took a deep breath. A call from her sister was always a surprise.

"So, start all over again, Cristal, and tell me exactly what it is you want me to do."

"It's easy, Jill. My friend, Hope Thomason, now owns the Seashell Cottage on the Gulf Coast of Florida, and she just needs someone to live at the cottage for the summer while we do our European tour, the one we've talked about for years."

"That's it?" It didn't sound like something difficult. In fact, it sounded like a great way to escape the memories of the past, thought Jill. School would be out in another week, and she didn't have any exciting plans for her summer break from teaching. Maybe some extended time on the Gulf Coast would do her good. But every time she tried to do something for her sister, it cost her emotionally, and often, financially. A requested lunch date would end up with Jill paying for it. What was supposed to be a fun event of shopping turned into a nightmare when Cristal pouted that the dress Jill bought was the one she wanted. Their relationship had always bordered on the toxic.

"There's one more thing. A friend of Hope's family, Greg Campbell, is an older man who's agreed to do some work on the cottage. He's staying in one of the guest rooms for a few weeks until the work is done."

"An older man, you say?"

"Yes. He and Hope's father are friends."

Jill let out a sigh of relief. Too many friends had been pushing her to start dating again. She had no interest in doing so. Not after Jay's death two years ago.

"Think about it. I'll call you tonight for your answer." Cristal cut off the call before Jill could ask any more questions.

Jill sat in a chair and stared out the window of the kitchen inside the small bungalow she called home in Ellenton, a small town in upstate New York. She should've sold it months ago. The memories she held of her life in the house weren't pleasant. She'd thought by clearing Jay's things out of the house following his automobile accident, she'd be able to chase away the unhappiness she'd known with him. But now the space just seemed empty. And lonely.

Her thoughts settled on her sister. Three years older than she, Cristal was the beauty of the family. Their mother had declared to anyone who would listen that Cristal got her beautiful features, naturally blonde hair, and bright blue eyes from a relative of hers, while Jillian looked like the Davis side of the family. The comparison was painful. Without the highlights she had to add every few months, Jillian's hair was a dishwater tan. Her hazel eyes held no trace of blue. Worst of all, Cristal's tall, willowy figure seemed to taunt Jill's shorter, curvy shape. It was a bad match-up all around. If it weren't so much like a well-known storybook scenario, it would be almost comical.

Restless, Jill got up and paced the kitchen. It wasn't their different looks that had made her relationship with Cristal so difficult. It was Cristal's tendency to manipulate others in order to get her own way. Jill knew how foolish it was to keep old wounds stored inside, but every once in a while, one poked through the shell she kept around herself. How could she forget that Cristal stole her date in college, the one guy she'd dreamed would be hers forever? It was just one of the ways

Cristal had hurt her through the years. A snort of disgust left Jill's mouth. She might not have even paid attention to Jay except Cristal thought he was a hottie. How was that for stupid rivalry?

Before she could go any deeper with that thought, the phone rang. Jill knew who it was before she even checked Caller ID. Her mother, Valerie Davis, had a nose for trouble. No doubt Cristal had phoned her for support.

"Hello, Mom," Jill said without enthusiasm.

"Hi, honey. Cristal called to tell me that she's arranged for you to have a very nice summer break. She's so thoughtful that way."

"She asked me to do her a favor so she and her friend can travel to Europe," Jill said calmly, still uncertain as to whether she should go ahead with the idea or even what it entailed.

"Well, if you don't do it, I'm sure they can find someone else to stay at the cottage. It sounds lovely. You should be grateful to Cristal for thinking of you," chided her mother. "A whole summer to relax."

It would be useless to argue. "Maybe you're right," said Jill. "I could use the break to get away." The idea suddenly appealed to her. This change in her normal routine might give her the opportunity to think things through, make some major decisions about her life, give her a fresh start. God knew she'd been in an emotional rut even before Jay had been killed.

"Splendid," her mother said with satisfaction. "I'm glad you'll help your sister out. It would mean so much to her. She and Hope have been planning this summer tour for a long time, and poor Cristal has been working very hard."

"You mean as a hostess at the club in Miami?"

"Now, Jillian, she does the best she can, and with her looks, she doesn't need to spend her time teaching school."

"Oh? Because I teach school ..." Jill stopped herself. She

didn't like the person she became when dealing with her family. Only her father had accepted her for who she was, and he'd died several years ago.

"I didn't mean that the way it sounded, Jillian," her mother said with a note of apology.

"Look, I have to go," Jill said. "I'll let you know what I decide."

"Please do. I care about both of you and hope that someday you girls will get along."

Jill sighed. "Goodbye, Mom." Though the day was ruined by the familiar routine with her mother, the idea of escaping to a place far away became tantalizing.

Later, while looking up information online about the Seashell Cottage, Jill filled with excitement. The pictures of it were lovely. It was not simply a cottage; it was a beautiful, three-bedroom, three-bath house that sat overlooking a wide, sandy beach. The house even had a screened-in pool.

Before she could change her mind or overwork the thought that something must be wrong if her sister was involved, Jill punched in Cristal's cell number and, when prompted, left a message.

"Hi, Cristal. Jill here. I've decided to stay at Seashell Cottage for the summer so you and Hope can travel. At the end of next week, when school is out, I'll drive down to Florida. I should be there by June 8th and can stay until late August. Let me know if those dates work with you and Hope." Hating confrontation, she paused and took a deep breath. "And, Cristal, thanks for thinking of me."

That evening Cristal called. The noise of music and partying in the background made it difficult to hear, but the message did get through that Cristal was thrilled Jill would stay at the cottage. "You'll see. This summer is going to be good for you, Jilly. For both of us, really."

"I hope so," said Jill honestly. She was more than ready for a change.

Ten days later, Jill pulled up to the Seashell Cottage and felt tears of gratitude sting her eyes. It was beautiful. When she stepped out of her car, the salty air filled her nostrils. Without waiting to explore the house, Jill ran onto the beach holding her arms in the air as if to embrace this new existence. The sand, warm from the sun, caressed her skin through her open-toe sandals. She removed her shoes and tossed them into the air. It was going to be a carefree, barefoot summer.

Walking up to the water's edge, Jill stuck her foot into the lacy froth and sighed. The water was delightful. The cries of seagulls above her drew her gaze to the sky, and she watched as a trio of pelicans skimmed the surface of the water looking for food.

Jill clasped her hands together and let out a satisfied sigh. She'd been so right to come here. Already, she felt as if some of her old, silent secrets were itching to break free. This summer, she wasn't going to be Jay's widow, Cristal's younger sister, a kindergarten teacher, or a reliable volunteer at the library. She was going to find the person who hid inside her— the one that had been broken.

"Hello. You must be Jillian Conroy," said a deep voice behind her.

Jill whipped around to face a pleasant, red-cheeked, older man, wearing jeans and a gray T-shirt with "Smith's Hardware Store" printed across the chest. She smiled. "And you must be Greg Campbell, the handyman Hope hired for the summer."

"That I am," he said, returning her smile. "You're just in time. I've been here for a week and have left some things for you to do."

"Oh?" Jill managed to say while hiding her surprise. Cristal hadn't mentioned any tasks.

"Yep, the laundry is piled up, and I'm tired of fixing the same old meal night after night. I heard you were a great cook."

Jill gripped her fingers together and mentally watched her plans shatter and fall to the ground like pieces of broken shells. "And what else have you been told about me?"

"That you were excellent at taking care of people, that in exchange for being here, you're going to cook and clean for me and my nephew, Brody."

"Your nephew?"

"Yep. He's arriving tomorrow." He bobbed his head. "I'm happy to help you with your luggage."

"Thank you, that would be nice." Jill used years of training to maintain her composure when what she wanted to do was reach across space and shake Cristal silly. This set-up was so typical of her sister. The offer of a Florida vacation was a ruse. Apparently, she was to cook and clean for the work crew. She should've known better.

Once they got her bags settled in one of the bedrooms, Jill had a chance to look around. She realized though everything was attractive, the pictures shown online were outdated. The walls and wooden trim needed a fresh coat of paint, along with other refinishing touches throughout the interior. That was the reason, no doubt, Hope had hired Greg and his nephew for the summer. It was a wise time to do it. Jill guessed the cottage was booked for most of the rest of the year.

In the laundry room, a pile of dirty clothes sat on the floor near a front-load washing machine. Hiding her displeasure, Jill sorted through them and put a load of dark things into the machine, using the last of an almost-empty bottle of detergent. She drew a deep breath. A trip to the grocery store was in order. She wondered what other discoveries awaited her. Sure enough, when she checked the refrigerator, she found a half-empty six-pack of coke, a hunk of cheese, and not much else. Her stomach rumbled. Even though she was tired from the drive, she gamely set about listing groceries she'd need to purchase. She'd passed a Publix supermarket not far from the cottage.

Greg had retreated to one of the bathrooms and was working on new grouting when Jill approached him.

"I'm going to the supermarket. Anything you need? Anything you're allergic to?"

Greg got to his feet and faced her. "No need for anything special for me, thanks. As I said, I'm glad you decided to take this job."

At his warm smile, Jill's irritation fled. Though Cristal had made it sound like a vacation, not a job, she wasn't about to blame him. He seemed like a nice man. "I'll do my best. I'm used to cooking for only myself."

"Not married?" Below a thatch of gray hair, Greg's blue-eyed gaze settled on her.

"Widowed. For two years."

"I'm sorry. Such a shame. My Annie's been gone for five years now. Life isn't the same without her. Brody, my nephew, is alone too. Divorced."

Jill simply nodded. If Jay were still alive, maybe she would've gathered her courage and she'd be divorced too.

On her way to the store, Jill called her sister.

Cristal answered with a cheery, "Hi, there! You in Florida?"

"Yes," Jill said carefully. "I had no idea I was hired to cook and clean for Greg Campbell. His nephew is going to be staying at the cottage too. Did you know that?"

"I did hear something about him coming, but I figured it was no big deal for you to take care of them. After all, you have to buy food and cook for yourself. How's the cottage? As pretty as the pictures?"

"Seashell Cottage is lovely. Right now, Greg is working on refreshing the interior and will be busy this summer doing other things. Still, it's a wonderful property, and the location is superb."

"That's all that matters. Enjoy. Hope and I are at the airport, ready to fly out. Can't wait!"

Hearing the click of the phone in her ear, Jill drew a deep, steadying breath. It wasn't worth being irritated. What was done, was done. She'd move forward and have the best summer ever. She'd loaded her iPad with lots of books and would enjoy a few weeks away from kids. She loved her young pupils, but a break from them sounded fabulous.

Back at the cottage, Greg eagerly helped her unload the groceries. "Looks like we're going to have some tasty meals," he said happily. "That's good because Brody just phoned. He and Kacy are coming in tonight instead of tomorrow. They should be here within a half hour."

Without crushing its contents in her hands, Jill carefully set down the carton holding a dozen eggs "Who's Kacy?"

Greg gave her an apologetic look. "She's Brody's eight-year-old daughter. A bit of a handful, which is why Brody has her for the entire summer. His ex needs a break."

She heard a tinge of sarcasm in his voice and sank down onto the nearest kitchen chair. Her summer wasn't going to be anything like she'd envisioned. It had just gone from bad to worse.

###

Jill was in the kitchen browning onions, sausage, and hamburger for spaghetti sauce when she heard a vehicle pulling into the driveway. She removed the pan from the burner and went to check on the arrivals.

Following Greg out of the house, she watched with interest as a striking young man climbed out of a black truck, gave a wave, and went around the front to open the door for his daughter.

A pink-sneakered foot hung in the air before the girl jumped down onto the ground, landing with a thud. Dressed in a pink-flowered sundress, she reminded Jill of a little doll with her light-colored curls and bright-eyed, full-cheeked face.

"Here we are," said the man to his daughter. "It's going to be a great summer. I promise."

"Doughnuts every morning, like you said?" The little girl, who showed the physical signs of eating too many sweets, gave her father a sly smile.

He shrugged as he answered, "We'll discuss it. Now, let's go say hello. You remember Uncle Greg, don't you? And this is ..." He stopped talking as he met Jill's gaze.

She couldn't help staring at his coffee-colored hair, classic features, and the smile that crossed his face above a slight cleft in his strong chin. A shiver crossed Jill's shoulders as they continued to stare at one another. This man's green eyes drew her in as if they were old friends, not people meeting for the first time.

"Hello. I'm Jillian Conroy," she finally said, feeling a bit foolish for the length of time that'd had passed between them.

"I hate the name Jillian," Kacy announced, crossing her arms in front of her body and glancing from her father to Jill.

"That's rude, Kacy," admonished her father, giving her a warning look. He turned to Jill with a smile. "Hi, I'm Brody. Brody Campbell, and this is my daughter, Kacy. She's staying with me for the summer."

"So, I've been told," Jill answered calmly, watching Kacy grab hold of one of her father's hands with both of hers. Recognizing the girl's claim on her father, Jill gave her an encouraging smile. "Hi, Kacy. I think you're going to have fun here. Wait until you see the beach."

Kacy made a face at Jill as Brody turned to his uncle and clasped him in a bear hug. "Hi, Greg. Great to see you again. Glad we can work together here for the next couple of weeks. I think it'll be helpful for Kacy."

"No! I already hate it here," said Kacy, her lower lip protruding into a classic pout that she obviously knew very well.

"Aw, honey. We're going to try our best. Remember?" Brody said quietly.

Observing the interplay between the two of them, Jill clamped her teeth together. The summer was bound to be even worse than she'd initially thought. The idea of packing up and leaving was tempting, but she'd somehow make things work. This was her own fault. She should've known better than to trust her sister.

CHAPTER TWO

Kacy strolled into the room as Jill was setting the table for dinner. "What are we having?"

Jill gave her a smile of encouragement. "Spaghetti. It'll be ready soon. Are you hungry?"

"Ugh," Kacy said, curling her lip. "Is there meat in the sauce? I don't eat meat."

Jill forced herself to remain pleasant. "In that case, you can have noodles with butter or cheese. I'm also making a nice, green salad, giving you plenty of choices."

Kacy's mouth turned down. "My mother makes me eat salad all the time. I'm not going to eat any salad while I'm here."

From her teaching experience, Jill knew how important it was to set boundaries early on. "I'm not here to supervise what you eat, but as long as I'm in charge of the cooking, I'll fix a meal, and people can eat it or not."

"Really?" Brody said, giving her a teasing smile as he walked into the room. "Greg told me you were a good cook."

Picking up a spoon, she said, "I don't know about that. I'll do my best, but I'm not going to prepare special items for individual meals."

"Fair enough. Maybe I can help. I make a mean omelet and a great ham sandwich."

Kacy pulled on his hand. "Remember, Daddy, I'm a vegan. Like Mom."

Though Brody smiled, his nostrils flared slightly. "While you're with me we're going to forget Mom's routines.

Remember?"

"Oh, right. That's why I'm going to get doughnuts every day."

Brody wrapped his arm around Kacy. "Not every day. That's not the deal. But we're going to have fun this summer and not worry about so many rules. Understand?"

Kacy stared up at him uncertainly. "I guess so. But I'm not eating the spaghetti sauce. *She* put meat in it." Kacy gave Jill a look filled with daggers.

"I told Kacy she can have butter or cheese on the noodles, and I'm also serving a nice, green salad," Jill said calmly. She wasn't going to react to Kacy's negative behavior.

Kacy's lips formed the pout that was becoming familiar. "I don't want that for dinner. I want something different. I want dinner at My Burger Place."

Brody paused. "Well, maybe since this is our first night, you can do that for dinner this one time." He turned to Jill and gave her an apologetic shrug. "Guess I'll be late for dinner tonight."

The triumphant look Kacy shot her annoyed Jill, but she schooled her features. She'd dealt with enough spoiled kids and too-eager-to-please parents to understand that Brody and Kacy would have to work things out for themselves. Babysitting an eight-year-old was not part of her duties. She'd already been given the tasks of cooking and cleaning.

After Brody left with Kacy, Jill called to Greg.

He came into the kitchen, sniffed, and smiled. "Something smells delicious. Do we have time for a glass of wine before dinner? Annie and I used to like to do that. I've stored a few bottles here in the kitchen."

Surprised but pleased, Jill nodded. "That sounds lovely. I

haven't had much of a chance to be outside, and I hear that sunsets here are spectacular."

"It's too early for sunset, but it's a beautiful part of day—a time to gather thoughts. Give me a minute and I'll open a nice pinot noir."

"My favorite," said Jill, realizing how few peaceful moments she gave herself.

Later, sitting outside looking at the waves moving into the shore for a frothy kiss before pulling away again, Jill felt her tension ease. She turned to Greg. "How long have Brody and his wife been divorced?"

Greg shook his head. "A couple of years. Allison found someone new, a doctor who made a lot of money in the stock market, and that was that. Never did like her much. She's one of those women who has to look perfect all the time. She's already damaged Kacy, making her feel ugly because she's a little hefty."

"Yes. That's why food is an issue." Jill shook her head. "I understand Brody has to work it out on his own, but, Greg, I'm not going to be played by either one of them. Besides, I had no idea that I would have any duties here except to look after the property."

Greg gave her a knowing smile. "I've known Hope Thomason for years, along with her parents. She's pretty spoiled, and very used to getting what she wants. Sounds like she might have tricked you into this."

"Oh, no, it wasn't Hope. It was that sister of mine," Jill said.

"Tell me a little about yourself," Greg prompted. "A beautiful, young woman on your own. Such a shame your husband died."

Jill took a sip of her wine and sighed. "Actually, as it turned out, he wasn't the nice guy I thought he was. Not after we'd been married for a few months and he'd had too many beers.

Then, he became someone I didn't like at all, someone who said horrible things to me." She felt her eyes widen. "Oh, my God! I haven't told many people that."

"Maybe it's time you did," Greg said simply. "Secrets have a way of eating into your heart."

Jill was quiet. In many ways, she supposed that's what had happened to her. Keeping her secret had changed her, made her lose enthusiasm for many things. She'd turned down dates from decent guys, opted out of hen parties, and all but hidden in her house these past two years. What in hell was that all about? Maybe, like Greg said, it was time to deal with it. Maybe, while she was away, she'd even talk to another professional about what she'd kept hidden.

"How about serving dinner now, to give us time to see the sunset afterwards?" Greg said.

"Sure, let's do it," said Jill getting to her feet.

As they walked toward the kitchen, Jill studied Greg out of the corner of her eye. She guessed he was in his seventies. With laugh lines at the corners of his eyes and an easy smile, he exuded a sense of contentment she found attractive. Though he'd said he was lonely, he obviously found pleasure in the little things in life like a nice glass of wine and evening sunsets.

She served dinner, and they sat down together. They were in the middle of their meal when Brody and Kacy returned.

"Did you have a burger?" Greg asked Kacy.

She beamed at him. "And fries and a coke. My mother never lets me have any of that stuff."

"She deserves a treat now and then," said Brody.

Kacy bobbed her head enthusiastically. "Tomorrow, we'll go to Chicken Lickin' for dinner."

"No, we'll eat here," Brody said quietly. "We're not going out to dinner every night. This was a special treat."

Kacy's eyes teared up. "But you promised, Daddy."

"No, I didn't. I said for tonight only." He turned to Jill. "Is anything left here for me?"

"Yes. It's nice and hot," she replied. "Help yourself."

"It's delicious," added Greg, giving her a smile.

"Nooo!" You're supposed to eat with me. Not *her*," cried Kacy.

"You've had your special meal. Now, it's time for me to eat," Brody said, getting a plate and serving himself at the stove.

Kacy screamed, "I hate you!" and left the room crying.

Carrying a plateful of food, Brody slid into a chair at the table, his cheeks aflame. "Sorry about that. I'm trying my best to cope. Food is an issue, along with several other things."

"I understand," said Jill with genuine sympathy. "I'm a kindergarten teacher. I sometimes see similar behavior from the kids at school whose parents are divorced or who are going through a hard time. It can help to talk to a psychologist."

He studied her. "That's what I am—a school psychologist for my school district in Pennsylvania."

"Oh, I didn't realize ..." Jill stopped talking when she noticed a look of sadness form on Brody's face.

"It's a field I really love." Brody set down his fork. "Allison, my ex, thought I should do something else, something that would bring in more money. But I know how much some of these kids need someone to talk to. The problem is, I seem to do better with them than with my own daughter."

"Now, Brody, you know it takes both parents working together to help a child through a difficult time. You have the exact opposite experience. Allison isn't about to listen to you or anyone else. If Annie were here, she'd tell you the same thing."

"Yeah, you're right. I've tried to talk Allison into letting me have Kacy full time, but she thinks it will tarnish the image she tries to present to others of being a devoted mother. It's hard to understand how some people can hide who they really are ..."

Jill glanced at Greg and then said, "You don't have to explain to me. I know about such things, such people."

Brody's gaze focused on her. "I'm sorry," was all he said, but Jill felt as if he'd seen inside her to the place where she'd stored her secret. Smiling brightly in an attempt to move on, Jill said, "Greg and I are going to watch the sunset. Maybe you and Kacy would like to join us?"

His mouth full, Brody nodded.

It was quiet as they finished their meals. As soon as they were done, Jill stood. "I'll do the dishes and join you on the porch." She wanted to avoid further conversation. She had the awkward feeling that with her confession about knowing people who hid their true natures, Brody already knew more about her than a lot of people back home. They'd never suspected that in the privacy of their home, Jay Conroy turned into a foul-mouthed bully when he'd had too much to drink. To them, he was the polite, attentive husband he pretended to be. And he never hit her, so there were no outward bruises to tell her story. The longer it had continued, the more silent she became.

Remembering all she'd gone through Jill twisted a piece of paper towel in her hands and wondered if she'd ever feel truly okay about herself again.

Outside, Jill found Greg in one of the two rocking chairs on the porch. Brody and Kacy were sitting on the wide seat of the old-fashioned porch swing hanging from a couple of wooden beams. The yellow orb of the setting sun was just beginning to slip below the horizon, sending streaks of orange, red, and purple into the sky like glittering bands of a tiara crowning the sun.

Jill sighed at the beauty of it and took a seat in the empty chair next to Greg. Gazing up at the sky, hearing the steady thump of waves hitting the sand, a sense of peace wrapped around her.

When the sun was totally hidden and darkness filled the sky, Brody stood. "Time for bed, Kacy. It's been a long day, and tomorrow will be busy."

Kacy crossed her arms in front of her. "I'm not going. My mom lets me stay up until I tell her I want to go to bed. She says it's easier that way."

"Well, you're with me, and when I say it's bedtime, I mean it," Brody said calmly and held out his hand.

Uttering an exaggerated sigh, Kacy took it, and they left the porch.

"Do you think Allison allows Kacy to stay up as late as she wants?" Jill asked Greg. In spite of her vow to stay out of that family's problems, she was curious. She'd once thought she wanted a houseful of children, but that idea had faded after her marriage with Jay. She'd never subject any children to him and his cruelty. Besides, she was well aware that raising children or teaching them wasn't easy. She was exhausted physically, mentally, and emotionally from dealing with the children in her classroom. Now that she was off for the summer, she was looking forward to having as much free time to herself as possible.

"To answer your question, I wouldn't be surprised if there is a bit of truth to what Kacy said about staying up late," Greg commented. "Allison doesn't like the trouble and work of parenting. She didn't even want Kacy. She wouldn't consider having more children, like Brody wanted."

"Oh, I'm sorry. That must be so hard on all three of them."

"Annie and I never had children—couldn't, you see, which is why Brody is so special to me. My brother, rest his soul, died when Brody was still in his teens, and Annie and I sort of took over for him." Emotion flooded Greg's face, giving his skin a light-pink hue.

"How sweet of you," Jill said, bringing even more color to Greg's cheeks. She looked up to find Brody standing in the doorway. "How's she doing?" she asked, interested in spite of herself.

"She's tired enough from the drive to fall asleep." Brody stepped onto the porch and sat once more in the swing. He turned to Jill. "I don't know what arrangements you made to be here, but I'm wondering if you could help me with Kacy. I'll be busy working with Greg. And though I've enrolled Kacy in a day camp nearby, I might need you to keep an eye on her for an hour or so in the afternoon."

Jill paused, unsure how to answer. Her plans didn't involve being a caretaker for a child. "How about checking with me each morning to see if I have plans for the afternoon? I've been given the task of cooking meals, so late afternoon might work on occasion."

"Jill had no idea that we'd all be here or that she was supposed to cook and clean for us," said Greg. "A misunderstanding of sorts."

Brody's eyes widened. "Oh, I didn't know. Well, I suppose I can ask one of the camp counselors to suggest a babysitter."

"Let's see how each day goes," said Jill, not wanting to be difficult. "I need to be able to be on my own as much as possible. This is, after all, what I thought was going to be my summer vacation."

"I understand," said Brody.

They sat quietly staring out at the water. In the darkness, the waves had a phosphorescent glow as they crested, emitting flashes of brightness.

Jill pointed. "Look! It's because of ..."

"Plankton," Jill and Brody said together.

Laughing, Jill said, "Great minds think alike."

Brody grinned at her. "Or nerdy science lovers."

A warm glow filled Jill. Maybe this summer she could simply be friends with a man. A man she could trust not to hurt her. A man she'd keep at a distance.

CHAPTER THREE

The next morning Jill was in bed when she heard a commotion in the kitchen. She got up, wrapped a lightweight robe around her, and hurried to see what was happening.

Brody looked up as she entered the room. "Sorry about all the noise. I was trying to put away the dishes when this pan dropped on the floor. I thought I'd get some coffee going."

"I'm supposed to be cooking for you guys. Give me a minute to get dressed."

Brody shook his head. "You don't have to do that. I can be in charge of breakfast. That way, you can sleep in."

Jill's jaw dropped. "You'd do that for me?"

He shrugged. "Why not?"

"But ..."

"It's all right, Jill. I'm an early riser."

Jill's mind spun. She couldn't let him do it unless ... "Okay, in exchange, I'll take charge of Kacy in the afternoon when she gets out of camp. You're here for only a couple of weeks, you said. Right?"

"Yes. Greg figured it would take us only three to four weeks to get the work done. Unless we uncover something we didn't expect."

"Okay, then. Deal?" Jill held out her hand. The idea of being able to rise when she wanted was so satisfying.

"Deal." His hand curled around her fingers.

She shivered as tingles of energy raced up her arm, and quickly pulled her hand away.

A bright smile spread across Brody's face.

That afternoon, when Brody brought Kacy back to the cottage after picking her up at camp, Jill greeted her. "Hi! Glad you're home. Guess we'll be doing things together in the afternoons. Shall we go down to the beach?"

Kacy shook her head. "I'm staying here with my dad."

"I found some coloring books in one of the kitchen drawers. Do you want to get them out?"

"No. That's for babies." Kacy gave her a challenging look.

Jill glanced at Brody and shrugged. "Okay, I guess I'll go to the beach, maybe wade in the water." She started for the door.

"You'd better go with Jill, Kacy," said Brody. "I'm going to be busy working."

"She's not my mother," said Kacy.

"Not by a long shot," Brody quickly agreed, giving Jill a wink. "She's a nice person who's helping us out."

"Okaaay," Kacy said. "But I don't like her."

"I expect you to be polite, Kacy," Brody said firmly. "I'm going back to work. Have a fun time with Jill. See you later."

After her father left, Kacy faced Jill. "Okay, if we bring a snack?"

"Sure," said Jill. "I'll grab a bunch of grapes and we can head out." Though Kacy was being difficult, Jill realized she was hurting.

As they walked along the beach, waded in the water, and looked for shells, Kacy remained mostly quiet. Jill didn't mind. She knew it would take time before they got to know one another.

Later, as they returned to the cottage, Brody met them at the front door. "Have a good time?" he asked Kacy, swinging her up in his strong arms.

"Uh huh," Kacy said, glancing at Jill.

Jill smiled. "Quiet walks are sometimes best. Now, I'd better start dinner."

"Thanks," said Brody. "I'm ready. In fact, I could eat a big bear. Or maybe a dinosaur."

"Me too!" said Kacy, laughing when her father tickled her, bringing a smile to Jill.

Jill headed into the kitchen feeling better about her new duties. Besides, the last half of the summer at the cottage would be hers alone.

Jill lay in bed the next morning, grateful for the opportunity to stay there. In the background she heard the low, quiet voices of Brody and Greg, then Kacy's higher-pitched whining. She rolled over and hugged her pillow. It felt wonderful to have her own space. Besides, mornings were not her best time.

After Brody and Kacy left the house, Jill climbed out of bed and went into the bathroom to take a shower. The warm water sluiced over her skin in silky strokes. She lifted her face to the stream of water raining on her, contentment rolling through her. Today, she'd walk the beach and scout the area a bit before settling down with a book.

As she dried off, she studied her reflection in the glass door of the shower. Though not tall and thin like her sister, she was average in height and curvy in the right places. At first, Jay had really liked that about her. She turned and looked into the mirror over the sink. Straight hair was in fashion. Hers swept her shoulders and was the right length for a quick, easy ponytail. She swept it away from her face and studied her hazel eyes and what her mother called the Davis nose. Straight and narrow, it seemed more suitable with age. At thirty-two, she was learning to be less critical of herself. She didn't have Cristal's blonde beauty, but she knew she wasn't ugly. Better yet, she was healthy.

She put on a swimsuit, pulled on a pair of shorts over it, and walked barefoot into the kitchen. Greg was sitting at the kitchen table going over some drawings.

"Good morning," Jill said cheerfully. "It looks like it's going to be another beautiful day."

"Yes, enjoy the outdoors this morning before it gets too hot," said Greg.

Jill helped herself to coffee. "Brody has agreed to get breakfast going each morning. In exchange, I'll watch Kacy in the afternoon."

Greg nodded. "Yes, he told me. Sounds like a pretty fair deal."

"I hope so," said Jill. "Kacy is going to be a real challenge. I know what it feels like to have others make you believe you're unattractive."

Greg's eyebrows shot up. "Another secret?"

"Nope, everyone knew I was the ugly sister, the one with the Davis looks. A neighbor used to call me 'the unpretty one.'"

"If you don't mind my saying so, there's nothing wrong with the way you look. Besides, appearance shouldn't matter so much."

"To little girls, it matters a lot," Jill responded quietly. From the refrigerator she helped herself to a container of yogurt.

Sitting opposite Greg, she said, "How does a chicken casserole sound for tonight?"

"Excellent. We're going to work outside this morning and then avoid the afternoon heat by working in one of the bathrooms. I'll be ready for some hearty food this evening."

"Okay, then that's what I'll fix."

Jill was standing at the sink rinsing dishes when Brody walked into the room.

A smile curved his lips as his gaze washed over her. "Got Kacy off to a good start at camp. At least I hope so."

"It may take her a while to settle in. Give it time."

He nodded. "My thoughts exactly." He turned to Greg. "Have you decided where we're going to start this morning?"

"Yes. We'll go ahead and drain the pool so we can work on cleaning it up and repainting it."

"Okay. I'm ready any time." Dressed in cut-off jeans and a white T-shirt that showed off his muscled physique, he looked ... well ... super sexy.

Jill turned away to finish the dishes and then went to get her sunglasses and suntan lotion. The next order of the day— a walk on the beach.

She stepped outside and breathed in the warm, salty air. It felt wonderful to be away from home. She walked onto the beach and wiggled her toes in the sand, feeling as free as they. No more secrets. No more hiding in a house. No more hoping that nobody would think she was a loser like Jay had screamed at her over and over again. If, by the end of the summer, she could go home without a lot of her emotional baggage, the job here would be worth it. Even if it meant taking care of Kacy for a while each day.

Her spirits lifted as she walked along the edge of the water.

Jill's steps slowed as she thought of Kacy. She knew hurt when she saw it, even if it was hidden behind a lot of bratty actions. Somehow, as long as she had to spend time with her, she'd help this little girl.

In the distance, a wooden pier beckoned to her. Jill picked up her pace.

She stepped onto the long wooden structure and walked

out to the end, listening to the gentle slap of the water against the bollards supporting it.

Several people—men, women, and children—were fishing. The quiet surrounding them was broken now and then by a triumphant cry as one of them pulled a fish from the water. *Such a seaside thing—fishing*, she thought, and decided to see if the cottage had any fishing poles she could borrow. After sitting and watching the action, letting her thoughts drift and her muscles loosen, Jill checked her watch. Realizing she'd been gone for over two hours, she headed back.

Brody and Greg were standing in the empty pool checking the interior when she arrived at the cottage.

"What are you doing?" she asked.

"We've scrubbed the surface, caulked, and patched it," said Greg. "Now we have to wait for a day or two until it's dry. Then, we'll paint it."

"Ready for lunch?"

"Perfect timing," said Brody, patting his stomach.

"Coming right up." She turned to go back inside the house when she heard a yelp behind her. She whipped around.

Greg was lying on his side at the bottom of the stairs in the empty pool holding his right arm. "Ow! Damn! I think I've broken my arm."

"What happened?" cried Jill, scrambling down the pool steps to reach him.

Still holding his arm, Greg sat up and gave her a sheepish look. "I stumbled on a step."

"Well, let's see how badly you're hurt," Jill said, observing him carefully. "Other than your arm, do you hurt anyplace else?"

Brody knelt beside them. "Your legs, hips, back are okay?"

"Yes. I landed on my arm when I fell." He shook his head. "I can't believe I misjudged the distance."

Brody nodded with sympathy. He clapped Greg on the back. "Now let's get you up and to a doctor. I want a professional to take a skilled look at you."

Once Brody had helped Greg to his feet, he talked quietly to him and threw his arm around him to aid in climbing up the stairs.

"Are you okay? Not dizzy or feeling sick?" Jill asked, following them out of the pool, searching for any signs of distress.

"Nope, just this arm of mine. Hurts like hell, but that's it." Greg's arm was bruising already and was twisted at an odd angle. Otherwise, he looked fine.

"I'll take him to the hospital," Brody said to her. "I'll give you a call if any complications arise."

"Okay. I'll text you my contact information. Keep in touch. I'll have sandwiches here when you get back."

Jill walked with them to Brody's truck and watched anxiously as Brody got Greg settled into the passenger seat with his seat belt on. Then Brody got behind the wheel and with a wave to her, he pulled out of the driveway.

Still shaken by what had happened, she sat in one of the rocking chairs on the front porch and drew a deep breath. Greg's sudden fall was a reminder of life's surprises.

Later, she was in the kitchen making the casserole for that evening when her cell chimed. She checked caller ID and picked it up. "Hi, Brody. How's Greg?"

"He's doing as well as can be expected. They've taken X-rays. It's a fairly routine break to correct. However, because of his age, it's going to take longer to heal than usual. He's going to be in a cast for a few months."

"Oh, no! What is that going to do to your work schedule?"

"That's something we'll have to work out together. Greg says there's still work he can do, but, honestly, I don't see how.

I can do a lot of it on my own, but that means I'll spend the whole summer at Seashell Cottage."

"I see," Jill said, uncertain whether to be happy or bothered by this news. "We'll have to sit down and talk about it when you two get home."

"We're going to be here for a while. Will you do me the favor and pick up Kacy at camp at four o'clock? I'll text you the directions. You'll want to speak to Ms. Melanie or Ms. Susannah about what happened. You'll also need to be on their list of people approved to pick up Kacy. I'll take care of that from this end."

"All right. Consider it done. Tell Greg I'm thinking of him." She got off the call and checked the time on her phone. She had two hours to read. If she was lucky.

As luck would have it, she'd just finished the first chapter of her book when her cell chimed. She frowned. *Camp Sunnyside.* She clicked onto the call. "Hello?"

"Hello. Is this Jillian Conroy?"

"Yes. Is everything all right?"

"Good afternoon. I'm Melanie Heckinger, one of the owners of Camp Sunnyside. I understand you're to pick up Kacy Campbell. Is that right?"

"Yes. Her father asked me to do that this afternoon."

"We would like you to pick her up now. We've had an incident here at the camp involving her, and she wants to go home."

"Oh? What happened?"

"A boy called her a name, and she hit him. He ended up with a bloody nose."

"Can you tell me what he called her?" asked Jill, pretty certain she knew the type of thing he'd said.

"He called her Humpty Dumpty and told her she was so fat that if she ever fell down, she'd break open just like an egg."

"Oh, my! That's bad." She wasn't about to encourage Kacy, but those words were mean enough to make any child want to strike back.

"We've talked to each of them, and now we're asking both sets of parents to pick them up and talk to them about the cruelty of name calling and how important it is to be kind. We pride ourselves in providing an open, safe atmosphere here at Camp Sunnyside. Before being accepted at camp, each child and his or her parent had to sign an agreement stating they would support our cause."

"All right. I'll be there shortly." Jill wrote down directions from those Brody had texted her and shut her book. Another Kacy challenge.

CHAPTER FOUR

Jill drove between the pillars of the driveway leading beyond the sign that clearly said, "Camp Sunnyside". Located between Treasure Island and St. Pete Beach, the camp's main building looked like a '50s-style home. Off to one side, a large, open-air structure with no walls offered protection from the sun for a number of kids who were working at tables on what appeared to be a variety of projects.

After parking the car, she studied the house. Built of concrete blocks painted sea blue, the one-story house welcomed visitors with a tiny front porch flanked by posts that held up a section of roof. To either side of the front entrance a window with white shutters looked out to the front. A palm tree sat at one corner of the house, its fronds making a kind of music as an onshore breeze steadily moved the air. Hibiscus bushes and a variety of colorful flowers softened the front of the house.

Tidy and well-maintained, the house and front yard appeared untouched by the number of children Jill guessed had walked in this space. A concrete walk lined with weathered-white, broken seashells led her to the front porch where she rang the doorbell.

A pleasant-faced woman with short gray hair and bright blue eyes opened the door. "Ah, you must be Jillian Conroy. I'm Melanie. Please come in."

Jill stepped through the entrance and gazed around. An office was to her right, a small sitting room to her left. From the front hallway she could see the kitchen at the back of the house where another gray-haired woman was working.

"Let's go into my office," said Melanie. "We can talk there."

Melanie's office was small but attractively furnished. One wall was lined with shelves that contained a mixture of books and colorful handcrafted items Jill assumed had been made by campers. In the center of the room, two side chairs faced a desk. A tall, gray-metal filing cabinet nestled in the corner behind the desk, and in the center of that wall hung a large, framed picture of a boy with a dog and puppies.

"Is that a Norman Rockwell print?" Jill asked, drawn to it.

Melanie smiled. "It's called 'Pride of Parenthood.' I love it. Here at Camp Sunnyside, we believe kind parenting should be available to all children. Pretty much as this print shows."

"Very nice." Jill sat in one of the chairs facing the desk as Melanie settled in a chair behind it.

Melanie cleared her throat. "I understand you're an acquaintance of the family."

"Yes. I just recently met Kacy and her father. It's a long story, but I'm doing a favor for the owner of Seashell Cottage and didn't know I'd be sharing the cottage with them."

"So, you're unaware of the difficulties Kacy has had in the past?"

"Personally, yes. But I've been told of a difficult situation she shares with her mother. Food issues are among the challenges."

Melanie nodded. "Yes, I gathered that. Anything else I should be aware of before we go to Kacy? She's in our outdoor building now. I've asked her to work on writing a note to tell Justin she was sorry."

"I can't think of anything. Her father is very open about her troubles. I'm sure you should be able to talk to him easily about any issues. He's with his uncle at the hospital at the moment. But I'll have him give you a call as soon as he's free to do so. Do you have a business card?"

Melanie handed her a yellow card with a sun design. Two names were listed under the camp's name as co-owners—Melanie Heckinger and Susannah Magellan.

"You own the camp?" Jill couldn't hide her surprise. Melanie was the perfect image of an old-fashioned, comfortable grandmother, not a businesswoman.

The corners of Melanie's lips lifted into a smile that reached her eyes. "No one is more surprised than I. Following a divorce, I wasn't sure what I'd do with my life. I met Susannah on the beach right after she was widowed. She was at loose ends and wondering what to do with her house. We got to talking, and this is what we came up with. It's worked out very well. We both live in the same condo complex down the beach."

"Is that Susannah in the back, working in the kitchen?" Jill asked.

Melanie laughed. "Yes, that's Susannah, though people first meeting us think I'm the one who works in the kitchen." She patted her stomach playfully.

Jill couldn't help smiling. She would have thought the same thing.

"How long have you had this camp?"

"This is our eighth summer. We also have camp hours during holidays and on weekends. And sometimes nearby hotels use us for the children of their high-season guests."

"Do you have staff?" Jill couldn't help her curiosity. She loved the idea of two women setting up a business like this. It made her realize she could be independent and break free from the past if she could come up with something creative on her own.

"Oh yes. We have four other full-time staff members. We're looking for a fifth. And from time to time, we hire part-time people for special activities like music, snorkeling, and the like. Right now, we have sixty kids of varying ages signed up for the summer. More will be added as time goes on."

Jill took a deep breath to calm her racing mind, and then blurted, "I'm a kindergarten teacher in New York State. I've also taught fourth grade. I'd love to work in an environment like this."

Melanie's eyes widened, and the skin at the corner of them crinkled with pleasure. "Let me get you an application. I'd be most interested in talking to you." She reached into a side drawer of her desk and handed Jill a piece of paper. "Fill it out and then let's talk about it. We're fussy who we hire. Naturally, any such decision is up to both Susannah and me."

"Thank you very much." Jill folded the paper carefully and tucked it into her purse.

"Now, let's go see what Kacy has done with that note," said Melanie, rising to her feet. Her eyes twinkled with humor. "I shouldn't say this, but I think you'll understand that a part of me was pleased that Kacy fought back. She simply has to find a new, better way to handle teasing."

"What about the underlying problem?" Jill said.

"The weight?" Melanie gave her a thoughtful look. "I have a feeling the less said, the better. Here at camp, we work with kids on food choices and exercise in very subtle ways. Kacy is smart enough to see how it can work for her, if she wants. It takes a while, but most kids love Susannah's healthy meals."

"You provide meals?"

"Oh, yes. Breakfast for some, lunch for all. Healthy snacks. It's just one of the benefits of a camp run by old-fashioned grandmothers."

Jill smiled, intrigued by all she'd heard.

"Come. On our way out, I want you to meet Susannah."

They walked into the kitchen.

Susannah was a surprise. Tall and thin, with long gray hair tied behind her head, she looked more like a model for a modern grandparent magazine than a camp owner who loved to cook for kids.

When introduced, Susannah's brown-eyed gaze swept over Jill with a look of approval.

"Susannah, Jill is interested in being a staff member here. I've given her an application. She's going to fill it out and call for an appointment."

"Nice," said Susannah. "You have a lovely aura. I think working here will be helpful not only for you, but for all of us."

Melanie let out a nervous laugh. "Susannah is a student of the universe, as she likes to say."

"I usually am not so outspoken about my ability to see into the future, but I knew the minute I saw you that you'd end up working here. Things like this sometimes occur to me. I hope you're not put off by that," Susannah said, giving her a quiet smile.

Jill had questioned so many things in her life that she'd always been cautious about talking to people like Susannah who seemed to see into the future. Oddly, though, Susannah made Jill feel comfortable, as if this is what she should be doing and was just discovering it now.

"Well, though it seems pretty settled, we'll still need you to follow procedure and fill out the form and meet with us," said Melanie.

"Oh, yes, Melanie. That's right." Susannah flung an arm around Melanie's shoulder. "Melanie is the one who keeps this a thriving business. I don't know what I'd do without her."

As they smiled at each other, Jill had the feeling that Susannah had saved Melanie from an uncertain future as much as Melanie had helped her. They were such interesting people the thought of working with them was enticing.

When Jill followed Melanie to Kacy's place at a table in a far corner by herself, Kacy looked up at Jill with surprise.

"What are *you* doing here?" Kacy said, frowning.

"Ms. Melanie asked me to come and pick you up early. I guess you know why," Jill responded calmly.

"Why don't you tell Jill what happened? It's best to get that out in the open," prompted Melanie.

Kacy let out an exaggerated sigh. "Justin Kinley is a bully and I hate him!"

Jill waited for Melanie to speak.

"Hate is much too dramatic," Melanie said. "Think of another word."

"Okay, he's a bully and I really don't like him," said Kacy, challenging Melanie with a look.

"Better," said Melanie. "Have you written the note as I asked?"

Kacy shoved a piece of paper across the table to Melanie. "There. I said it, but I'm not sorry. It's not nice to call people names."

"I agree," said Melanie, "which is why you should be receiving a note from him. He's had a hard time in his family recently, so I'm hopeful the two of you can find a way to stop hurting one another. Once you or someone else uses words to hurt, you can't take them back. Punching isn't the right way to handle those words. Right?"

Kacy looked down at the ground and nodded.

"Ms. Melanie has asked me to take you back to the cottage," said Jill. "Your dad is not able to do it."

"Thank you, Jill," said Melanie. "Kacy, gather your things. Thank you for the note for Justin. We'll see you tomorrow."

"I'm not coming back," said Kacy, giving Jill a sideways glance.

"I'm sure that's something you and your father can figure

out," said Jill. "Now, it's getting late. And I need to tell you about Uncle Greg. He's broken his arm. We need to make sure everything is ready for him at the cottage."

"He broke his arm? Really?" said Kacy, diverted from fussing over whether she'd be coming back to camp.

"Yes, we'll find out more about it after we get home."

Jill waited while Kacy got ready to leave. And when they went out to her car together, they maintained a peaceful quiet between them. Jill saw that Kacy was buckled into the backseat and then went around the car to the driver's seat.

"I'm not coming back to camp," said Kacy, giving her a defiant frown as Jill drove away from it.

Jill studied her in the rearview mirror. "I understand you don't want to, but I don't think it's right to quit because someone hurt your feelings. By not coming back, you've made Justin think he can get away with his nasty remark. Do you see?"

Kacy frowned. "You're not my mother!"

"No, sweetheart, I'm just here for the summer helping a friend, you, your dad, and Uncle Greg."

"Oh." Kacy was quiet for a moment. "Sometimes Dad has friends who think they're going to be my mother. I don't like that."

"I can imagine, but don't worry. Like I said, I'm just here for the summer." Jill wasn't at all surprised to learn that Brody had been dating women who were more than willing to take on the role of his wife. He was an attractive man who seemed like a nice guy and a father concerned about his child.

When she pulled into the driveway of Seashell Cottage, Brody's truck was there. Anxious to see how Greg was doing, Jill parked the car and got out.

Kacy ran ahead of her along the walk to the front porch shouting, "Dad, I'm not going back to camp!"

Brody met them at the door. "What's this?" He looked from Kacy to Jill.

Kacy raced inside.

"I suggest we discuss it later," Jill said. "How's Greg?"

Brody sighed and shook his head. "He has a fracture of a bone in his forearm, his ulna, and is in a cast. The good news was it wasn't a severe break. The bad news is that it usually takes three to six months for the bone to heal completely, and he won't be able to do much work with it until then."

"Oh dear! Working with his hands is how Greg earns a living. And what about this job?"

"We're all going to sit down and discuss it tomorrow. Right now, he's on pain medication and has been told to rest. 'Falls like that are very hard on older people,' the doctor said."

"Yes, poor Greg. I'll go see what I can do for him."

She started to go inside when Brody said quietly. "Can we talk about Kacy now? She's home early. Why?"

At the anxious expression marring his face, she said, "Okay, let's sit down out here. There's a lot I want to tell you." They sat in the rocking chairs and turned to one another.

"I received a call from the camp asking me to pick up Kacy early. It seems a boy called her Humpty Dumpty and told her she'd break like an egg if she fell down. Kacy rightfully was angry, but, unfortunately, she punched him in the nose and made it bleed."

Jill ignored the flash of humor on his face and continued. "I talked to Melanie Heckinger, one of the owners of the camp, and she had both Kacy and the boy who taunted her write apology notes to one another."

"Did Kacy do it?" Brody asked, looking concerned.

"Yes, but she told us she doesn't want to return to camp."

"Hmmm. I hate the idea of Kacy being taunted," said Brody. "Her mother verbally beats her up about her weight. I don't want other kids to do it too."

"As a teacher who's dealt with similar behaviors, I don't think it would be wise to let her quit. Also, Melanie told me all about the camp's philosophy in handling children like Kacy, and I was so impressed with it and the camp that I'm going to apply for a job there."

"Honestly? I thought this was your vacation," said Brody.

"I was looking forward to time alone," Jill admitted, "but after seeing the camp and talking to Melanie and her co-owner, Susannah Magellan, I'm intrigued by the idea of doing something different with children. I'm not sure where it will lead, but I'm willing to do a little experimentation with it. Melanie and Susannah have instituted a subtle program to get kids to eat healthy. I think it might help Kacy. And the atmosphere of kindness is something all kids need."

"Okay, if you say so. I'll make it clear to Kacy that she needs to go back. Especially now with Greg unable to do the work around here, I'll be busier than I'd thought."

When he rose to leave, Jill reached out to touch his arm. "Please don't tell her I'll very likely be working at the camp. She's threatened by the idea of me. Apparently, she's worried about other women becoming her mother."

Brody's sound of disgust was surprising. "Another idea from her mother. At one time, Allison asked Kacy to let her know if I was dating anyone seriously. Maddening, but true."

"I see," said Jill, realizing how complicated this man and his family were.

CHAPTER FIVE

The next morning, after Brody had dropped Kacy off at camp, Greg, Brody, and Jill sat in the kitchen to discuss the situation with Greg's injury and its impact.

"The doctor said I can do some light work with my hand as long as there's no lifting or other stress that puts weight on that arm," Greg said. "I was counting on this job to carry me through the summer. My fall clients will understand if I'm a little late in helping them open or close certain properties. I can still oversee them, but I won't be able to do upgrades or heavy maintenance on any property until at least September."

"Or later, Greg. It depends on the healing of that arm," Brody reminded him.

"What about this project?" Jill asked quietly.

Greg glanced at Brody.

"I made plans to stay for only two weeks, three weeks max. But I think it might be worthwhile for Kacy if we spend the whole summer here, and we all help her see a new outlook on her life. You can assist me on the repairs and other work on the cottage, Greg, but I'll do most of the work. We can't let your business disintegrate. You've built it into a nice operation."

Greg's eyes watered. "That would be great, Brody. I sold my house before coming here, thinking I'd stay at the cottage this summer and then decide where I want to live. I've looked at a couple of condos close by that I like."

They both turned to Jill.

"Is it all right if we spend the entire summer here with you at Seashell Cottage?" asked Greg. "I know it's not how you had envisioned your stay here."

Jill gave up on the idea that her summer would be a peaceful, restful one. "It's fine. I don't want this injury to ruin your business. And you're right, Brody. This could be a valuable summer for Kacy."

"We'll draw up a list of priorities and go from there," said Brody.

Greg nodded his approval. "Okay, then. I'll do as much as I can to help you."

"I'll help with Kacy as much as possible, but like I mentioned yesterday, I'm applying for a job at Camp Sunnyside. I'll try for part-time and see if that will work."

The three of them smiled at one another.

"Sounds like a plan," said Greg, his eyes becoming suspiciously moist. "I appreciate it."

"There's just one stumbling block. The agreement with Allison was for me to be in Florida for two weeks and then back in Pennsylvania, in case she wanted to see Kacy." Brody's sigh said a lot. "Trying to work out any deal with her is difficult, but I'll call her now and see what I can do."

After Brody left the room, Greg asked Jill about the camp.

As Jill talked about the philosophy of the camp, seeing the kids, and some of the facilities, her enthusiasm grew. "I think it will give me a new perspective on teaching. Or even doing something different."

"Fantastic. I'm acquainted with Susannah. She's a nice person."

Jill couldn't help the smile that crossed her face. Susannah and Melanie seemed as different as possible, both in appearance and in approach. Susannah's head seemed in a cloud, while Melanie was all business—a grandmother used to being in control. Yet, somehow, it seemed to work.

Brody entered the room wearing a frown. "It took some doing, but I think Allison will go along with my plan to spend all summer here with Kacy. For Allison, it's a control issue, not one of concern for Kacy. Believe me, I know."

"As much as there might be conflict between them, I haven't heard Kacy say anything bad about her," said Jill.

"Yes, they have sort of a co-dependent relationship. I'm trying to get Kacy to understand what it means to care for and about others." Brody lifted his shoulders in a shrug and let them drop. "One baby step at a time, right?"

She nodded and gave him an encouraging smile. "Each one important."

Greg stood. "The pool is the priority today. As long as it's dry, we need to get it painted. The days will only get hotter, more humid. And, too, Kacy might enjoy splashing in the pool after we get it done."

"She needs swim lessons," said Brody. "Allison is afraid of the water, which is why Kacy is not yet a strong swimmer."

"It's so important. It has been shown that if kids don't learn to swim by the time they're eight or nine, there's a high probability they'll never learn," Jill said, commiserating with him. Hearing herself speak, she stopped and silently reminded herself that she shouldn't get involved. If Kacy was going to be in the house with her all summer, it wouldn't work if she acted as if she were trying to replace her mother. Kacy had made that clear to her.

She got to her feet. "I'm going to fill out the application and go to the camp to talk to Melanie and Susannah. I should be back in time to make a nice lunch for you guys."

"As I said earlier, I make a mean sandwich," Brody said. "And if you're going to be working, you don't have to worry about us."

A sense of relief swept through Jill. Jay had always

expected her to fix all of his meals, telling her it was her job. She hadn't thought much of it during their short marriage, but now she saw how manipulative, how controlling that was.

"Thank you," she said to Brody, wondering what issues he'd faced with Allison. If she was as difficult as Jill thought, he hadn't had an easy time of it.

Brody smiled, took hold of Greg's free arm, and they left to go outside.

Jill went into her room, glad for the privacy and the small computer desk there. As she filled out the application, her thoughts drifted.

She'd always wanted to be a teacher, like her father. Her mother might have subconsciously put her down for having the Davis physical features, but no one could deny that Jill and her father shared a love of learning, the same subtle humor, and a true bond of affection unique to the household. Jill was, as her mother had often complained, his little princess.

As always when she thought of her father, Jill's heart clenched with sadness. She was ten when he dropped dead in the school parking lot from a brain aneurysm. The whole town mourned the English teacher and basketball coach they loved. But nobody hurt as much as she.

Jill set her pen down, got up, and stared out the window at the water rolling into the sandy shore in a peaceful rhythm as timeless as the Gulf itself. She grabbed her sandals and headed out to the beach, needing to feel the kiss of nature on her cheeks, the soft sand between her toes. Her father would be pleased she was attempting a new teaching role with the kids at Camp Sunnyside. She felt her eyes moisten. He was the only person she'd always been able to count on for support. She'd thought Jay would take over for him. He dazzled her with love and affection when they met and for a while afterward. But after a few months of wedded bliss, the real Jay emerged, constantly looking for ways to discredit her, eradicating her self-confidence like flesh-eating bacteria.

Jill lifted her face to the sun, allowing its warmth to defeat the chill that had filled her at the thought of her ex. She'd been foolish to marry him. *Stupid! Stupid! Stupid!*

She clasped her head in her hands and shook away the awful feeling, reminding herself that Jay was no longer around to hurt her.

With purpose in her stride, she marched up the beach. The past was behind her, and she wasn't about to repeat it. Her thoughts flew to Brody and Kacy. As she'd told herself many times already, they were dangerous for her because beneath her actions, Kacy was a child who needed someone to help her discover and accept how beautiful she was. And Brody? He was a handsome guy who wouldn't have any trouble finding dates or someone to marry.

Her pace slowed. She faced the water and breathed in the moist, salty tang of the air. The cries of seagulls and other birds filled the air. She loved the authenticity they gave to the scene around her. Everywhere people were sitting on the beach, walking it, or swimming in the water beside it. She laughed as one toddler dragged a plastic pail full of sand behind him, while another shoveled sand with great concentration. Construction workers in the making.

She walked back to the house feeling refreshed, entered her room, and went into the bathroom to put more suntan cream on her face. Jill stared at herself in the mirror. Her tresses, having been caught in the moist breeze, were frizzy. She'd always worn her hair long because that's how Cristal wore hers. Now, though, she wondered what she'd look like with short, easy-to-care-for hair. Before she could change her mind, she went to her computer, found a salon online, and punched in their number. When the receptionist offered her an appointment later that morning due to a cancellation, she took it. If she was going to make some changes in her life, she'd start with this.

She called Melanie and arranged to meet her late that afternoon.

Satisfied that she was moving forward, Jill went outside to check on Brody and Greg. Brody was using a roller to apply paint to the dried surface of the pool walls. Greg was trying to paint along the upper border.

"Here," said Jill. "Let me help. I have some time before I have to leave for an appointment."

Brody looked up at her with surprise. "You're going to paint in those clothes?" He was wearing only swim trunks. "I figure the less you wear, the better."

"I'll be right back," said Jill. She dashed into her room and put on an old T-shirt and the bottom of her least-favorite bikini.

As she hurried back to the pool both men grinned their approval. "That's better," said Greg. "This epoxy can be messy."

Jill took the paintbrush from Greg and set to work on the opposite end of the pool from Brody. She liked to paint. The blue paint was harder to work with, but she gamely kept at it until Brody came up behind her.

"Good job! Now, I'll take over. Thanks."

As she stepped back, she tripped over the long handle of the roller Brody had been using.

A strong hand gripped her arm, holding her upright. "Gotcha! We don't want any more accidents in this pool."

His warm fingers around her shot sensation through her body. To cover, she smiled and moved toward Greg. "No more accidents. Right, Greg?"

He laughed. "Right."

She climbed out of the pool and went into the cottage, well aware that two sets of eyes followed her every move.

Later, sitting in the stylist's chair at Henri's Salon and Spa, Jill wondered if she'd made a mistake by making this appointment. Long, straight hair was the vogue for so many young women. She'd always loved how it looked on Cristal.

The stylist, a male named Frederick, circled the chair studying her features. He stood in front of her and smiled. "I think something like the pictures I've seen of Jennifer Lawrence. A sexy pixie look. With your fine features you can get away with it. Very new. Very you."

Jill drew a deep breath. Could she do it?

Frederick waved his hand at her. "Sweetie, it's going to be fabulous. I promise. We'll add a few highlights in the right places, and you won't believe how fab you'll look."

His smile was so bright, so encouraging, she said, "Okay. Let's do it."

He began snipping hair quickly, spinning the chair from side to side. "Don't look, sweetie. I won't be through with you until after we've shampooed and rinsed. Then I'll make the final cuts." He turned the chair away from the mirror.

He hummed as he continued cutting and putting highlights in her hair. Hummed, that is, between the words that flowed easily out of his mouth. It turned out Frederick was a wealth of information. He knew all the best places to eat.

He waved a comb in the air. "Gavin's at the Salty Key Inn is one of my favorites. Great story behind that property. Even better food."

Jill made a mental note of it. She didn't intend for the summer to go by without treating herself to some nice meals in restaurants.

After she'd sat reading while the highlights took hold, Frederick shampooed her hair. Jill sat in his chair, clutching her hands in her lap. She looked so ... different. Her wet hair clung to her skull. Her stomach roiled. Had she done something she'd regret?

"Don't worry," Frederick said in a soothing voice. "It's always a shock at first. Trust me, sweetie. You're going to love it."

He blew her hair dry and then started texturizing her hair for body, working quickly. Each snip of the scissors in his hand sent another thread of worry through her.

When he was through, he stood back and grinned at her. "See? I told you. You look stunning."

Jill blinked in surprise at the image in the mirror facing her. Her eyes looked larger, and her cheekbones more pronounced. She'd worried her hair would be too short, but the way he'd styled it made it the perfect length, framing her face beautifully.

"Thank you, Frederick! I love it!"

He smiled and nodded. "I knew you would." He gave her a quick hug. "See you next time, sweetie."

"Yes," she said, patting her hair gingerly. "I'm already planning on it."

Jill left the salon feeling better not only about her appearance but, more importantly, about the way she was beginning to make some life changes. On the spur of the moment, she called Melanie to see if they could reschedule their meeting for tomorrow morning.

She was going shopping.

When Jill returned to the house with a handful of shopping bags, she found Greg napping in his room with his door open and Brody placing blue painters' tape on the trim in the living room.

"Things are going to be a mess for a while," he said, keeping his back to her. "I'm going to start painting this room tomorrow." He patted a strip in place and turned to her. "It's supposed to rain so—Wow! Look at you! What happened? I mean, you look great ..."

At his obvious discomfort, a chuckle escaped Jill's lips. "Thanks." Her cheeks burned. His reaction both embarrassed and pleased her.

He looked away and turned back to her. "Like I said, I'll start painting the living room tomorrow. Hope it won't disrupt anything for you."

"It should be fine. I'm going for my job interview tomorrow morning. Maybe I'll end up working there right then. They seemed in such a hurry to hire people."

He studied her. "I did a lot of research on the camp before I signed up Kacy. I like it a lot, and I like the idea of someone like you who's taught school being involved. What a great summer job! I once thought of doing something like that."

Jill smiled. He had such a positive attitude. No wonder Brody was great with kids.

She went into her bedroom to unpack her purchases. She'd gone a little overboard, but she hadn't bought any new clothing in years and realized it was time for a change there too. Her purchases were contemporary and fit her new image. She realized at thirty-two she'd been acting and dressing like an old lady. The store clerk who'd helped her with her selections was as pleased as she by the choices she made.

One of her favorite items was a sundress in a tropical pink with big white flowers. The bougainvillea-pink color gave the classical style a new twist. White jeans, short denim shorts, and other items were needed additions to her limited wardrobe. Now that she was on this new path of upgrading her appearance, she wondered if being in an unhappy circumstance had made her give up on the simple things like a nice wardrobe. She vowed to look at any opportunity that might help give her a new, positive spirit.

CHAPTER SIX

The next morning, Jill took a last look in the mirror. She'd applied a little eye shadow and mascara and liked the effect. As Frederick had implied, she was beginning to see herself in a different way. Not the ugly, younger sister of years ago, but a woman with a new outlook. It felt wonderful.

She said goodbye to Greg and Brody and left for the interview with a new enthusiasm for the future.

Later, sitting with Susannah and Melanie in their office, Jill explained that she'd love to work at the camp on a part-time basis, that she felt a commitment to her job at the cottage.

Melanie and Susannah glanced at each other, then smiled at Jill.

"No problem," said Melanie. "Susannah already warned me that this would happen. As it turns out, the teacher we offered a job to a few days ago has accepted our offer. He'll work full-time, so this is perfect. You'll be what we call 'a traveling teacher,' going from one project to another. You may even be called upon to help in the office."

Jill grinned. An idea had already been forming in her mind, a thought she'd put on hold for a while.

After they worked out hours and wages, the women all rose. "I'm so glad you're coming on board," said Susannah, giving her a hug. "I knew you would, but it's always nice to see my intuitions come true."

Melanie squeezed her with enthusiasm. "This summer is going to be the best. I just know it."

Susannah arched an eyebrow at Melanie, but said nothing.

They arranged for Jill to begin work tomorrow, and gave her a number of things she'd most likely need for the job, including a water bottle, suntan lotion, a baseball hat with the camp logo on it, and three yellow T-shirts with the camp logo on the front and the word "staff" printed across the back in bright blue letters.

"We like to keep things sunny around here," said Melanie, patting the yellow, folded shirts as she handed them over to Jill.

Jill smiled. As Melanie said, it was going to be the best summer she'd had in a long time. She almost felt like a camp kid again.

"Tomorrow, you'll meet Jed. He's a really great guy with a very interesting family," said Susannah, and Jill knew from the way Susannah had closed her eyes that there was a whole lot more to the story. It made the idea of working there even more intriguing.

On the way out to her car, Jill saw Kacy sitting with a boy at a table in the open-air building. She hurried on her way. She wanted the opportunity to break the news to Kacy about her working there when they had some privacy to talk.

At the cottage, Greg and Brody were working in the living room painting the edges of the wall close to the trim.

"Hey! What are you doing, Greg? I thought you were supposed to give your arm a rest."

He looked up at her and grinned. "My arm is resting just fine. I've figured out a way to hold the paintbrush without adding stress."

"Of course, it's taking him forever to do his side of the room," Brody teased.

Jill smiled at the camaraderie between them. They obviously loved one another. As Brody went back to work, she wondered about his history.

"You get that job?" Greg asked her.

"Yes, I'll be working at Camp Sunnyside Monday through Friday from 11 o'clock until 4. I can't wait to start tomorrow."

Brody turned around. "Congrats. Sounds like a great schedule."

"I had to make sure I had time to supervise the two of you," she quipped.

Both Brody and Greg burst out laughing.

"No way," growled Brody playfully, looking adorable as he teased her back.

Jill changed into shorts and a T-shirt and wandered out to the beach to gather her thoughts. She liked the idea of being able to walk the beach. Back home, her "beach" was a small park on the opposite side of town.

She stopped to pick up a seashell and studied it, amazed that such a beautiful thing was sitting on the sand waiting for someone to discover it. She gazed out across the Gulf, feeling a calmness wash over her as she watched the ebb and flow of the waves. A new life, like the seashell she'd found, was waiting for her to discover.

She was no longer afraid of the thought of starting over. She'd once seen a quote that read something like, "A strong woman can change her future." Now was a perfect time to do it, she thought, hope rising within her. It occurred to her then she didn't want to go back to her small town. Cristal could be the one to keep an eye on her mother, not that her mother needed or appreciated the things Jill tried to do for her. And the house? She'd put it on the market as she should have done a long time ago. She lifted her hands to the sky and shouted, "Yes!!"

Sandpipers and other birds scurried away.

Seeing how she'd startled them, Jill laughed. She'd surprised herself too.

Walking quickly, Jill's mind worked in tandem with her steps. She had a lot to take care of over these next few weeks. She could hardly wait to get going.

When she returned to the cottage, she fixed lunch and carried her sandwich to her room. There, she did online research on the area schools and then made a call to Pinellas County Schools. She was teaching kindergarten in New York, but she was willing to take any grade if it meant she could get a job. After reviewing the available positions, she filled out an application online. Then she called Sandra Dixon, a friend of hers back home who sold real estate. Her house was in excellent condition and could be shown as is. And if Sandra wanted to stage it for a fee, she was willing to pay for it.

After Jill explained what she wanted to do, Sandra said, "I'm so surprised, Jill, but I'm pleased for you that you've decided to make some life changes. I just didn't think you'd leave town to do it."

"Being away even this short time has given me the chance to think things through. Or maybe it's being able to step out onto the beach every morning that's given me a new perspective."

"I'm going to miss you, Jill. You're one of the few people I and everyone else can depend on to help with any problem. I'll get back to you with facts and figures, and we'll put the house up for sale quickly. Do we need to clear the house of items of value, personal papers, or the like?"

"Actually, I took care of those things before I left, so my mother couldn't snoop when I was gone. Valerie Davis does like to gather information, as she calls it."

Jill and Sandra laughed together.

They said goodbye, and then Jill sat at her desk and started to make a list of things she'd need to do. She realized the house might take time to sell. While it was perfect for a couple or a small family, it wasn't suitable for most larger families in town.

Jill's stomach whirled on the way to the camp to pick up Kacy as Brody had asked. She had no idea how Kacy would react to the news of her working there.

When she arrived at the camp, cars had lined up in the driveway and were slowly moving toward the front entrance of the house, where Melanie and Susannah were helping children into cars.

Kacy frowned when Jill pulled up to the front.

"Here's your ride, Kacy," said Melanie. "Hurry, get in. Others are waiting."

Kacy stood in a now familiar pose, arms crossed in front of her. "My dad picks me up. Not her."

"Today, Jill is picking you up," Melanie said smoothly, opening the car door and gently moving Kacy forward. She waited until Kacy had buckled into the seat in the back of the car and then she stepped away. "See you both tomorrow!"

"Are you going to pick me up tomorrow?" Kacy whined.

Jill smiled and spoke calmly. "I'm going to be working here at the camp, so I'll probably take you home with me most days."

"I don't want you at the camp. It's *my* camp. Not yours!"

"It is yours as a camper, and mine as a staff member, Kacy," Jill said. "It's a great camp for both of us."

"It's not fair," said Kacy.

Jill didn't bother to respond. It would only give Kacy another opportunity to fuss.

"Whatcha do to your hair?" Kacy asked in the silence that followed. "You cut it off. Girls are supposed to have long hair."

"Really? Who told you that?"

"My mother. She won't let me cut my hair. She says my face is too fat to have short hair."

"I see," Jill commented. If given enough time, she hoped to instill in Kacy the idea that she was fine as she was. If, by chance, the activities and diet at the camp helped Kacy lose a little weight, that would be great, but no way was she going to oversee what Kacy did or did not eat. It was none of her business.

As soon as Jill pulled to a stop in the driveway, Kacy unbuckled her seat belt, got out of the car, and started running for the front door, crying, "Dad! Dad! Where are you?"

Jill sighed. She knew what was coming. As she entered the house, she could hear Kacy.

"No, Dad. You're supposed to pick me up. Not Jill."

"Jill is doing us both a favor by picking you up and spending time with you before dinner. I need to be able to keep working to help Uncle Greg so I can have time with you in the evening."

When Brody saw Jill, he waved her over. "Hi! I'm just telling Kacy how important it is for me to have time to finish up projects for Greg."

Jill glanced at Kacy and nodded. "Yes, your father and I made an agreement. There are a lot of fun things we can do. I checked this morning and found plastic buckets and shovels for making sandcastles, and net bags for shelling."

"Sandcastles?"

"Or anything else we want to make. I don't live near a beach, so I want to be able to do these things while I can."

Kacy studied her for a moment. "Okay."

"Let me figure out what we're having for dinner, and we can head out." Jill smiled. "In fact, any time you want to help me cook, you can."

"Really?" Kacy's eyes lit with excitement. "My mother

won't let me help in the kitchen."

Jill and Brody exchanged meaningful looks.

"While you're with me, you can learn to cook with Jill," Brody said. "Remember, we're going to try new things."

"Okay," said Kacy. "I want to make cookies."

"We're getting dinner ready now, but another time we can do something else," said Jill. "First, though, we'd better take advantage of the beach. Get your bathing suit on and I'll meet you by the front door with our towels and everything else we need."

Jill left before Kacy could fuss about the plans. She and Brody had talked earlier about the need for Kacy to spend time outdoors.

Jill quickly changed her clothes, grabbed her sunglasses, suntan lotion, and towels, then packed them into a large canvas beach bag into which she'd earlier placed the sandcastle building supplies. She stepped into the kitchen and stopped.

"Hi, Kacy! What are you doing?"

"I'm hungry," Kacy said, munching on a cracker.

"Okay," said Jill, reaching into the refrigerator. She turned and handed Kacy a bunch of grapes and two bottles of water. "Let's pack these and a beach blanket in our bag and be on our way."

Kacy followed Jill to the front door, helped her with the bag, and they walked out onto the sand.

"Wait up for me!" Kacy cried, hurrying to catch up to Jill.

Jill turned and smiled, happy that Kacy had bought into the idea of their being outdoors. For an eight-year-old, she spent too much time playing video games or watching television.

Gray clouds hovered at the horizon giving the illusion of mountains in the distance. Jill took several deep breaths, inhaling the salty air in welcome gulps.

"Whatcha doing?" Kacy asked, staring up at her with a puzzled expression.

"I'm breathing in the fresh air," Jill said. "Go ahead. Try it."

Kacy sniffed. "I don't want to."

Jill set down the bag and spread the blanket on the sand, "Okay, I'm going to see what shells I can find. It's high tide, so it isn't the best time to go shelling, but we can look."

"I want my snack now," said Kacy.

"Later," said Jill, and headed down the beach.

From behind her, a child's voice said, "Can we make animals out of shells like I saw in a store?"

Jill couldn't hide her smile. "Sounds like fun to me, Kacy."

Kacy hurried to Jill's side. "Okay, then. I'll look for shells too."

Bending over to see better, they moved slowly along the water's edge looking for gifts of shells from the Gulf waters.

"Look!" cried Kacy, grinning as she held up an almost-perfect scallop shell. "We can use this."

"Sure," Jill said. "It's an excellent beginning. We can collect a lot of shells. When you're ready, we'll glue some of them together to make different things." She held out a net bag, and Kacy proudly put her shell into it.

After a while, Kacy said, "I'm bored and hungry."

"Let's go back," Jill said. "I'll race you to our blanket." She took off in a trot without waiting for Kacy. If she was not mistaken, Kacy wasn't about to let her win any race.

Sure enough, huffing loudly, Kacy caught up to her and then raced past her when Jill slowed her pace.

As Jill approached the blanket, Kacy stared up at her with a gleam in her eye. "I beat you!"

Jill laughed at the triumph in Kacy's voice. She was fine with it. This little girl needed a chance to excel. "Yes, you did!"

"Can we have our snack now?" Kacy asked.

"Sure." Jill handed Kacy the bunch of grapes. "Help yourself, but leave some for me. I'm hungry too."

It was quiet as they ate their grapes and stared out at the water.

Jill broke the silence. "I'm not going to be at the camp all day, Kacy. I'll be there only from eleven o'clock in the morning until four in the afternoon when it's time to leave. And I promise you, I won't interfere with what you're doing. I'll be too busy helping other people. I just wanted you to know that."

Kacy studied her and then nodded. "Okay."

Jill handed her a bottle of water. "Here. You might need this."

Kacy accepted the water and frowned. "Why are you being nice to me? Because of my Dad?"

"What? No. I try to be nice to everyone because it's the right thing to do. I'm sure your father is a very decent man, but I'm not interested in being more than friends. I've got plans of my own."

"Yeah? Like what," said Kacy, suspicion coating her words.

"Wow! You really are worried about him, aren't you?" Jill said with sympathy.

"My mother told me to tell her if Dad starts dating again. She doesn't like it when he goes out with someone she might know."

"Oh, I see," said Jill, hiding her dismay. *Was Allison making her child act as a pawn of sorts between her divorced parents?* "Well, your mother doesn't know me, and I don't date your dad, so it looks like it's very safe for you."

Kacy remained quiet.

Jill patted Kacy's back. "I've heard your father say this is going to be a different kind of summer for you. Maybe you don't have to worry about what your dad does so much while you're here. What do you think?"

"And we don't have to tell my mother?" A grin spread across Kacy's face.

Jill shook her head. "We're not hiding anything, we're just going to have an easy, friendly time of it while we're at Seashell Cottage."

Kacy studied her, and then a huge smile lit her face, sending a gleam of happiness into her blue eyes.

Tears smarted Jill's eyes, but she blinked back the threat of them. The joy on Kacy's face was worth all the patience it would take for this to be the best summer for both of them.

CHAPTER SEVEN

When they got back to the cottage, Greg and Brody were sitting on the porch waiting for them.

Kacy raced up the stairs and over to her father. "Jill and I are going to make shell animals." She held up the net bag she'd carried. "I've got my first shell."

Brody grinned and swept Kacy into his lap for a hug. "That's great. I can hardly wait to see them."

"Yes," said Kacy. "And I don't have to worry because Jill doesn't want to date you."

"Oh?" Brody said, glancing up at Jill.

"We had a talk," Jill said, hating how her cheeks felt on fire. She sent a silent message for him to drop the subject.

Sensing her discomfort, he bobbed his head in acknowledgement. "What are the two of you cooking up for dinner?"

"I'm not cooking tonight. I'm too tired," said Kacy, plopping down onto the porch swing.

Brody and Jill exchanged glances. Jill guessed Kacy had heard that line quite often at home.

"Well, I've got a shrimp dish to put together. Why don't you guys relax with a glass of wine or a beer while I get changed and get the meal started. It shouldn't take long."

"I don't like shrimp," Kacy announced, rocking back and forth in the swing.

"You have to take only a taste. If you don't like it, there will be rice and a green salad for you to eat." Jill left the porch before Kacy could begin a routine of fussing.

Later, in the kitchen, Jill was setting the table when Brody walked into the room.

"So, you don't want to date me?" He grinned at her. "That ends all chances of my persuading you that behind this boring person is a knight in shining armor waiting for a chance to swoop you up onto my white horse."

Jill laughed and then quickly sobered. "Apparently, it's been a concern of Allison's that you not date anyone she knows. She's put a lot of pressure on Kacy about many things. To comfort her, I said I had no intention of dating you, that I had plans of my own."

"I see," Brody said. "I appreciate what you're doing for Kacy, but we can't let an eight-year-old dictate what we will or will not do." He shook his head. "Allison isn't easy to deal with. Staying here a few extra weeks might be beneficial for all of us." He gave her a smile and left the room.

As Jill prepared the meal, her mind spun. *Boring?* Brody was anything but boring. And he was right. She couldn't let a child make decisions for her. Still, she had no intention of dating Brody or any other man until she had herself in a better place emotionally.

After dinner, Jill sat on the porch talking to Greg. The meal she'd carefully prepared had become a battleground with Kacy constantly testing her father over the food she claimed she didn't like. But when he stood firm, she meekly ate rice and salad, after eating one small bite of a shrimp.

"Guess we're all part of a new experience for Kacy," Greg said quietly. "But it's important for her to see that none of us is going to put up with bad behavior."

"It's a shame that eating a meal has become a war zone," said Jill. "Nicely prepared food is such a pleasure. I haven't done much cooking for myself lately, but I'm going to change that now that I have people to eat it."

"My Annie was an excellent cook. Homestyle, nothing fancy, but delicious."

The note of sadness in his voice prompted Jill to reach over and give his hand a squeeze. "She sounds like a lovely person."

He nodded and then spoke in a gruff voice. "The best part of me, she was."

Jill sighed softly. That's the kind of relationship she hoped to have one day—a husband who loved her and would treat her with respect, someone who would never scream at her, call her names, threaten her with a raised fist. She rocked in her chair and stared out at the dark waves rolling in to meet the shore.

"Did you used to live close by? Is that how you met Hope's parents?" Jill asked Greg.

"I met her parents at a social event many years ago. Richard and I hit it off right away, and his wife, Rebecca, and Annie became friends. Richard's sister, Louise, left Seashell Cottage to Hope. Louise was a single woman who'd lost her beau in Vietnam. Never did marry."

"What a lovely inheritance," Jill said. Her family had always had enough money to take care of them, but not much more than that.

"Yeah, I love this property. At one time, I thought it might come into the family. Brody and Hope dated for a while. Then Allison came along, and everything changed."

"How so?" Jill knew she was prying but couldn't stop herself from asking.

"Allison is a stunning woman who knows what she wants and gets it. She wanted Brody from the moment she saw him. Annie and I were there to see it happen. We tried talking to him about it, but the two of them were dead set on getting married right away. He hadn't given himself enough time to see her for the self-centered person she was. When Allison realized that his being Dr. Campbell didn't mean a lot of money, she left in a hurry, taking Kacy with her. Just about broke his heart to have Kacy on a part-time basis and her living with her mother."

"Sometimes it's difficult to see people for who they are," Jill said recalling how foolishly she'd chosen to marry.

A noise behind them stopped Jill from saying more. She turned to find Brody and Kacy walking onto the porch.

"Story time is over, so Kacy would like to say goodnight to everyone," said Brody evenly.

Clinging to her father's hand, Kacy said, "'Night." She turned to her father and said in a loud whisper, "Okay, Dad?"

"Yes, that's fine, Kacy. Now to bed."

They left together, and a few minutes later, Brody returned to the porch alone.

"Get her all settled?" Greg asked.

"Yes, I'm trying to set up a new routine with her. It'll take some time for her to get used to it, but she needs to have a regular schedule. Allison doesn't stick to one." His voice changed, became sad. "She told me it's too much work."

Greg held up his broken arm wearing a cast. "Perhaps my accident will turn out to be a very useful thing. Giving you more time here with Kacy might be just what she needs."

"We'll see," said Brody. "Kacy's a great kid when she lets herself go. But her mother has made her feel so inadequate it's going to be tough to get through the walls she's building around herself, walls that should never exist for a child her age. You can imagine how infuriated it makes me."

"Especially because of the work you do with other kids," said Jill. Looking back on her own childhood, she recognized the wall she'd built around herself in Cristal's presence.

Brody turned to her and smiled. "Thanks for spending time with Kacy. It means a lot to her."

"You're welcome. She's excited about making shell animals, and we're going to build sandcastles too. I think it'll be fun."

He studied her for a moment. "You're a very nice person. I'm glad you're here."

Heat crept into her cheeks but she couldn't stop it from happening. The look he gave her said a lot more than his words. She prayed the feelings he stirred inside her wouldn't show on her face.

Through the louvers on the windows, sunshine was making lemony stripes on the floor when Jill awoke. A new sense of excitement filled her as she contemplated the day. The idea of working with Melanie and Susannah made her feel more secure about the choices she was beginning to make. She ruffled her hair and got out of bed, feeling freer and happier than she'd been in ages.

She pulled on a pair of shorts and a T-shirt and padded into the kitchen. Brody and Greg were working outdoors, but Brody had left the coffee pot on, and the aroma of coffee played with her senses in a pleasing way. After she poured herself a cup, she headed out to the front porch and sat looking at her surroundings.

The sun glistened on the crests of the waves with a brightness that created shimmering light around them. Nearby, the fronds of a palm tree whispered in the breeze. Puffy white clouds, like dollops of whipped cream, floated above the earth.

Jill sighed with pleasure. She sipped her coffee feeling more certain than ever she was making the right decision to move away from her hometown. She already loved Florida—the beaches, the temperature, the lifestyle. Even if she didn't get a teaching job she wanted right away, she felt confident she could find work until an opening came along.

Her peaceful moment was shattered by the sound of her cell phone. She checked caller ID and felt her stomach clench. *Her mother.* Reluctantly, she clicked onto the call.

"Hello."

"Jillian Elizabeth Davis Conroy, what are you doing selling your house? What an unpleasant surprise! Are you crazy? Where are you going? What are you doing? You didn't talk to me about this. How do you think I felt when Barbara Becker asked me about it the other day after she saw the 'For Sale' sign in your yard?"

Jill allowed her mother to rant for a few moments, wondering why she'd put up with such behavior for so long. Fate had given her a reprieve from a controlling, abusive husband. It was up to her to escape some of the same behavior from her mother. Funny, she hadn't thought of it as abusive, but now she did. This was why she'd put up with Jay's behavior. She was used to being treated as if her thoughts didn't matter. She was a grown woman. She didn't need to answer to her mother or anyone else about making the decision to move—a decision that was becoming smarter and smarter.

"Are you through?" Jill asked as calmly as she could when anger bubbled inside her.

"You ought to consider such a move carefully, Jill. You've been gone less than two weeks. What are you going to do about a job? You can't just leave. Several parents are counting on you to teach their children. You know how well-respected you are at that school. You need to think about the responsibility you have to those families."

"Mom, stop. Listen to yourself. You're treating me like a child. I'm an adult capable of making my own decisions. I've made the choice to move and that's what I'm going to do."

"But what about me?" her mother cried. "You're the one I can depend upon if I need anything. Cristal's so busy she never comes home."

"Well, perhaps it's time she did," said Jill, "because I'm not changing my mind." She watched seagulls circling in the sky. Their shrill cries sounded a lot like the harping voice of her mother.

"I'm coming down there to talk some sense into you," her mother said.

"I'm sorry, but all the bedrooms are taken," Jill said with satisfaction.

"What? I thought you were going to be there by yourself."

"Without my knowledge, Cristal arranged for me to cook and clean for the two live-in workmen and an eight-year-old girl."

"Oh, I didn't realize ..." her mother said.

"I should have known something like this would come up, but this time, I don't mind. They're nice people, and I believe I can help the little girl with some issues. As it turns out, she and I have a lot in common."

"You should reconsider what you're doing. You've lived all your life here in Ellenton. You might be unhappy living elsewhere."

Jill corralled her temper. "I'm looking forward to the change, Mom. It's time for me to take control of my life."

"Are you doing this because of Jay?"

"I'm doing this because I need to become free from the past, from Jay and everyone else."

"Well," her mother huffed. "I've always stood by you, Jillian. Maybe it's time you stood by me."

"Maybe I need to stand on my own," Jill said. In the past, she'd usually done her mother's bidding. "I've got to go now. We'll talk another time." Before her mother could protest, Jill cut off the call.

Sitting back in the rocking chair, Jill drew deep breaths to slow her racing heart. As she'd explained to her mother, it was time to make some changes. Surprised by her newfound determination, Jill smiled. Damn! It felt fantastic to stand up to her mother. She could almost picture her father giving her a thumbs-up sign.

Jill set down her coffee cup and walked out onto the beach, which was empty in front of the house. She stepped into the water, allowing it to swirl around her ankles. As the waves withdrew, they took some of the sand with them, giving Jill a soft massage on her feet. She closed her eyes and gazed up at the sky, letting the heat of the sun smooth away the frown on her face. She drew slow breaths in and out, trying to time them to the rhythm of the waves. Soon, the angst that had caused acid to bubble in her stomach eased.

Allowing nature to intrude into her life was such a positive force she felt the sting of tears. Communing with the universe in this way gave her a sense of self and a new definition of destiny. She recalled something from Shakespeare, something a friend had once mentioned to her. "It is not in the stars to hold our destiny, but in ourselves." *Yes, I will do it.*

She walked down the beach with a new spring in her step. *If I had wings, I'd fly*, she thought, feeling as if she could.

When she returned to the cottage, she went into her room and called her real estate agent.

"How are things going, Sandra?" Jill asked. "I know the market has slowed somewhat. Is that affecting my house?"

"Actually, it's not. The fact that your house is on such a large lot is a big factor. It's perfect for a couple I know who are away at the moment but have promised to look at it when they return."

"Oh, that sounds promising."

Sandra was quiet and then she said, "I got a call from your mother. She had no idea you were selling the house."

"Yes, it was quite a surprise," Jill said. "But I've told her I have no intention of changing my mind. And I'll be as flexible as possible with timing when anyone makes an offer. Frankly, I just want out of the house."

"Big changes, Jill," said Sandra. "I'm happy for you. I really am."

"Thanks," she said. Sandra had stayed in touch with her after Jay died, but even she didn't know the secrets Jill had kept inside.

CHAPTER EIGHT

Jill filled with excitement as she parked the car at the camp and got out. In many ways, this was the beginning of a whole new way of life for her. If things went well, she wouldn't wait any longer to call the school at home and resign.

As soon as she walked through the door, Melanie approached her. "Glad you're here. The kids are restless this morning. I want to introduce you to Jed Carter. You can work with him on beach activities and help with swim lessons."

"Okay. That sounds like fun."

Melanie smiled. "Jed is a great guy. He teaches history and is the baseball coach at a local high school."

Susannah approached them. "I think you're going to love his family too. In fact, I know you will."

"Nice," said Jill wondering what Susannah saw of the future this time. She'd spoken with such confidence.

Melanie led Jill out to the front of the house and onto the beach. A tall, lanky man saw them, waved, and strolled over with an easy gait.

"You must be Jillian," he said, smiling. He held out a hand, and she took it, surprised by the size of it. The twinkle in his eye and his quick smile made his ordinary face come alive.

"Jill, this is Jed Carter, our new athletics director," said Melanie, beaming at him.

Jed laughed. "It's a big title for the job I do, but I love kids, and this is a nice break from high school."

"You coach baseball?"

"Yep. I was a pitcher in the minor leagues and never made

it to the big leagues. But I learned a whole lot about the game and am willing to share that."

"Dad! Dad!"

Jill turned to the sound of the voice and was surprised to see Kacy trailing after a girl with bright red curls, who was running toward them.

"Ah, that would be my daughter, Emily," Jed said, smiling.

She came up to them. "Dad, meet my new friend Kacy. She's here for the summer."

Kacy joined them and stood by Emily's side. Standing shoulder to shoulder, the two of them were adorable together. Emily's blue eyes sparkled as she smiled at her father, making her rather ordinary face seem beautiful.

"Hello, Kacy. Where are you from?" Jed said.

Kacy glanced at Jill and then said, "I'm from Philadelphia, PA."

"PA?" said Emily. "Why not PB?"

"PB and J?" Kacy said, and the girls broke into giggles.

Jill and Jed rolled their eyes and laughed.

"You'd better get back to your group, girls," Melanie said, still chuckling. "Love it when you kids make new friends."

The girls ran off holding hands. Watching them, Jill's heart filled with tenderness. She knew how special it was to find a friend.

"Cute kid. Who is she?" Jed said.

"Kacy is the daughter of one of the two workmen staying at Seashell Cottage with me for the summer," Jill explained. "I'm just getting to know them. Greg Campbell has a contracting business in the area. His nephew Brody, who is Kacy's dad, is helping his uncle with the project."

"Got it. I'm glad Emily and Kacy are getting along. We're fairly new to the area ourselves, and Emily's had a hard time finding friends, partly because things are chaotic at home, and we haven't been able to step in to help."

Melanie turned to Jill. "Jed and his wife, Niki, have triplets who recently turned one."

"Oh, my! Yes, things must be *very* chaotic at home."

Jed laughed. "Niki's family is here. That's why we moved here from up north. Each time someone comes to the house, they end up with the care of one of them. The neighbors and new friends love it. Especially the empty nesters and grandparents in the neighborhood."

"Well, I'll leave the two of you to oversee the activities. I understand you've set up a beach volleyball tournament, Jed."

"For the older kids. The younger ones are taking swimming lessons in the pool." He turned to Jill. "I thought you might like to help Kelly with that."

"I'll introduce Jill to her," offered Melanie.

"Thanks," said Jed. He gave them a little wave and walked away toward the volleyball court set up in the sand.

"Wow! You said his family was interesting, but triplets? I don't know how anyone could handle that," Jill said to Melanie.

"Both Jed and Niki are laid-back people. I'm sure that helps a lot," said Melanie.

At the swimming pool, Melanie introduced Jill to a tall, big-boned young woman with dark hair cut very short and deep-brown eyes that brightened with pleasure when Melanie said, "Here she is. Kelly Summers, meet Jill Conroy."

"Glad to meet you," Kelly said. "I heard I'd have a helper today."

Melanie beamed at them. "Jill just joined the team as a part-timer, working from eleven to four during the week."

"Wonderful! You're going to love it here. I'm working with eight-year-olds now who need to learn how or improve their swimming."

Jill darted a glance at the pool. Kacy was one of the eight girls lined up on the pool deck in bathing suits. "I'm ready any time. I've got a bathing suit on beneath the shorts and shirt."

"Okay. That'll work," said Kelly. "I've got extra towels here, but you'll have a chance to dry off because we sit and talk after we swim. Some kind of therapy you might say, in an effort to make sure everyone feels part of the group."

"Great idea," Jill said, liking the camp more and more.

"See you later," Melanie said. "I'm off to hide out in the office. Jill, sometime this afternoon, we'll sit down and talk about how you can help me there."

Jill returned Melanie's wave and took off her shorts and shirt. The suit she wore was one she'd splurged on at the end of summer sales a year ago. She'd thought the hot-pink, one-piece with cut-outs was daring at the time, now it seemed suitable in this tropical-like setting.

Kelly led Jill over to the group. "Hi, girls. This is my new helper, Jill. Can you all say hi?"

Jill was relieved when Kacy became part of the welcoming chorus. She had no intention of letting any of the kids know that she and Kacy lived together. That was Kacy's news to share, if she chose to do so. At the moment, Kacy was trying very hard to ignore her.

By the time the swim session was over, Jill was exhausted. Helping one little girl deal with a fear of getting her head wet had taken a whole lot of patience. Then, Emily had wanted Jill to watch her swim, while Kacy pouted off to the side.

Jill got out of the pool with the others and wrapped a towel around herself. The sun was a welcome warmth, coating her body.

"Okay, girls. Gather round while we all catch our breaths,"

said Kelly, waving them closer, into a circle. "I also have some carrot sticks for those who need a little snack."

"No cookies?" asked one of the girls.

Kelly smiled. "Not after we've just given our bodies a nice workout. And, girls, be sure to drink plenty of water."

The girls, many of them munching on the carrot sticks, sat in a circle as directed. Sitting with them, Jill noticed that Kacy didn't reach for a carrot until Emily did. Then, she like Emily, took two.

"We have a new member of the group today. Emily, do you want to tell us a little about yourself?"

Emily's fair cheeks turned pink, but she nodded. "My dad is in charge of all the games. That's why I'm here. I've got two little brothers and one sister. They're triplets, and they can be a whole lot of trouble. My dog, Mollie, just had four puppies. Three girls and one boy." She shook her head. "I don't want any more babies at my house."

"You've got puppies! Can I see them?" squealed Kacy.

"Yes!" the other girls cried.

"My mom said they have to stay with their mother. They're just babies now. But by the end of the summer, my dad might let me bring them here."

"Sounds like a plan," Kelly said, interrupting the groans that followed. "Let's see. Who else would like to tell us something about themselves?"

Jill waited for Kacy to say something, but she looked down at the ground and remained silent.

The clanging of a bell broke through the silence.

"Lunch time!" cried one of the girls. "C'mon!"

The eight girls headed for the open-air pavilion like a flock of scurrying geese.

"Thanks for helping out," said Kelly. "It's valuable for each of the girls to have some undivided attention. It's so much more than just swimming lessons."

"Yes, I think so too. Even at their young age, girls can be so cruel to one another."

Kelly looked into the distance and nodded. "You can imagine what kind of teasing I got. To be this size and gay to boot. What a deadly combination."

"I can imagine how hard that was for you," Jill said with genuine sympathy. She might have been hurt and frustrated by the constant comparisons between her and Cristal, but it was nothing to what Kelly must have gone through as a child.

"Thanks for saying that. Time is changing things, but it can still be difficult. Fortunately, I have a wonderful partner who's helped me believe I'm okay as I am." Kelly's eyes filled. "It's been a blessing."

"I'd love to meet her sometime," Jill said. "I'm thinking of moving here and want to get to know as many people as I can. I already am a fan of Melanie and Susannah."

Kelly laughed. "They're as different as can be. Susannah owned the house here until Melanie bought it with some of the money from her huge divorce settlement. It was a good thing, too, because Susannah's husband left her with a whole mound of debts. Guess he was a gambler."

"Oh. She didn't see that coming?"

Kelly grinned, then sobered. "She can see some things into the future, but she sure missed that one. I've known Susannah since I was a small girl. She and my mother are friends. That's why I know so much about her."

Jill's mind was spinning. It seemed a very small community. Is that what she wanted?

"C'mon. Let's go to lunch. Susannah has a knack with food, making the simplest thing taste marvelous."

"A little magic, perhaps?" Jill said, arching an eyebrow.

Kelly chuckled. "Maybe so. Maybe so."

They walked together to the pavilion.

Observing the gathering of children laughing, talking, and eating, Jill's heart filled. She felt comfortable here. Though she hadn't wanted children with Jay, she wanted to spend time teaching them. Tomorrow morning, she'd call her school in New York, alert them that she'd decided to move, and then follow up on applying for jobs in Florida.

At the end of the meal, Jill stood with two other staff members she'd just met, chatting easily with them. Jennifer was the arts and crafts director, and Mike was in charge of water sports, under Jed's direction.

Jed approached her. "Is it okay if Kacy stops by my house on your way home so she can see the puppies. Emily invited her." His lips curved. "Besides, I think you and Niki would really hit it off."

"Sure. That sounds like fun." The meal she'd planned could wait until another day. Tonight, they'd have burgers for dinner, and maybe Brody or Greg would be willing to grill them outside.

Perfect!

CHAPTER NINE

A few miles inland in a pleasant, family-oriented development, Jed and Niki's two-story house stood out among so many one-story homes. The tan stucco exterior was brightened by a wide front door painted turquoise.

Jill pulled up in front of the house, shut off the engine, and turned to Kacy. "We can't stay too long. I'm sure Emily's mother is busy with the babies."

Kacy frowned. "I want to see the puppies."

"Yes, I know."

They walked up to the front door, passing by a triple stroller and a small bicycle parked next to the walkway. Before they could ring the bell, the door was thrown open and Emily stood there, a puppy wiggling in her arms.

"Hi, come on in. Mom and Dad are in the kitchen."

Jill and Kacy stepped inside.

Emily shut the door behind them. "Hurry, Kacy. The puppies are playing in the pool room. Follow me."

Jill tagged along behind them, observing the large open space to one side that appeared to be a huge family room. On the other side of the hallway, she noticed a bathroom and what looked like a den with shelves lined with books on either side of a large TV screen. Emily led them to the kitchen and then continued walking with Kacy to a room at the very back of the house next to sliding-glass doors that opened to a pool surrounded by a sizeable patio.

"Hi," said Jed. "Glad you could make it." He faced Jill holding a little girl, whose strawberry blonde hair obviously came from her mother, who was lifting a baby boy out of a highchair.

Emily's mother turned to her. Of average height, she was a pretty woman with soft red curls, hazel eyes, and a bright smile.

"Hi, I'm Niki." She rubbed the baby's stomach. "This is Luke. Jed is holding Nina, and Mark is the one in the middle highchair over there. He's about to throw a tantrum if I don't feed him. Here, will you hold Luke for me?"

Before she could explain that she didn't have much experience with babies, Luke was handed to her. Holding him awkwardly, Jill said, "I'm not used to little ones this age."

Niki smiled at her. "Believe me, you're doing just fine. As soon as I finish with Mark, we can put the babies in their play area and sit and talk."

Luke started to fuss. Not knowing what else to do, Jill jiggled him in her arms and began making silly noises for him. His face lit with pleasure. She laughed when he reached up and squeezed her nose.

"Better watch out," warned Jed. "Luke loves to tweak noses. Sometimes it hurts."

Jill took hold of Luke's arm and made circles in the air with it, keeping his hand as far away from her nose as possible. Even with suntan lotion on, her entire face was sunburned from the afternoon in the sun. Caught up in the game she was playing with him, Luke shrieked with joy and waved his free arm in the air.

From his place in his highchair, Mark imitated the noise, and then Nina joined in, delighted to be part of the chorus of shrieks.

Trying to imagine what life with triplets must be like on a daily basis, Jill started to laugh. "How do you do it?" she said, looking from Niki to Jed.

They exchanged amused glances and turned to Jill. "One minute, one hour, one day at a time," said Niki. "When Emily was born, I was careful about every little thing. With these three, I've learned that babies are a lot more adaptable than I thought."

Kacy entered the kitchen and trotted over to Jill. "Can I have a puppy?"

"I can't answer that. It's up to your parents, not me. But let's take a look." Jill turned to Niki. "Okay if I take Luke to look at the puppies?"

"Sure," Niki answered, "but hold on tight. He'll squirm and try to get down."

Jill followed Kacy into the next room and watched four little fluffy bundles of white and gray fur jostling each other while their mother looked on.

"How adorable." Jill leaned over to get a closer look and was almost pulled off her feet by the squirming boy in her arms. "Whoa! Hold still, Luke."

Jed swept into the room behind her. "Here, I'll take him. Niki's parents are due to arrive soon to help out. Go ahead and get a look at the pups. I'll give you a super deal if you take one." He took Luke in his arms and grinned at her.

"Are you going to get a puppy?" Kacy asked, her voice high with excitement. "Can I help you pick one out?" She pointed to a pup in the middle of a brawl. "That one. I want that one."

"Slow down," said Jill, chuckling softly. "First, I have to find a job and a place to live."

"You looking for a teaching job?" Jed asked, his eyebrows raised in surprise.

"Actually, I am. I've decided to make some changes in my life, and I'm looking for a teaching position at an elementary school. I'm a kindergarten teacher, but I've also taught fourth grade. Know of any jobs available?"

"I might," Jed said. "Let me check, and I'll let you know. If that doesn't work out, I'd suggest signing up as a substitute teacher."

"Yes, it might come to that." She'd tried substituting before and hadn't liked it.

Niki came into the room. "My parents are here, Jed. Would you please take Luke to them and give me a chance to talk with Jill?"

After he left, Niki said to Emily. "Why don't you show Kacy your room? Jill and I will be out by the pool if you need us."

The pups, exhausted now, curled up in a fluffy heap and settled down for a nap with their mother who seemed as calm to Jill as Niki was with her children.

Niki led Jill outside to a table protected by an umbrella, and they each sat in one of the four chairs surrounding it.

"Whew! A few treasured moments," said Niki, giving her a smile. "Now, tell me all about yourself. Jed has already mentioned meeting you and thought we'd like one another. It's been difficult for me to make new friends with the family situation as it is."

"I've been a schoolteacher for several years in the town where I live in upstate New York. I was married for two years, until my husband was killed in an automobile accident."

"I'm so sorry," said Niki softly.

Jill gazed at her sympathetic expression, drew a deep breath, and let it out slowly. She was done with hiding. "Actually, he was very abusive to me." It felt good to put it out in the open, freeing her from the past and the horrible secret she'd kept.

Niki reached across the table and squeezed her hand. "I'm glad you felt you could tell me."

"Thanks. I've kept it hidden for a long time. Now I'm trying my best to be honest about it. Especially because I've decided to move here to get a fresh start."

"Admirable," said Niki. "We lived outside of Boston in a small town along the south shore. I thought I might not like Florida, but I love it. It's a great place to raise children, and being able to be outdoors every day is healthy for them too."

"Jed mentioned you're here because your parents live close by."

An impish grin spread across Niki's face. "My mother nagged me until I got pregnant with Emily. And when no more pregnancies happened, she encouraged me to do IVF." Niki chuckled. "Now, I tell her it's only fair that I count on her to help. She loves it."

"Are you an only child?" Jill asked her.

"I have a brother a couple of years older than I am." Her hazel eyes gleamed. "In fact, I'd like you to meet him someday. I have a feeling you two might be compatible. He's single now too. His wife was very difficult, very selfish. As awful as it might sound, I'm glad he's rid of her."

Jill was about to comment when she was stopped by Kacy and Emily running toward them.

"Can Kacy stay for dinner?" Emily asked her mother.

Seeing the hesitation on Niki's face, Jill said, "Tell you what, girls, instead of that, why don't we invite Emily to Kacy's house for dinner?"

Niki smiled. "That would be nice."

"I'll bring Emily back home around eight o'clock."

Niki's face lit with pleasure. "Maybe Jed and I can have a quiet dinner by ourselves while my parents get the babies down for the night."

Jill turned to the girls. "Okay, it's settled. Emily will come to our house, Kacy, and stay for dinner."

Kacy's eyes grew wide. "You mean it, Jill? Emily can come for dinner?"

"Yes. Maybe this will be the first of many times," Jill said. Realizing this must not be allowed at home with her mother, she gave Kacy an encouraging smile, and stood.

"Guess the three of us should be leaving. I know two hungry men are there, waiting for dinner."

"Before you leave, come meet my parents," Niki said rising from her chair.

Following introductions to them, Jill learned that Dave Beachum used to work in the insurance business and was finding retirement a bit of a bore after being so busy. His wife, Carolyn, liked to be involved in community activities and kept busy with family while her husband played golf. Both adored their grandchildren.

At the end of their brief conversation, Niki said, "Jill's going to be moving here. I think Charlie should meet her."

Two sets of eyes turned to Jill.

Instead of feeling uneasy as she usually did when someone suggested that she be introduced to a man, Jill relaxed. Having a sister like Niki and with parents as pleasant as this, Charlie couldn't be a bad guy. And if she was going to make changes, she had to start meeting people.

Carolyn's gaze roamed over Jill. "Yes, she should meet Charlie," she said with a decisiveness Jill found flattering. "The two of them might get along just fine."

Kacy tugged on Jill's hand. "Can we go now?"

Jill smiled at Kacy's eagerness. "Emily, are you ready?"

Emily gave her mother a kiss before hugging her grandparents. "I'm going to Kacy's house for dinner," she announced proudly to them. "She's my new best friend."

"Very nice. For both of you." Carolyn beamed at her granddaughter, and gave Jill a quick wink.

The two girls raced out of the house and to Jill's car. At the sight of them, Jill's heart filled with happiness. She loved that

Kacy, who seemed so much like her, had already found a friend. She'd found a new friend too.

Jill pulled into the driveway of Seashell Cottage worried that Brody might consider her invitation to Emily as overstepping boundaries.

She parked the car and chuckled softly as Kacy and Emily raced around the house to the porch.

When she walked up to the front of the cottage, both girls were chatting with Brody and Greg.

Brody looked up at her with questioning eyes.

"Hope you don't mind ..." Jill began.

"It's great that you've invited Emily here," Brody said before she could finish. His glistening eyes told her how touched he was by it.

"I'm going to show Emily my shells," Kacy announced. "And then we're going to look for more. Okay, Jill?"

Surprised but pleased by the question directed to her, Jill glanced at Brody and said, "Sounds great. It's going to be a little while before I have dinner ready."

The girls dashed inside, leaving Jill alone with the men.

"I don't remember when I last saw Kacy this excited," said Brody softly. "I can't thank you enough."

"Emily and her parents are sweet people. They moved here several months ago from the Boston area, and with triplets in the house, her parents, Jed, and Niki, haven't had much time to socialize outside the family."

"Triplets?" gasped Greg. "That's a handful."

Jill sat down on the swing. "It's amazing. Both Jed and Niki seem like such calm, capable parents."

"I'd like to meet them sometime. Especially if the girls are going to be doing things together," said Brody.

"Maybe we can invite them over for dinner one night when Niki's parents are taking care of the triplets." As soon as she said it, Jill realized how far she'd come. She hadn't entertained at home for years. Jay had claimed he didn't like her friends, and after his death, she'd felt too incapable, too worthless to free herself from the way he'd made her feel.

"What's for dinner? Do we have time for a glass of wine?" asked Greg, getting to his feet.

"Yes, we do. We're having hamburgers. I hope one of you is willing to cook them on the grill while I put together the rest of the meal. Any takers?"

Brody raised his hand. "I'll do it. I owe you big time for making Kacy so happy."

Though she'd only done what she'd do for any little girl in need of a friend, a rush of pleasure went through her as his gaze settled on her with a look of approval.

CHAPTER TEN

The next few days flew by as everyone in the house got accustomed to their new routines. Kacy still had moments of stubbornness and defiance, but with a friend like Emily, she grew to understand that acting out wasn't the cool thing to do, and nobody in the house was going to let her get away with it.

At work, Jill discovered she loved helping Melanie in the office. When Melanie offered to lend her a number of books about child psychology, Jill eagerly took her up on it. One night, as Jill sat out on the porch, she decided to ask Brody what he thought about the book she was reading. Susan B. James had written a wonderful book about siblings and the problems they might encounter living in a family in which they felt they didn't belong. It had struck home with Jill, and she needed perspective.

When Brody joined her on the porch, Jill took that moment to reach out to him. "Do you mind if I ask you a few questions about the book I'm reading by Susan B. James?"

"Is that the one on siblings?" he asked, looking very interested.

"Yes. Melanie is lending me several books that I find intriguing. This is one of them. Do you know it?"

"Indeed, I do. It's one of my favorites. Families are fascinating. Sometimes helpful, sometimes not. When you think about it, you're born into a family. That doesn't always mean you like being part of it, or would ever choose a sibling for a friend."

"What she says makes sense, but thinking that way has

always made me feel guilty. Do you think it's healthy to be able to recognize those facts, or do you think they feed into something not necessarily nice within you?"

Brody studied her. "I believe it's okay to have those feelings. Dealing with some of the kids I work with in the school system, I find that many of them have reasons to feel that way. The disintegration of the family as a unit is very real."

"Society has changed," Jill said.

"Yes, it's changed a lot. I'm talking about families where parents are too busy, too lazy, or too addicted to substances to take the time to deal with their kids in a proper way."

Jill knew from the way he'd clenched his fists how sincere he was. "Have you ever had to confront parents or report child abuse?"

Brody nodded. "I've phoned Child Services about a few kids and have tried to talk to parents from time to time. Mostly, I listen and counsel kids in senior high school about choices. But you wanted to talk about siblings. Do you have siblings?"

"An older sister who is as different from me as two people could be," said Jill, hating the sound of defeat in her voice. "After reading the book, I wonder if it's best to get those differences out in the open and deal with them, or carry on knowing that neither one of us will ever be close to the other."

"Hmmm. I think it's always wise to get feelings out and deal with the consequences in a safe way." He grinned. "So, this sister of yours is ugly and dumb, huh?"

Jill laughed. "She's bright and beautiful."

"And?"

"And that's is all I'm saying now. But I'm going to think about our conversation, and when the time comes, I want to be able to sit down and talk to her about a number of things."

"Fair enough," Brody said easily. "I have no siblings and

always wished I'd had a brother. I was a late-in-life child and, unfortunately, both my parents are deceased. I guess you could say I'm a lonely only."

"Is that why you wanted more kids?"

"In part. But Allison wouldn't consider it."

"At one time, I thought I wanted a lot of children. But when I discovered the dark side of the man I married I knew I didn't want children with him." Jill paused, reconsidered, and blurted, "Now, I've begun thinking of it again."

Brody's gaze stayed on her, making her wish she hadn't been so open.

"Marriage is an interesting institution," said Brody. "You think you know someone, and after living with them for a while, you discover you don't know them at all."

Jill remained quiet. She knew he was thinking of his own marriage.

Brody shook his head. "Once was enough for me. I don't want to go through it again."

His words brought relief to her. They'd be staying in the house for the next several weeks, but there would be no need to impress, no need to be anything but who she was. He'd made his point with a quiet but emphatic tone she recognized.

A few days later, Emily and Kacy were drying off from swimming in the pool at the cottage when Kacy said, "I want short hair like Emily's."

Surprised, Jill sat up on the chaise lounge she'd been lying on. "I thought you liked your hair long."

Kacy shook her head. "Not anymore. Will you cut it for me?"

"If you going to get it cut, you need a professional to do it. But nothing can be done without your father's approval."

"Okay, I'm asking him now," Kacy said. She and Emily raced inside the house.

A few moments later, Brody and the girls headed toward her.

"Tell him yes, Jill," cried Kacy, jumping up and down in her excitement.

"What do you think, Jill? I know Allison likes Kacy's hair long, but I see how difficult it is to take care of after Kacy's been swimming, like now."

"The decision isn't mine to make, but I agree with you. It's difficult to handle those curls when they're wet or sticky from the salt air." She gazed from Kacy to Emily and back again. "It's also a friend thing," she said to Brody softly.

"Okay, Kacy, I say yes. Jill, do you know of someone who can cut a kid's hair?"

"I'm sure Niki does. I'll ask her." She lifted her phone and punched in the number. After explaining what was needed and getting the phone number of a woman who specialized in cutting children's hair, Jill thanked her and turned to Brody. "Niki says Ronnie at Kids' Kuts does a great job."

Brody gave her a little salute. "Okay, thanks. I'll give them a call."

As he headed inside, the two girls tagged behind him like chirping chicks following their mother.

Jill and Niki remained on the phone, chatting, until Niki was called away by the sound of crying.

But even after they ended the call, a warm feeling filled Jill. Niki seemed to enjoy their growing friendship as much as she.

The next afternoon, Jill sat in Kids Kuts waiting for Ronnie to finish with Kacy's hair. Brody's instructions were to do whatever was needed to make it easy to care for. Watching the long locks fall to the floor and the way the remaining hair curled softly around Kacy's face, Jill realized how right the new style was for her. Kacy's face, thinner now from the little bit of weight she'd lost, was beautifully framed by sun-streaked curls.

"All done," Ronnie announced, turning the chair around in a circle so that Kacy could get a look at herself in the mirror. "Like it?"

Kacy's eyes welled. "Yes, but my mother is going to be mad at me."

"Remember, this is a decision both you and your father made. While you're living in Florida, he wants you to be happy."

A smile crossed Kacy's face, chasing away her worried look. She patted her hair. "I like it. Now Emily and I are twins."

Ronnie and Jill exchanged amused glances, well aware the two girls looked nothing alike.

"Your hair suits you," said Ronnie. "You're going to be very happy you did this. It'll be a lot easier to manage."

"I love it," Jill said, smiling at Kacy. "I'm pretty sure your Dad will like it too."

Kacy hopped off the chair onto the floor and stared down at the piles of curls. When she looked up, her eyes were full once more.

Jill reached over and patted Kacy's shoulder. "Don't worry so. I'm sure your mother will understand."

Kacy shook her head. "No, she's going to be angry." She straightened. "But I don't care."

The ride back to the cottage was quiet. Kacy stared out the window lost in her own thoughts. Jill let it go. Brody would deal with his daughter's worries. She'd said all she could to reassure Kacy.

Moments after Jill parked in the driveway, Kacy was out of

the car and running to the front of the house. Jill stepped out onto the driveway. Unable to resist, she walked over to one of the bougainvillea plants nearby and bent over to admire a pink flower. She loved all the colorful flowers and greenery of this sub-tropical area. The tall palm trees were her favorite. She liked to listen to the sound of their fronds whispering in the breeze, as if they were sharing secrets with one another. She even liked how that sound turned to one of irritation at being disturbed when afternoon storms came along.

She looked up as Brody and Kacy came toward her.

Smiling, she said, "What do you think, Brody? Doesn't Kacy look adorable?"

"Yes, indeed." He wrapped an arm around Kacy. "Now, my little girl wants to show her best friend." His crooked grin sent light to his eyes. "We're going to Emily's house, but I'll be back in time for dinner. I'm looking forward to a nice relaxing evening. We're done with the painting on the inside of the house. We'll start on the outside soon."

"How is Greg doing with all this work?"

"He's working his best to be helpful, but it isn't easy for him with his arm in a cast. He's been trying to convince me to set up practice here and help him with his growing business part-time."

"Oh?" She was surprised by the idea.

"I told him no, maybe in the future, but not now. Not until certain things are settled." He glanced at Kacy.

Understanding the silent message, Jill nodded.

"Let's go, Dad." Kacy took hold of her father's hand and tugged.

"Better hurry," Jill said. "I know one anxious girl is waiting to see her friend's new look."

He laughed. "Women! They start this at such a young age."

"It's all for you men," she teased, and shared the laugh that followed with him.

She waved them off and walked down to the beach, flipped off her sandals and entered the lacy edge of the water warmed by the sun. The water surged and retreated, caressing her ankles with its salty touch. She gazed out over the blue expanse of water, feeling as if she were standing at the edge of her new life.

As nature carried on around her, Jill let her thoughts drift. Strange as it might seem to others, she measured her own progress for making changes in her life to Kacy's. A dominant, criticizing mother could do so much damage. She vowed to herself to be kind to any children she might one day have.

"Look out!" A sharp voice startled her out of her reverie in time to duck a frisbee headed right for her.

"Sorry," said a teenaged boy.

"No problem," she replied, reminded how quickly things could change. She headed back to the house, wondering what changes the future held for her.

Brody returned to the house alone. "Kacy's staying for dinner at the Carters' house."

"How'd it go?"

He smiled and gave her a thumbs up sign. "Emily loved seeing Kacy's new style and readily agreed to Kacy's idea that they were special sisters, if not twins."

"It's wonderful they've quickly become so close. I hope they always will be. They're adorable together."

"Yeah. Emily's a great kid. Jed and Niki are wonderful parents. I spent a little time talking to Niki. She really likes you, Jill."

"I like her too," Jill said. "She and I have already agreed to set aside time to do things together. In fact, as I suggested earlier, maybe we can invite Jed and Niki here for dinner."

Brody patted his stomach. "Speaking of dinner..."

She laughed. "Hold your horses, cowboy. I haven't quite decided what to serve. I was thinking of steak ..."

"I'll grill it," Brody said, cutting her off.

"Okay," Jill said. "It's a deal. Let me check with Greg."

"Where is he?" Brody said, looking around.

"In his room. He said something about getting cleaned up."

She left Brody in the kitchen, went to Greg's door, and knocked.

Greg opened the door with a flourish and stood there grinning.

Jill took in his freshly creased khaki pants, golf shirt, and the wetness in his hair from a shower. "Wow! You look great! Are you going out?"

"As a matter of fact, I am. Hope it doesn't ruin your dinner plans, but a friend of mine called and invited me to her house. I said yes."

"How sweet! Of course, I don't mind. Brody is going to grill a steak I bought on sale. There will be plenty left over if you change your mind."

He gave her a quick hug. "I'll be fine. You three go ahead and enjoy dinner here."

"Kacy's at Emily's."

Greg's eyes lit with mischief. "Then it's very convenient I'm going out. You two can have a nice evening together."

"You know it's not like that between us," Jill protested.

"Oh, yes. I forgot," Greg said, chuckling softly as he walked away.

She followed him into the kitchen.

Greg handed Brody a bottle of wine. "This is a very nice cab, perfect with a special steak dinner. You two enjoy a quiet evening together. I'm meeting a friend of mine for dinner."

"A female friend," Jill said, leaving her wondering why Greg was being so direct about making this dinner seem like a date. He knew very well she needed time to heal before she contemplated a relationship with another man. And Brody had made it very clear he had no intention of a serious relationship with anyone.

"A female friend, huh? You talking about Barb Mitchell?" Brody said to Greg.

"The very one." Color rose in Greg's cheeks. "She and Annie were such old friends."

"Yeah, well I think she wants more than that with you, Uncle Greg. Better be careful."

"We're friends. That's all. But I'm not one to pass up a tasty meal. She's a wonderful cook."

"Oh!" A soft gasp escaped Jill. She'd been trying hard to improve her cooking, but she needed more practice.

Greg grinned at her. "Don't worry, Jill, you're a wonderful cook too. I just need an evening out."

"Well, then, you'd better get going," teased Brody. "I have an enjoyable evening planned right here."

Smiling at the two of them, Greg gave a little wave and left the room.

Brody turned to her. "Well? Should we get started? I can't remember the last time I had time to spend an evening with a beautiful woman."

Jill decided to play along with him. "Or I with a handsome, kind man."

Brody opened and poured the wine into two glasses. Taking one, he handed it to her. The other, he lifted to his nose. "Mmm. Smells like berries. Let's see."

Jill took a sip, allowing the silky substance to slide down her throat slowly. She wasn't a connoisseur, but she knew excellent wine when she tasted it. This was delicious.

"What do you think?" Brody asked her.

"It's lovely. Maybe we'd better change up the meal a bit. If you take care of seasoning the steak, we can let it sit while I make a French dressing for the salad. And why don't I put together lemon and garlic roasted potatoes? It's an old recipe, and I think it'll be perfect with a meal like this."

"It sounds great," said Brody. "Let's sit on the porch and relax. It's been another long week, and it isn't over."

"Give me time to get the potatoes in, and I'll join you."

A short while later, Jill stepped out onto the porch and took a seat in one of the rockers. As always, sitting on the porch, gently rocking in her chair, Jill felt her worries melt away. The world seemed to be at a peaceful rest.

"Thanks for helping with Kacy today," said Brody in a chair next to hers. "You've been wonderful about spending time with her. I think it's paying off. Already, she's a very different girl from the one who first came here. I'm hoping it will continue. I've decided to ask Allison to allow Kacy to live with me."

"But Allison would have her some of the time, wouldn't she?"

"Certainly," said Brody. "A mother's presence is important. And as she grows, it will become important for Kacy and her mother to share all those girly things we guys know nothing about."

Jill pressed forward with a question that had been itching her mind. "What happened to Allison? Was she always as difficult as she seems to be? Kacy had a very emotional time when she first saw her hair. She was afraid her mother would be mad at her."

Brody let out a sigh. "Allison grew up poor, and she has several ideas about how certain people should look and act— things that were not part of her life. Money and material objects are important to her. She met Marcus at a medical meeting we attended and, believe me, when she realized how rich he was, she didn't hesitate to go after him. He jumped at the chance. She's a beautiful woman."

"Kacy's going through an awkward stage, but she's going to be beautiful one day, too."

"Yes, but I hope she will be a very different person from her mother." Brody stared out at the water. "It doesn't say much for my judgement that Allison and I even got together. And then I should've realized that I was never going to be able to give her all the things she wanted."

"That's a pretty harsh assessment of yourself," said Jill, remembering how easily she'd been taken in by a man who turned out to be the total opposite of who she thought he was.

Brody turned to her and smiled. "I'm glad we can talk candidly about our past. It's rare that I open up about it, and it feels exhilarating."

"Shall we take a walk? I find that feels helpful too."

Brody set down his wine glass and offered his hand to her. "Madame, will you walk with me?"

Jill laughed, rose, performed a small curtsey, and took his hand. "Thank you, kind sir."

They walked out onto the sand still warm from the heat of the afternoon sun. No words were spoken as they moved easily side by side, matching steps. Jill had never felt more comfortable with a man. Nothing was expected of her beyond friendship.

Brody turned to her and smiled. "Nice, huh?"

"Very nice," she replied, meaning it with her whole heart.

CHAPTER ELEVEN

As they returned to the house, the sun was beginning to lower toward the horizon. The clouds at the horizon were a pale-yellow, but would become brighter pink and orange when sunset took place.

"It's so humid today, I'm going to jump into the pool before fixing dinner. Okay with you?" Jill said to Brody.

"Sounds refreshing to me. I'm going to sprint ahead to get a few kinks out."

Jill watched him leave, observing his easy gait and tight butt. She wondered what it would be like to make love to him. Surprised by her unexpected thoughts, she pushed the outrageous notion aside.

Inside her room, she slipped out of her clothes and into her pink bathing suit. Her new life here would afford her the opportunity to do something as simple as this—a swim in the pool after a walk on the beach.

Her cell phone rang as she reached for a towel. She stopped to pick it up and saw a number she didn't recognize.

"Hello? Is this Jillian Conroy?" said a deep voice.

"Speaking."

"Hi, this is Charlie Beachum, Niki Carter's brother. I'm going to be in town, and Niki thought I should meet you. I'm wondering if I could take you to dinner next Friday."

Jill's fingers turned cold. She'd been on only two dates in the last year and they'd both been disasters, with her dates wanting more than she was ready to give. She was unsure she could trust again.

"I thought we'd go to Gavin's restaurant at the Salty Key Inn. Their food is great, and it's a nice place to sit and talk," he continued.

Jill reminded herself how important her growing friendship was with Niki and swallowed hard. "That sounds very nice. Thank you."

"I'll pick you up at seven, if that's okay." He sounded pleased, and Jill was suddenly glad she'd said yes.

"That's perfect. I'll be ready. Thank you."

"No, thank you! Niki would never let me forget it if I didn't call. And we all love Niki," he said, affection in his voice.

"That we do. See you Friday."

Jill clicked off the call, hoping she hadn't just made a mistake.

Outside, sitting in the pool, chatting with Brody, tension over the upcoming date eased. If she could talk like this with Brody, she shouldn't worry about her evening with Charlie. He'd only asked her out for dinner, for heaven's sake.

"How's the house hunting going?" Brody said to her now.

"I haven't talked with a local realtor yet. I'm just perusing the newspaper ads. Once my house sells, I'll begin to investigate in earnest. Summer is an excellent time to be looking."

His gaze settled on her with a questioning look. "You're really going to do it? Make a big change like this? It's a pretty gutsy move."

She stilled and then straightened. "Yes, it is, but one I need to make. I probably should've done something like this years ago."

"Understandable. It's so easy to get stuck in a situation and feel like there's no way out."

Brody stood up from the pool steps and took off, swimming the length of the pool and back again with long, smooth strokes. Watching him, she wondered how he could make the most difficult of tasks seem so easy. He was a wizard at fixing up the house, working quietly beside Greg, doing beautiful work naturally.

"Guess I'd better get out and start up the grill. I'm hungry. How about you?"

"Yes, and I could use another glass of wine. Like Greg told us, it's lovely."

She climbed out of the pool, self-conscious about her less than perfect body. But when she turned around, admiration gleamed in Brody's eyes as he studied her. Their gazes met. Heat flooded her cheeks. She'd never felt particularly attractive, especially after she was married. Seeing Brody's reaction, she felt like a shy teenager searching for a way to stay cool as the football captain passed by her in the hall at school. She reached for a towel to cover herself up.

He gave her an impish grin as he climbed out of the pool. "I've decided I like pink. You in that suit —" his words stopped abruptly at the ringing of his cell. He picked up his phone. "Hello?"

As Jill dried off, she couldn't help overhearing his end of the conversation. "Sure. I'll pick her up in the morning. Maybe Emily would like to spend the day here. I'll take the afternoon off so I can take them to the movies. Kacy mentioned it to me. Okay, see you then. Thank you."

Brody clicked off the call and turned to her with a wide grin. "Guess we have the whole evening to ourselves. Kacy is spending the night with Emily." The look he gave her made it clear he was delighted.

The fluttering in Jill's stomach felt like a flock of butterflies trying to break free. Standing there in only swim trunks, he looked adorable ... and so very sexy. She cleared her throat which had gone dry. "If you light the grill, I'll begin the rest of the dinner as soon as I change my clothes."

"Deal." He wrapped a towel around his waist and followed her inside.

Standing in front of the mirror in her bathroom she contemplated the image in front of her. Her body was not thin, not fat, but pleasantly rounded. By some standards, she needed to lose weight, but she was unlikely ever to be a model and, frankly, didn't aspire to be one. *How had it happened that women and girls never felt okay about the way they looked?* she asked herself. It didn't seem to bother men if they weren't "perfect."

She fluffed her hair with a towel and let it go every which way. Tousled is what Frederick had called it. She applied a little mascara and eye shadow, which he'd also told her completed the look. Her skin, she noted, was turning a soft brown from the sun. She'd never felt better.

Dressed in shorts and a tank top, she padded into the kitchen, looking forward to spending time with a man she liked.

He looked up at her when she walked into the room, and smiled. "I've poured another glass of wine for each of us, and the grill is lit. So, the rest is in your hands."

"Thanks. A simple salad sound okay? The potato casserole should be done soon."

After she checked the casserole, it seemed only natural that they both headed for the porch. As inviting as the beach was for a place to walk or run, the porch was the perfect place to sit and watch others and to enjoy their lush surroundings.

"What would you say if I was interested in setting up a

summer camp of my own one day?" said Jill. "I could teach for the school year and run a camp for special kids during the summer months."

His brow wrinkled with concern. "What do you mean by 'special kids'?"

"Kids who've been bullied, kids who need extra assurance about themselves, kids who need to enjoy some experiences to help build their self-confidence."

"Would you try to coordinate through the local school system?"

"Yes, that was my thought."

He cupped his chin with his right hand and gazed out over the Gulf where gulls were circling, their wings white against the darkening sky. "Something like that could be very valuable to certain kids. I work with older kids through the school, but on my own, I work with younger kids assisting one of my friends who coaches soccer. They would love an opportunity like that. You might even be able to write a grant to help with the funding."

Jill's pulse jumped with excitement. Doing something like this would make her life meaningful. She'd be reaching out to others while she healed herself.

The sound of the buzzer on the oven brought Jill to her feet. "The casserole is ready. Do you want to cook the steak while I fill water glasses and then toss the salad?"

"Sure." Brody got to his feet and followed her inside.

"Something smells delicious," he commented as they headed into the kitchen.

"A family favorite," Jill said.

Brody went to the counter where he'd left the seasoned steak. "I'm guessing this will take around ten minutes, give or take a minute or two. The grill is nice and hot."

"I'll be ready," she said, impressed by the way he'd accepted the role of grillmaster.

Living in the same house with Greg and Brody, Jill had a better idea of what her marriage should have been like. Both men were kind and supportive of her and didn't try to take away chunks of her self-esteem.

By the time Brody brought in the steak from the grill, the table was set, salad tossed, and casserole ready to serve. After letting it rest, he sliced the steak and served it.

Sitting opposite him at the kitchen table, sharing a wonderful meal, Jill vaguely remembered evenings like this as a young child.

"Nice, peaceful dinner tonight," Brody commented.

Jill smiled. "I was thinking the same thing, remembering what it was like when I was young. Back then, fussing children were not allowed at the dinner table. It was a peaceful time for all of us."

"Kacy's coming along, but she still tries to dictate what we will or won't have for dinner. I say serve a healthy meal and let her choose whether to eat it or not. It's obviously become such a game between her mother and her."

"At camp, she's doing a better job of eating what's put in front of her," said Jill. "Susannah is a wonderful cook of healthy, well-balanced meals."

"I've noticed that Kacy's already lost some weight," Brody said. "I'm pleased it's happening naturally."

"Yes. The pressure on kids to look a certain way is astounding. No wonder some children rebel against those expectations."

His gaze slid over her. "Were you one of them as a kid?"

"No." She shook her head. "I didn't even try. I knew I would never measure up to my sister, and instead of rebelling, I hid in my room. When I was older, I did my best to ignore her barbs and pretended nothing was wrong." She clapped a hand over her mouth. "God! I must sound like the biggest loser ever."

Brody reached across the table, took hold of her hand, and studied her with a sympathetic smile. "No, you sound like someone who's been hurt by the comparisons you talk about. The shame of it is that no matter what your sister looks or acts like, you needn't have worried. You are perfect just the way you are—a beautiful woman."

To hide her emotions, Jill drew in a quivering breath. "Wow! You're so skilled at your job. I bet your students love you."

He sat back in his chair. "Thanks. That means a lot."

"I'm serious. It's so easy to talk to you."

"It sounds so simple, doesn't it? Just sit and talk to someone. The thing is, behind every word is an experience, a concern, sometimes pain that has to be dealt with. It can take a long time to resolve certain issues."

"Oh, my God! You think I need a lot of help?"

He laughed. "No, I don't. I think you're already on your way to doing something about your past by forging ahead with a new future for yourself. I must say, I envy that. I sometimes feel stuck, but I don't want to move away from Kacy. If only Allison would let me have Kacy most of the time, she could travel more and be part of her husband's social business life."

"She married a doctor, right?"

"Yes, he's a plastic surgeon." Brody's mouth became pinched. "His job is making people look perfect. Allison's already had a surgery or two. You can see how this would tie into her insecurities and why she puts so much pressure on Kacy. It's disturbing, really."

They finished their meal in silence.

"How about a cup of coffee?" Jill said, rising from her chair.

"That would be great," said Brody, getting to his feet and

grabbing his plate. "Need any help? The Tampa Bay Rays have a game tonight. Want to watch it with me?"

"Sure. Go get settled in front of the television, and I'll bring your coffee to you."

She got the coffee maker going and then set to work loading the dishwasher. After sharing a meal with a man who appreciated her, she didn't mind cleaning up at all.

She poured them each a cup of coffee and went into the living room. Brody smiled at her and patted the seat on the couch next to him. "They're ahead 3-2. It should be an exciting game."

"You're a fan of theirs?"

"Normally, I root for the Phillies, but as long as I'm in Florida, I'm rooting for the Rays."

"Very fair of you," Jill teased.

He laughed. "Why not?"

They sat quietly until the batter for the Rays hit a home run. Then, both of them were on their feet shouting. Caught in the excitement of the moment, Jill turned to Brody.

He pulled her to him and gave her a hug. "Good game, huh?"

Heart pounding with alarming speed, she could only nod. His strong arms around her, the sexy, spicy smell of his aftershave had her trembling. For a moment, she leaned against his broad chest wishing she could hold onto this moment. He made her feel safe and daring at the same time.

He lifted her chin until she was looking into his eyes, their green color filled with longing.

He bent down to kiss her.

She froze, then melted as his lips met hers. She knew his kiss would be special, but the heat that went through her, settling at her feminine core was something she'd never known.

When he pulled back, he looked as dazed as she felt.

Shaken, she stepped away. "I've got a date on Friday," she blurted, trying not to react to the magical moment that had just happened between them.

"Really?" He gave her an impish smile, letting her know he was aware of how she was feeling.

She gave him a weak smile. "I thought it best to get that out there. I'm not interested in any relationships."

"But you're going on a date," he said quietly.

"It's a favor. For Niki."

"I see," he replied. "I don't think a kiss between us is going to ruin that date, do you?"

Jill pulled herself together. "No, of course not. And like I said, I'm only doing what Niki asked of me."

"Good." His handsome face brightened.

She stood still, wondering if he was going to try to kiss her again. When he sat down on the couch, disappointment pricked her.

He grinned up at her. "The game's not over, Jill."

"Oh, right." Jill lowered herself onto the couch beside him, her heart pounding so hard she wondered if he could hear it.

He turned to her, his expression tender. "I'm glad we have this time together." His eyes became green pools of desire as he leaned toward her.

"Me, too," she replied, before his lips met hers in another kiss that sent her emotions soaring.

CHAPTER TWELVE

After a restless night of imagining what else Brody could do with those lips of his, Jill awoke in an unsettled mood. She got up and splashed water on her face, hoping to wash away the turbulence in her mind. She told herself if she was going to forge a new life, she couldn't be involved with a man who was dealing with a difficult family situation and who would move back to Pennsylvania in a couple of weeks. Besides, she reminded herself, she owed it to Niki to meet her brother with an open mind.

Later, when she walked into the kitchen, Greg was sitting at the kitchen table.

"'Morning!" she chirped with effort. "How was your date last night?"

Smiling, he shook his head. "Having dinner with Barb Mitchell is no date. But she does have someone she'd like me to meet."

"Oh, really? Anyone you know?"

"She wouldn't tell me who it is, but I've agreed to come to her house next week where a group of her friends is gathering." His eyes twinkled. "At my age and all alone, how could I refuse?"

"Sounds very interesting. Where's Brody?"

"He went to pick up Kacy and Emily. This morning, we'll paint the little pool shed. He's going to take the afternoon off."

"I'm going to grab a cup of coffee and take a walk on the beach."

As she poured the steaming liquid into her cup, she

recalled how innocently last evening's coffee time had started, and how wonderfully surprising it had turned out be. Brody Campbell epitomized everything she was looking for in a man. But it was a case of too soon and in the wrong place. She sighed. Her timing had always sucked.

She set the mug down and leaned against the counter to steady herself. As much as she might want a simple summer romance, she couldn't allow herself to get involved with Brody.

"You all right, Jill?" Greg asked from behind her.

Turning to him, she nodded and forced a smile. "I will be. Thanks."

She grabbed the mug of coffee and took it outside where the birds, the flowers, and the steady movement of the Gulf water would settle her.

A couple of days later, Jill entered the house at Camp Sunnyside eager for another day. She hadn't felt this excited about a job in a long time.

Melanie greeted her with a smile and waved her into the office. "How about helping me with the financials? Susannah thinks it would be a wise idea for you to learn all about the business side of running the camp. It would give me more personal time."

Alarm ran through Jill. "Are you okay? Susannah doesn't see something awful in the future, does she?"

Melanie laughed. "Quite the opposite. She's predicting that I'm going to meet a man. Not that I trust her intuition. Believe me, I don't have any interest in marrying again. But I do think having you learn office procedures is something we should do for the camp."

Relieved, Jill nodded. "Okay, I'd like that. As much as I love working with the kids, I'm interested by all the work behind the scenes."

"Right after lunch, we'll begin. I know Kelly is counting on your help for the swim class. By the way, I think Kacy is doing very well. Something as simple as a haircut can make a difference at that age." Melanie chuckled. "She told me that she and Emily are true sisters, that they wanted to be twins, but instead are sisters of the heart. Adorable, huh?"

"It's very sweet. I can only guess what she's gone through at home and am cheering her on."

"Yes," said Melanie, resting her gaze on her. "I see how kind and encouraging you are to all the children. It's a nice trait."

"Thanks. I'll meet up with you after lunch."

Outside, Jill hurried over to the pool. The eight-year-old class was about to begin. Kelly, a trained instructor, didn't really need her help, but the two of them had formed a bond of friendship that Jill liked, and sitting with the girls to chat after their lesson had proved very insightful.

Today, the girls were preparing for a race among themselves.

"Remember," said Kelly, "this is a way to test how well you're doing, not whether you're pretty, or smart, or anything else. You're all improving, and that's what's important. Some of you will be faster than others. It'll be fun to see how that changes over time. Understand?"

The girls bobbed their heads and rocked back and forth on their feet restlessly.

"Okay, we'll start with four of you and then do the second half of the class with four more. Jill will time you."

Kelly handed Jill a stopwatch, a clipboard and pen, and directed her to the far end of the pool.

Jill had remained true to her word by not having too much interaction with Kacy, but she couldn't help a thread of nervousness that wove through her. Kacy wasn't a great swimmer in the class, but she'd been trying to get better. And living with her, getting to know her through their times together on the beach, Jill had grown fond of the sweet girl that sometimes hid behind Kacy's difficult behavior.

Standing at the end of the pool, Jill cried out, "On your mark! Get set! Go!!"

Three girls and Kacy dove into the water. Arms flailing, feet kicking, the four girls headed toward her. Emily led the group with Kacy at the end.

"C'mon, Kacy!" Jill cried.

As if she'd heard her, Kacy surged ahead but quickly slowed, coming in last.

"Great job!" Kelly said. "Who's the winner, Jill?"

"Emily came in first, Jenna second, Amy third, and Kacy fourth."

"Excellent. Now hurry out so you can cheer for the girls in the second race."

The girls scrambled out of the pool and ran to get their towels. Gathered in a group they watched as the second group dove into the pool. All but Kacy cheered them on.

Jill noticed but was too busy to say anything to her.

After the second group of winners was announced, Kelly gathered the girls together and urged them to sit in a circle.

"Great race, girls," said Kelly sitting beside Jill. "The biggest prizes go to Kacy and Skye."

"But I came in first," said a girl named Molly.

"Yes, indeed, and you will, of course, get a prize. But today's race wasn't about who came in first, it was about trying hard and doing the best you could. The person who comes in last isn't a loser. She's a winner for trying her best. Do you girls understand what I'm saying?"

"Does it mean we shouldn't want to be first?" said Molly,

looking confused.

Kelly laughed. "No, you're an excellent swimmer and should always try to do your best. If it means you come in first, that's great. But it doesn't mean that the others don't deserve recognition too. In fact, you're all getting the same prize. Why? Because I noticed that each of you tried hard. If you hadn't, you wouldn't get anything."

Jill handed them each a granola bar. "Congratulations, girls!"

"And now I'll give out the ribbons," Kelly said. "First prize is blue. Here you go, Molly and Emily." She handed out all the ribbons.

Jill watched Kacy study her yellow ribbon and then put it aside. And when the bell rang for lunch, Jill noticed Kacy left it behind.

Without making a comment, Jill picked up the ribbon and tucked it into her pocket. Hopefully, she'd have a chance to give it back to Kacy privately, so they could talk about it.

After the traditional buffet lunch, Jill headed into Melanie's office, pleased to be given this opportunity to learn. She'd been thinking lately of not going back to teaching in a school, but doing something different with kids, maybe even, as she'd mentioned to Brody, running a camp of her own.

Melanie spent time showing Jill the layout of the office, where files were, what forms were needed for each step of the process. "In today's world, we have to be very careful with private information in print or online. Because we offer scholarships, financial information is especially confidential."

Jill studied the unlocked drawer where files were placed in alphabetical order.

"You'll notice some folders are thicker than others. That's

because families whose children have success here usually send more than one child." Melanie smiled. "It helps to keep camp registrations filled. In fact, we sometimes have a waiting list."

"I've forgotten. How long have you been doing this? Everything seems so well organized."

"Almost eight years," said Melanie. "But I have some business experience and that's helped."

"Kelly mentioned how the camp started. It's really impressive to see how you two were able to come together to do something like this."

Melanie shook her head. "I don't know how we did it. Susannah and I are total opposites. Even now, all her spooky ideas of knowing about the future worry me. And Lord help us if she ever tried to run the business. But she's one of the sweetest, kindest people I know, and that goes a long way with me."

"A fabulous cook too," said Jill.

"That too," agreed Melanie. "And so much more."

As Jill looked through the materials, she discovered that some of the promo information was outdated. "Do we need to get fresh photographs and more up-to-date info for these?"

Melanie picked up one of the brochures and frowned. "Yes, we do. Maybe that's something you can work on for us. We should consider a new theme, too. 'Sunny Days and Ways For Kids' doesn't quite do it."

"Okay, I'll work on it. I like to create new ideas."

"I'm so glad you decided to join us," said Melanie. "I'll leave you here becoming familiar with the office routines. Tomorrow, we'll work on the financials. I've given you a lot to think about. Now, I've promised to check on the summer showcase."

"Summer showcase?"

"Yes, at the end of the summer we hold an open house and have the campers demonstrate the skills they have learned, and we also have a talent show for those campers and staff who want to participate. It plays a big part in bringing everyone together. You're welcome to enter too."

Jill laughed. "Thanks."

"You might want to talk to Susannah about it," Melanie said in a breezy manner as she left the room.

Jill felt goosepimples scurry across her shoulder, and shivered. She didn't like Susannah knowing things ahead of time. Besides, Jill knew she sounded like a yowling cat when she tried to sing.

When she arrived at the cottage, she noticed Brody's truck missing and let out a sigh of relief. She knew she was acting foolish, but she still didn't know how to deal with the feelings he'd opened up. It was sometimes awkward to be around him. Jill realized he was waiting for a signal from her as to how he should proceed, but she was too confused to be clear with him about it. Besides, tonight she had a date with Charlie.

Greg was in the kitchen when she walked in.

"Hungry?" she said, smiling at him.

"Getting there. Thought I'd sit on the porch for a while. Want to join me?"

"Sure. It sounds delightful. Charlie Beachum is going to pick me up at seven o'clock. It will be nice to relax a little before I have to get ready for our date."

"A date? That's a big step for you isn't it?" His smile was kind.

"Yes, it is. I've avoided dating for so long, but if I'm going to make changes, I need to do this."

"Seems to me a certain someone right here might be

interested," he commented.

Jill frowned and gazed out the window, searching for the right words.

When she turned to Greg, he smiled. "A little awkward, is it?"

Pleased he understood, she nodded. "Brody has a lot of family issues and will be returning to the Philadelphia area in a couple of weeks."

"I see," Greg said, but Jill had the impression he'd held back a lot more than he'd allowed himself to say.

"I'm going to fix myself a glass of iced tea. Would you like some?" Jill said, happy to end the conversation about Brody.

"Thank you. That sounds wonderful."

Jill poured two glasses of the iced tea she kept in the refrigerator, handed one to Greg, and followed him out to the front porch, where she settled into one of the chairs with a sigh.

"Busy day?" Greg asked.

"Yes, the girls in the swimming class had a race this morning. Kacy won fourth place and she was not happy about it." Jill pulled the ribbon out of her pants pocket. "In fact, she left this behind."

"Guess it wasn't showy enough."

"But Kacy tried very hard and has improved her swimming. I'm really proud of her."

Jill jumped when she heard a voice behind her say, "You're proud of Kacy? For what?"

Kacy followed her father onto the porch.

"You scared me," said Jill. "I didn't hear you slide the door open."

"Yeah, guess you were busy talking," Brody said, lowering himself onto the swing. "What were you saying about Kacy?"

Kacy slid onto the seat of the swing next to him and gave

her a quizzical look.

Jill decided to make this a teaching moment for Kacy. "I was telling Greg how proud I am of Kacy." She rose and held out the yellow ribbon to Kacy. "I think you forgot this. Kacy was in a swimming race this morning and did well."

"No, I didn't! I came in last," cried Kacy, folding her arms in front of her, refusing to take the ribbon.

"Two groups of four raced the length of the pool," Jill explained to Brody. "The purpose was to see how much they've all improved. And Kacy did very well. She's learned a lot and is a much better swimmer. In fact, all the girls have done so well, Kelly is thinking about doing some water ballet with them."

Kacy's eyes lit up. "Ballet?"

Jill smiled. "That's right. You can be proud of yourself, Kacy. You and all the girls."

Kacy reached for the ribbon. "I can't wait to do ballet. Mom wouldn't let me take classes."

"This is different from regular ballet class," Jill said. "But I think you'll like it."

"I'm going to put this in my room. Okay, if I use my computer?" Kacy said to her father, getting to her feet.

Brody nodded. "Yes, and then I'm going to take you and Uncle Greg out to dinner. Jill has a date."

Kacy looked up at Jill, crestfallen. "You do?"

Touched by a show of caring, Jill nodded. "With Emily's uncle."

"Oh," said Kacy, before hurrying inside.

In the awkward silence that followed, Brody said, "Thanks for helping Kacy understand you don't have to be number one to be a winner."

"You're welcome," Jill said, thinking it was a good lesson for herself.

CHAPTER THIRTEEN

As the time drew closer to seven o'clock, the nerves inside Jill started to thrum. She reminded herself it was only a date, a favor for a friend.

When, at last, she heard the doorbell ring, her nerves did a tap dance throughout her body. She was glad that Brody, Greg, and Kacy were not in the house to witness how scared she was. She glanced at herself again in the mirror. Her turquoise sleeveless dress fit her nicely and looked great with her tanned skin. Wisps of her hair, bleached by the sun, caressed her face and accented her hazel eyes. Her new, cubic zirconia earrings sparkled in her ears.

Taking a steadying breath, she headed for the door.

Through the glass, she saw a tall, lean man with auburn hair waiting patiently for her. She felt a smile cross her face as she opened the door.

When he saw her, his eyes lit. "Hello, I'm Charlie Beachum. My sister sent me here," he joked.

Jill felt her nerves steady, and laughed. "She called me an hour ago to make sure I'd be ready."

"Sounds like her," he chuckled. His gaze swept over her. "You look great. I hope you're hungry because Gavin's is supposed to be fantastic."

"I've heard great things about it. I'm starving."

He grinned. "I'm glad you're not one of those women who doesn't enjoy dining out."

She returned his smile. "Let me get my purse, and we can leave."

He waited by the door while she hurried into her bedroom. Anticipation of a pleasant evening together replaced her nervousness. Charlie seemed a very nice man, relaxed and easy to talk to. He wasn't bad-looking either. He and Niki shared some features; she had bright red hair while his was a dark auburn in a spiky style. His lean body was well shaped with broad shoulders.

She closed the door behind her and he led her to a gray convertible. "I put the top up so the wind wouldn't mess with your hair."

"Thanks. Another suggestion from Niki?"

He grinned. "She wants this date to go well. Niki really likes you."

"She's been great to me. Some day when I get up my courage, I'm planning on giving her and Jed a night off."

"Triple trouble plus Emily? Pretty scary," Charlie commented, making Jill laugh.

A short while later, they drove through the entrance of the Salty Key Inn and to the rear parking lot by Gavin's.

"I looked up some information on the restaurant," Jill confessed. "It's a great story about the three sisters who own it. And maybe we'll see Petey the Peacock, the bird that roams the property of the Salty Key Inn."

Charlie got out of the car, walked around it, and held the door for her as she tried her best to exit the passenger side gracefully.

He took her elbow, and they made their way to the entrance. Twinkling lights in the shrubbery led the way. The trunks of nearby tall palm trees were wrapped with the same kind of twinkling lights, creating a soft glow around them.

When they stepped inside, Jill took a moment to look

around at the wood paneling, crystal chandeliers and wall sconces, and elegant furnishings.

A hostess greeted them, then led them to a table in an alcove next to a window overlooking a small garden of colorful hibiscus, bougainvillea, oleander, and other tropical plants.

"How beautiful," Jill murmured as she was seated.

"Your waiter will be right with you," the hostess said, and walked away.

"Yeah, if the food is as great as this place looks, we're in for a treat," Charlie said. "Shall I order wine?"

"That would be nice," Jill said. "Greg, one of my housemates, has introduced me to some nice wines, and I'm enjoying it."

The waiter came over and introduced himself. "Good evening, I'm Mike. Anything to drink besides water? We have bottled imported water, either still or bubbling, or tap water."

Charlie looked at her.

"Bubbling water would be lovely."

"For me, too, but I'd also like to get a bottle of wine," said Charlie.

The waiter handed Charlie a leather-bound folder. "I'll send the wine steward over. In the meantime, you might want to look at the food offerings to help you make your wine choice. As noted, we offer fresh entrées each night, so no specials are listed."

Jill accepted a menu from the waiter and quickly became absorbed in the selection of food.

"What do you think? Fish or meat?" said Charlie. "It all looks delicious."

Jill smiled. "I'm going to go for the Glazed Sea Bass with a Ginger-Butter-Cream sauce. It sounds yummy."

"I'm going to do the scallops. Guess I'll go with a white wine."

The wine steward came over to the table. "How may I help you?"

While Charlie talked to him about wine selections, Jill tuned out and gazed out at the garden. Lit mini lights woven among branches and plants made the setting seem like a fairyland. She let out a sigh of contentment. She'd forgotten what it was like to go out for a meal like this. Jay had considered a meal in an elegant setting like this a waste of money.

She was still smiling when she turned to Charlie. "I'm sorry. You were saying?"

"I just wanted you to know I'm already enjoying this evening. Gourmet food and excellent company. You can't beat it."

The wine steward brought over the bottle of wine Charlie had ordered, gave him a taste, waited for his approval, and then poured some wine into a glass for Jill before putting the bottle into an ice bucket in a stand next to Charlie's seat.

"Enjoy," he said, giving them a little bow. "It's a nice sauvignon blanc from Chateau Ste. Michelle in Washington."

Charlie lifted his glass in a salute to her. "Here's to a pleasant evening."

Jill took a sip of her wine and smiled with appreciation. "Delicious. It's a treat for me to be out like this."

"Niki tells me you're going to be moving here from New York State. That's quite a difference."

"I hope so," Jill answered honestly. "I'm ready for a change. How about you? Where are you living?"

"I'm in the Boston area for my job with an IT consulting company. I love living there on the North Shore. It's home to me, even with my family now living here in Florida. Something about the city is special." He grinned. "And being a Red Sox fan, how could I leave?"

She laughed with him. "The other night, Brody and I cheered for the Tampa Bay Rays."

"Brody? Is that the guy living in the house with you?"

"One of them, yes. His uncle, Greg Campbell, is the man the owner hired to work on some renovations of the cottage. After Greg injured his arm, Brody has had to take over for him. But staying the extra time is Florida is great for his daughter, Kacy."

"Ah, Kacy, Emily's friend. I heard they're cute together. It's nice for Emily to have a friend when the 'T's,' as I call the triplets, take up so much of her parents' time."

"Both Niki and Jed are amazing parents. They have a lot more patience than I'd have in the same circumstances."

"Niki has always wanted a lot of kids. I'm sure she didn't think she'd get them in quite this way, though."

"How about you? Do you want kids some day?"

Charlie frowned. "My ex-wife and I tried, but it didn't work. We never pursued it. At the moment, I don't want to even think about it."

"Understandable," Jill said, changing the subject. "Niki told me you're quite a sailor."

The unease on Charlie's face was instantly replaced with a smile. "Yes, I crew on a sailboat, a 43-foot ketch out of Marblehead. It's the best way I know to relax completely."

"I've been to Boston just once. It was beautiful."

Charlie winked at her. "You'll have to come visit sometime."

Jill smiled, but wasn't exactly sure what the invitation meant. "When are you leaving to go back north?"

"Tomorrow. We have a race on Sunday, and I can't miss it. I just came down here to see my parents and check on Niki. I wanted to be sure everything was okay."

Their appetizers came.

Jill had ordered the herbed tomato tart; Charlie had opted for the beef carpaccio.

Conversation ended as they dug into their food.

After a few bites of the seasoned tomatoes drizzled with a blue cheese cream on a crispy triangle of pastry, Jill couldn't hold back a groan of pleasure.

"Mine's delicious too," said Charlie, chuckling.

Soon after their appetizer plates were cleared away, their main courses arrived.

Jill took a bite and smiled. "This sea bass is fantastic. What a marvelous blend of flavors! Thank you."

"The scallops are delicious too," Charlie said. "The wine is perfect with them."

As Jill continued to eat her meal and chat with Charlie, she felt enveloped by an almost tangible feeling of well-being. She knew then that no matter what, she wasn't going back to New York State to live. She made a mental note to call Sandra to see what, if any, news she had on the sale of her house.

The conversation between them remained easy. Harmless really, thought Jill. She liked Charlie and was grateful he was such a sweet companion.

They shared crème brûlée and ordered coffee.

"What a perfect meal," said Jill. "It's inspired me to be a little more adventuresome at home. After my husband died, I hardly cooked at all. Now, I'm feeding two hungry men who aren't fussy and a little girl who doesn't like anything."

"My mother is a great cook. We've always eaten well," said Charlie. He smiled at her. "It's nice to be with someone who enjoys good food." He signaled the waiter for their check.

Jill excused herself to go to the ladies' room. As she strolled through the tables of diners, happy conversations filled her ears.

Inside the ladies' room she admired the tile and the brass

faucets in the shape of fish. Gavin's might be understated from the outside, but the interior was gorgeous.

When she exited the room, she saw Charlie standing by the door talking to the hostess, a pretty young blonde. He turned and smiled as she walked over to him.

"All set?" he asked her.

She nodded. "I'm ready to go if you are."

"I am. "He took her arm. "I was just asking the hostess if any of the Sullivan sisters work here in the restaurant."

"Do they?"

"Apparently so. Especially for large parties."

"I'd love to meet them. They've done such a wonderful job with the place."

The ride back to the cottage was quiet. Jill's nerves kicked up at the thought of how the evening might end. Would he kiss her? Should she invite him in? What about Brody? These and other thoughts buzzed in her mind, like a pesky gnat she couldn't chase away.

In no time, Charlie pulled into the driveway and parked beside Brody's truck. He turned to her. "I had a great time. Can I call you again when I'm in town?"

"I'd like that," Jill said honestly. She hesitated. "Do you want to come in? It's such a lovely evening."

"Thanks, but I'd better be going. I've got an early flight."

He leaned over and gave her a sweet, short kiss on her cheek.

Surprised, she looked at him.

He gave her a sheepish smile. "Guess I'm a bit skittish. Come here." He drew her to him, and this time his warm, sure lips met hers in a kiss that told her he definitely cared. When he drew back, he studied her for a moment and smiled. "I'll walk you to the door. And, next time, I'll arrange to be here longer."

She waited as he hurried around the front of the car to open the door for her.

On the porch, he turned to her. "Goodnight. I'll call you when I'm back in town."

He waited until she stepped inside, then gave her a little wave, and left.

Jill closed the door behind her and leaned up against it, unsure how she felt about Charlie. She definitely wanted to see him again. Maybe she'd know better then.

She stepped into the living area and stopped. Brody was on the couch in front of the television sound asleep.

On tiptoes, she went over to one of the side tables next to the couch and picked up the control for the television.

As she turned it off, Brody stirred and cracked open an eye. "Wha' time is it?"

"Bedtime," she said softly. It was an early night for some, but Brody worked hard every day and was used to early-morning risings.

He sat up and rubbed his eyes. "How was your date?"

"Good," she responded.

He gazed up at her and grinned. "Glad it wasn't terrific."

Smiling to herself, she left him and went to the privacy of her room to sort out her feelings.

CHAPTER FOURTEEN

The next morning, as Jill was pouring herself a cup of coffee, Brody came into the kitchen.

"Hey, thanks for waking me up last night. I probably would have slept there all night. Guess all this physical labor is getting to me."

"No problem. What are you working on now?"

"Landscaping. We need to trim back some of the bushes next to the house so we can paint there. Greg thinks we should also replace some of the plantings." He gave her a wry look. "Funny how many projects he's coming up with. Guess he really wants me to stay."

Jill swallowed the sip of coffee she'd taken. "Would you consider moving here?"

"At the right time, perhaps. But I'd have to make sure it wouldn't mess with custody rights for Kacy. She's really changed for the better since being here, and I don't want her to go back to her old ways."

"Yes, that would be a shame."

He grabbed a bottle of water out of the refrigerator and a paper towel to mop his brow. "Guess I'd better get back to work before it gets even hotter."

Jill finished her coffee and headed outside to walk the beach. She loved this time of day. The beach hadn't yet filled up, and she could stroll along the shore without constantly having to bypass other people.

Her cell rang.

She lifted it out from the back pocket of her shorts and

checked caller ID. *Niki.*

"Hey, there!" Jill said. "Time away from the 'T's' as Charlie calls them?"

"Yeah, the babysitter just arrived. Speaking of my darling brother, I think Charlie has a thing for you. He didn't come right out and say it, but when I asked how the date went, he smiled the kind of smile that means a big 'Yes.'"

"He's very nice. We're going to go out the next time he's in town."

"And?" Niki persisted.

"And I really liked him. But he seems very settled in his life in the Boston area."

"Yeah, I know, but my parents and I are hoping he'll relocate here. That's why I wanted him to meet you."

"Oh, girl, that's a big challenge," Jill said. "We've gone on only one date."

"I know, I know. Jed tells me to butt out, but it would be so perfect if the two of you got together."

Jill laughed. "You're such a romantic. Speaking of that, remember I've offered to babysit the kids if you and Jed want to go to a movie or something."

"Thanks. We may call you last minute sometime."

"That will work," said Jill. "Until then, maybe we can meet some afternoon for coffee or a glass of wine."

"Let's see how it goes," said Niki. "If the babysitter is still alive, one day soon, I'll ask her."

Jill laughed as she hung up. Life at the Carter household was a zoo.

Two days later, when Jill entered the house at Camp Sunnyside, Susannah hurried over to greet her. "Jill! Just the person I need to talk to. Melanie's on the phone. Come on back to the kitchen with me."

Jill followed Susannah into the kitchen and inhaled the delicious aroma of baked cookies.

"May I?" she asked.

Susannah grinned. "One, no more. Big kids and little love these granola chocolate cookies, and I don't have time to make more."

Under Susannah's watchful eye, Jill lifted a cookie to her mouth and took a bite. "Mmm," she murmured. The chocolate mixture was delicious—soft and crunchy at the same time.

"Have a seat," Susannah said, indicating a chair at the kitchen table.

Observing her serious expression, dread filled Jill. Was Susannah about to give her bad news? Something about the future?

Susannah sat opposite Jill and studied her for a moment. "I know this may sound strange, but the moment I saw you I knew why you were here. Melanie is going to want to spend less time at the camp, and I need to know if you'd be willing to step into her shoes."

Jill swallowed hard. "Is this because of something bad?"

Susannah smiled and shook her head. "Quite the opposite. Besides, Melanie doesn't need the money, and she's getting restless to have more time to herself. But, as I'm sure she told you, I can't run the business end of things. I will need someone like you to help her."

Jill sat back in her chair and let out a long breath. "Wow! To tell you the truth, I've been thinking about having my own camp. Something for kids in need of support, kids who have been bullied, that kind of thing."

"Exactly," said Susannah. "And not just for summertime."

"I still would want to teach school until the camp really took off. Would you be willing to accept that?"

"Sure, because I know it's going to be a success," said Susannah.

"Because you see it in the future?"

Susannah laughed. "No, because I know how talented you are. Melanie has said you'll do fine."

"But I'm just beginning to learn ..."

Susannah held up a hand to stop her. "No need to worry about it. I trust Melanie's word."

"Well, I guess that means a lot. Still, I'll want to go over the numbers and the rest of the details before I give you any answer. How much time do I have?"

A smile spread across Susannah's face. "I haven't a clue."

A snort sputtered out of Jill. It wasn't the answer she expected.

Kelly popped into the kitchen. "There you are, Jill. Ready to help me?"

Jill jumped to her feet. "I'm coming right now."

By the time her session at camp was over and she and Kacy were headed home, Jill knew she needed time on the beach.

"Shall we go shelling today?" she asked Kacy.

"Yes, I want to find an olive shell so I can make a dog."

"Ah, you've been reading the shell book I gave you."

Kacy grinned. "I know lots of shell names now."

"Well, then, you can teach me."

Kacy's face brightened. "Okay. You ask, and I'll tell you."

"Sounds perfect to me," said Jill, thrilled by Kacy's interest in shells.

At the house, Jill found Greg and Brody stretched out in lounge chairs by the pool.

"Busy day, huh?" she said, giving them a teasing smile.

"Truly was," said Greg. "Brody has been finishing up the planting. I've been doing my best to help him, but this dang arm is driving me crazy. I'm no help at all."

Jill glanced at Brody. He looked as exhausted as Greg. "How about the two of you taking a walk along the beach with Kacy and me? It's a wonderful way to relax."

"Count me out," said Greg, "but Brody might like it."

"What about it?" Jill said, thinking the fresh air and relaxation on the beach might do him a world of good.

Brody groaned and got to his feet. "Okay. I'll meet you out front."

Jill hurried inside to change into her bathing suit.

Kacy was already in her bathing suit, standing by the front door, holding onto the shell book and the net bag for collecting them.

"Wow! I guess I'd better hurry. Your dad is going with us."

Kacy's eyes widened. "Really?"

"Yeah, better grab a towel for him when you get one for yourself."

Jill left her and went into her room pleased Brody was being included in doing something special for Kacy.

She changed her clothes, dabbed more suntan lotion on her body, and put on a light cover-up over her swimsuit. She packed a towel in her beach bag and grabbed three waters from the refrigerator before heading outside.

Brody and Kacy were waiting for her.

The three of them set off on foot.

"Let's set our things down here and walk north, away from the crowd in the other direction. We'll have a better chance of finding unbroken shells," Jill suggested.

"I'm looking for an olive shell," Kacy announced. She opened the book Jill had given her and pointed out the shell to her father.

"Okay, that's what I'll look for too," he said. "How about if I find something else? Will you tell me what it is?"

"Yes. I'm learning all about them," Kacy said proudly.

"Excellent," said Brody, beaming at her, then turning to Jill. "It's great that we're all becoming friends. I like it."

Kacy frowned at him. "But, Dad, she's going to marry Uncle Charlie. Emily said so."

Jill's breath left her in a rush. "What?"

Kacy gave her a smug look. "Emily told me her Uncle Charlie really likes you, and her mother wants you to marry him."

"Huh? This is the first I've heard of this," said Brody, looking as surprised as she felt. "Is it true?"

Jill sighed. "What's true is that Niki wants that to happen. It doesn't mean it will."

"When is Charlie going to be back in town?" Brody said.

"I don't know. He spends a lot of time in the summer helping a friend on his sailboat. That's why he had to leave early the morning after our date." She smiled. "It sounds like such an exciting hobby. I've never been on a sailboat."

"Are we going to look for shells or not?" said Kacy impatiently.

"Oh, hon, sorry. Let's do it now," said Jill.

They headed down the beach, each looking intently at the numerous shells scattered along the shore by the waves as they moved back and forth over the sand.

Sometime later, Kacy shrieked, "I found one!" and came running over to where Jill and Brody were bent over searching for shells.

Jill straightened. "Let's see it."

Kacy held up a shell. "It's almost perfect!"

Jill and Brody looked at it carefully.

"I like the fact that it has a few markings on it. It makes it real," said Brody.

"Me too," said Kacy. She handed it to Jill. "Will you hold onto it for me?"

"Sure. Do you want to keep looking or do you want to make a sandcastle? The tide is low and it's a perfect time to do it."

"Sandcastle!" cried Kacy. "I'll get the buckets and shovels."

As Kacy ran ahead, Brody turned to Jill. "It's wonderful to see her like this."

"Yes, it's been only a couple of weeks, but it's made a huge difference. I'm glad Kacy was able to stay here with you."

Brody made a face. "Allison called. She and her husband had a quarrel. I'm not sure what the fight was about, but Allison is worried about their future. I told her to just take it one day at a time."

"What does all this mean for you and Kacy?"

He shook his head. "I don't know. Allison is so unpredictable that it's hard to keep up with all her demands."

"Well, like you said, take it one day at a time. Guess that's all you can do."

"Yeah. I've got a lot of things to think over." The sadness in his voice touched Jill.

She reached over and took hold of his hand. "You're a great guy. Better things are bound to happen."

"If life were only that simple."

Jill was about to say more when Kacy returned with the two plastic buckets and four shovels Jill had bought earlier.

"I want a big, big, big castle, Dad," Kacy announced.

"Okay. I know a lot about construction. We'll make it the best ever. Jill will help too."

Kacy glanced from her father to Jill and frowned.

"I'll start by drawing out the area. You two start filling the buckets," Brody said cheerfully, ruffling Kacy's curls. She picked up a bucket and marched away.

Jill and Brody exchanged smiles. Jill understood why Kacy was worried about competing for her father's time. That's how she'd felt about her mother when her sister was around. She wanted to tell Kacy not to worry, that she and her father were not going to get together, but she thought of their kisses and decided to say nothing.

Moments later, when Jill knelt on the sand beside Brody, patting the sand into the shape he wanted, she wondered what it would be like to make a life with him. Living in the same household here in Florida had proved to be much easier than she'd first thought.

He nudged her. "Whatever you're thinking about must be good because you're smiling. But we need you to get back to work."

A burning sensation that had nothing to do with the sun crept up her cheeks. "Sorry, just daydreaming, I guess."

"I want to make a special room for me. A princess room," said Kacy. "And one for you, Dad."

"What about Jill? She's working on the castle too."

Kacy bit her lip and studied her. "Maybe you can have a room outside the castle. Then I wouldn't have to tell Mom."

Jill noticed the anger that flashed across Brody's face and quickly said, "Sure. I could stay in a guest house on the property."

Kacy's face brightened. "Yes, that's it. We'll make it pretty too."

As Kacy went back to work, Jill sent Brody a silent message to say nothing to Kacy about the guest house. Later, she and Brody could talk about it.

Kacy shaped a mound of sand in a round hill. "There! That's where you are, Jill. Emily and her triplets are going to be inside the castle with me. And one of the puppies, too."

"Where am I going to be?" Brody said. "Somewhere inside?"

"Yes, you and Mom and I will live in the big part of the castle." Kacy beamed at her father.

Brody frowned. "I don't think that's going to work, Kacy. Mom and I don't live together anymore, remember?"

Kacy looked down. "I remember," she mumbled. "I wish ..."

"It's okay. I understand. But Mom is living with Dr. Henderson now." Brody spoke in a quiet reassuring voice.

"I don't like Marcus Dear."

Jill and Brody exchanged looks of surprise.

"Is that what you call him?" Brody said to Kacy.

She shook her head. "No, that's what Mom calls him."

"Well, if you want to put Mom and Marcus in the castle, I'm sure there's room," Brody said.

Kacy's lower lip jutted in a look of defiance. "No, I'll leave them out."

"How about I help drizzle sand on the castle to decorate it," said Jill. "Want to help, Kacy?"

"Drizzle? What's that?"

"Let's fill the buckets with water and bring them back here, and I'll show you," Jill answered, happy to be able to divert Kacy's focus. Brody's look of relief told her he was glad too.

Once Kacy saw Jill scoop very wet sand into her hands and let it drip through her fingers for a decorative touch, Kacy was enchanted by the idea. As more and more touches were added, the mounds of sand were transformed from ordinary to fancy.

Watching the joy on Kacy's face as she worked hard to decorate the castle, Jill's heart filled with affection. Kacy was struggling with her parents' divorce and her mother's treatment of her, but she still had a child's innocence that touched her.

When at last Kacy was ready to leave the beach, Brody and

Jill gathered their things while Kacy ran ahead. Left alone, Brody turned to Jill and placed a hand on her shoulder. Looking into her eyes, he said, "You're a very sweet woman. Do you know that?"

Suddenly shy, she didn't know where to look.

When his lips came down on hers, she stiffened, then responded, unable to resist the sensations rolling through her.

"Hey! What are you guys doing?" Kacy's voice shattered the moment.

Jill jerked away from Brody.

"I'm thanking Jill for helping us make the castle," said Brody gently. "Any more questions?"

"No," said Kacy. "Can we go swimming now?"

"Sure," Brody said, and turned to her. "Ready, Jill?"

Trying not to notice the way his body had responded to her, Jill nodded. She needed to cool down too.

CHAPTER FIFTEEN

The next morning, Jill got a call from the county school system requesting an interview for a third-grade position. Elated, she arranged to meet with them later that morning, and quickly called Melanie to tell her she'd be a little late to work.

She printed off a copy of her resumé and reviewed it. Looking over the information, she was proud of the work she'd done with kids, but it seemed a little pathetic that she'd gone from childhood to adulthood, to marriage and widowhood all in the same place. Those last years had been so unhappy. She remembered how down she'd been, how trapped she felt in an existence that was devoid of joy. In the weeks since she'd been in Florida, her whole life had changed. Gratitude filled her. For once, her sister had done her a real favor.

As she was getting dressed for her interview, her cell rang. *Sandra.*

"Hey there," Jill said to her real estate agent. "Happy news, I hope?"

"Good news and bad. Which do you want first?"

"How about the bad," said Jill. "Then the other will seem wonderful."

"Okay, the bad news is that when an inspection was done on your house, they found an area that showed evidence of termites."

"Termites? Oh, my god! Is the house falling down?"

"No, no, nothing like that. But the back porch needs to be

rebuilt. Termites at one time got into the underpinnings. Otherwise, the rest can easily be addressed. There is no present activity."

Jill swallowed hard. "How much is it going to cost to rebuild the porch?"

"That's the good news. The couple interested in buying the house are willing to make that part of the sales agreement. He's a carpenter and can do the work himself, but he wants to be fairly compensated for it. I've suggested selling the house to them at a lower price, which means their mortgage would be lower. That would help them and be an easy way to resolve the issue. What do you say?"

"How much lower?" Jill asked.

"Fifteen thousand dollars. That would be fair market value anyway. Prices have been dropping. I suggest you accept the offer quickly. The reduction in price would take care of any other problems associated with what they've found."

"Let's do it!" Jill's excitement was heartfelt. The house represented the last vestige of her marriage.

"Okay, then. I'll draw up the papers and fax them to you. Do you have a fax number?"

"Hold on. I'll give you the number at the camp where I'm working." Jill picked up the card for Camp Sunnyside and read the fax number to her. "How soon do they want to move in?"

"That's another piece of luck. They're flexible, but I would suggest moving your things out of the house as soon as possible. If necessary, we can ask if they'd be willing to have you rent the house to them until, say, the middle of September when you'd have to have all personal items removed and the house cleaned."

"Okay. I'll have a better sense of timing soon. I have a job interview this morning and should know more then."

"Congratulations, Jill. It sounds as if things are going your way. Talk to you later."

Without waiting for much of a response from her, Sandra hung up, leaving Jill stunned at how fast things seemed to be moving.

She hurried into the shower. If she was lucky, the day would continue in like manner.

Later, her head spinning with ideas, Jill left the school building, pleased by how the interview had gone. Equally as important, she liked the superintendent, the vice principal of the elementary school where she'd be teaching, and a third-grade teacher who worked there. Though she wouldn't have much time to set up her classroom, the teacher she'd be replacing had left the room more organized than she'd thought.

She hurried to the camp to tell Melanie and Susannah.

As Jill entered the camp office, Melanie said, "I've received some paperwork for you. Looks like you might have sold your house." She handed Jill a number of pages off the fax machine.

"That's what I need to talk to you about," said Jill facing them. "I need time off to pack up my things. I thought I'd leave on Friday and be back on Sunday."

"Heavens! Is that enough time?" sputtered Melanie. "It would take me months to pack up my belongings."

In that moment, Jill made her decision. "I'm only going to pack up personal items, no furniture or bulky items. I'm going to start fresh here."

Susannah smiled and nodded at her. "I believe that's going to prove to be a very wise choice."

Jill held up a hand. "I don't want to hear why you're saying that."

"No problem," said Susannah. "Sometimes I can see the future; sometimes, not."

Melanie laughed. "You gotta love her. She sure keeps me on my toes."

Jill joined in the laughter and then became serious. "I should also tell you that I got a teaching job this morning. I'll be at Palm Creek Elementary, teaching third grade. If you want me to continue to work for the camp, I can do that too."

"Yes, we do," said Susannah. "Just like we discussed."

Melanie gave Susannah a quizzical look, then added, "I agree."

"What about housing here?" Melanie said. "You'll need to find a place to live, won't you?"

"I'm not sure what to do," Jill said. "I might rent a place until I decide exactly where I want to live."

"That should give you enough time to find something suitable for the long term," said Susannah.

"Why don't you take the rest of the day off to get organized," Melanie suggested. "Tomorrow, you can go back to your regular schedule. And then you can leave for New York." She gave Jill a warm hug. "I'm so happy things are working out for you. We love having you as a part of the team here. Right, Susannah?"

"Yes, indeed." Susannah beamed at her and hugged Jill in a quick embrace.

A tall, attractive woman with gray hair worn pageboy style greeted Jill with a warm smile the moment she walked into the Palm Rentals and Realty office. "Hi, Jill. I'm Kay Branson. Melanie called to ask me to take special care of you. I understand you need a rental while you decide where you want to buy. This is a perfect scenario for us because we do both rental and sales transactions."

"Great. I'm house sitting the Seashell Cottage at the moment, but my stint there will be over at the end of the summer." She'd thought of asking Hope if she could stay longer at the cottage and dismissed it.

"Why don't you come into my office? We can talk there. Coffee? Tea? Water? Lemonade?"

"I'm all set, thank you," Jill said, hurrying behind Kay who was striding down a long hallway. They entered a corner office with a clear view of the building's landscaped yard. As she settled into the chair Kay offered her and waited for Kay to be seated at her desk, Jill stared out the large glass window at the bounty of colorful, tropical flowers and bushes.

"Well," Kay said, settling back in her chair and studying Jill, "where should we begin?"

"Do you have any house-sitting opportunities?" Jill asked. "I don't have any furniture and I'm hoping not to buy any until I have a place of my own."

"I understand. When you mentioned your stay at Seashell Cottage, a thought came to mind. Several of the properties we list are owned by snowbirds who spend just a few short winter months here. There's one in particular that's quite lovely. It's small—two bedrooms, office, living/dining area, nice big kitchen, patio with small spa pool, and a lovely location in a golf course neighborhood that has a couple of community swimming pools and lots of outdoor activity. The owner is extremely fussy about who rents it. Fill out our rental questionnaire, and we'll take it from there."

"In a couple of weeks, I'll be starting my new job teaching third grade at Palm Creek Elementary. I need a place convenient to that."

"If you get approved, this will be a perfect location for you. It's within a mile of the school. Here, let me show you pictures of it online. If it's of interest, I can give you a tour."

Kay swiveled one of her two flat-screen monitors around so that Jill could get a look.

"Each building contains four condos, two upper and two lower ones. The one I'm talking about is on the right bottom. As you can see, the grounds and facilities are kept in meticulous condition. As a bonus, each condo has its own private garage, as well as an outdoor, covered parking space."

A picture showing a handsome building next to a golf course oozed charm and comfort.

"The interior shots are up-to-date and appear exactly as they are," Kay said, clicking through photographs.

Pleased with everything she saw, Jill said, "Yes, this looks perfect. I'd even pick the same furniture myself." Her gaze darted to the rental price and she gasped. "Three thousand dollars a month? There's no way I could ever pay that."

Kay held up a hand to stop her. "That's just a number we've put there to keep non-serious renters away. I have the authority to set the price for the right person. The original owner has died, and this rental is part of her estate. Her daughter now owns it, but has no interest in living there."

Jill looked at the questionnaire she'd been handed. "Is it all right if I fill out the information here in the office?"

Kay smiled. "Of course. Why don't we move you into our conference room? You can help yourself to refreshments there and take your time. It will be well worth it, I promise you."

After getting settled at the wide mahogany conference table, Jill began the task of filling out the paperwork. As she'd done when she'd reviewed her resumé, Jill thought of her life. It seemed so empty, so gray before coming to Florida. Her present life was as colorful as the bougainvillea, oleander, and palms that made her world seem bright and promising.

Under additional comments, Jill wrote: "I would love to be

able to live here. I respect all the original owner did to decorate and care for the home. From the photos I saw, she and I share very similar tastes. As a friend of mine might say, it's as if destiny has brought me here."

Satisfied she'd done her best to present herself well, Jill signed the paperwork and went to find Kay.

Kay looked up from behind her desk. "All done?"

Jill nodded and handed her the papers. "When do you suppose you'll have an answer?"

"It shouldn't take long, two to three days at the most, if I can reach the owner. If for some reason it doesn't go through, there are plenty of other properties. But I have a feeling this is perfect for both you and Catherine."

"I'll be leaving for New York to pack up my things in the next day or so, but I'll keep in touch."

"As will I," Kay said, shaking Jill's hand. "Safe travels."

On her way to Seashell Cottage, Jill called Sandra. After exchanging greetings, Jill said, "I'm not going to take any of the furniture with me. Would the new owners be interested in buying any or all of it? If so, I'll make them a deal they can't believe." When he'd moved in with her, Jay had told her she had no taste and insisted on all new furniture he'd selected, erasing all traces of what she'd chosen, making it his place, not hers. Jill had always hated it.

"I'll ask them," said Sandra. There was a pause, then Sandra said, "Oh, Jill, I can't believe it's all happening this fast. I'm going to miss you!"

"Thanks," said Jill. "It's been unreal. Things are moving so quickly that it almost seems as if it was pre-ordained. I'm very happy about it. I should have done this a long time ago, but my mother was insistent about me being there for her sake, and I didn't want to disappoint her."

"For that reason alone, I'm glad you're making the move.

Who knows? You may find me camped on your doorstep every now and again," joked Sandra.

"I'd love it," Jill said, pleased by the idea they still could be friends.

As she clicked off the call, excitement pounded through Jill. It was happening! If she didn't already love her name, she might change that too, from Jillian to something more exotic. But her father had always loved calling her Jilly Bean, and she still clung to that memory.

She checked her watch. Time to swing by and pick up Kacy. She called Brody's cell, and when there was no answer, she spoke to Greg.

"Hi, Greg. Where's Brody? I wanted to check in with him to make sure he knew I'd pick up Kacy from camp."

"He's not here, but I'm sure he'd appreciate it. He's busy with ... something."

Greg's evasiveness worried her. "Is everything all right?"

He sighed. "I don't know why I'm not supposed to say anything about it, but he's signed up for sailing lessons."

Even as tears stung her eyes, Jill felt a broad smile spread across her face. She knew exactly why he was doing this. "Don't worry, I won't mention it."

She clicked off the call and hugged herself, wishing she could hug Brody. Nobody had ever made a sweeter gesture to her. She'd treasure it always.

CHAPTER SIXTEEN

A board the commuter plane that serviced small airports in upstate New York, Jill gazed out the window at the miniature scene below her. It was funny, she thought, how surroundings at ground level seemed so large, so all encompassing, but appeared inconsequential in the scheme of things when seen as such a tiny part of the world.

On the ground, her life would return to a familiar pattern she was thankful to be able to escape. Jill vowed to stay strong against her mother's disapproval. She'd already listened to her mother complain that Jill was giving away her house, she owed her mother more consideration than this, and her father would disapprove of her actions. The last comment hurt more than the others, but Jill remained stoic.

When the pilot announced they were about to land, Jill's stomach did a dive that had nothing to do with the airplane. Beneath the determination to stay strong, old patterns of loss, inadequacy, and a need to please others threatened her. *Was it possible that in a matter of a couple of months, I can make enough changes to be the new, freer person I want to be?*

Without wanting to, she found herself thinking of Brody's daughter. She promised herself she would make this change as quickly and as easily as possible to prove to Kacy that she, too, could have a different life.

Jill searched for her mother among the greeters clumped together at the security gate, waiting for arrivals. She stopped in surprise when she saw a woman who looked much too old to be her mother. The woman waved, and, suddenly, everything snapped back into place and her mother looked like her usual self.

Jill rushed forward and hugged her. "Hi! Thanks for coming to pick me up."

"Of course," her mother replied. "Do you have luggage?"

"Just this." Jill held up a backpack filled with all she'd need for this short trip.

Her mother shook her head. "I don't know why you think you can be packed up in just two days. You have a houseful of things."

"Not anymore. I'm selling the house furnished. That way I don't have to move anything big."

Her mother stopped and stared at her. "Are you serious? But you and Jay bought new, beautiful furniture when he moved in."

"Another reason to let someone else have it," said Jill filled with satisfaction.

"Humph, I don't know why you think you can waste money that way."

Jill held back words. There was so much she could say, but she knew it would fall on deaf ears. Her mother would never believe that Jay was abusive to her. He'd hidden it well in front of others.

"Where did you park the car?" said Jill, standing at the entrance to the parking garage.

"2 B, not far from here."

Jill followed her mother to the car, still silent even as her thoughts flew in circles. She knew it was time for her to speak up or be thrust back into her old life.

After she stowed her backpack in the backseat and she was settled in the passenger seat, she turned to her mother and said quietly, "You've never believed nor have you tried to understand why I was so unhappy with Jay. After being away,

I realize more than ever how emotionally abusive he was to me. That's a big part of why I'm looking forward to making these changes in my life. And how I choose to make them, is really none of anyone else's business."

Her mother's face turned red. "Well, I ..."

Jill laid a hand on her mother's arm. "I'm not saying this to start a fight. I'm just making myself clear in a way I haven't been able to do before now. I appreciate all you've done, keeping an eye on the house."

Her mother sat back and studied her. "What a surprise you've turned out to be, Jillian. It's going to take some time to get used to the new you, but I'm going to try." Her eyes welled. "I've really missed you."

"I'm not abandoning you, Mom. I'm just finding my independence, and I plan on keeping it."

"Yes, well, I guess I'd better get you to your house. Do you know where you're going to live in Florida?"

"No," Jill said with unconcern. "It won't be a problem. I'm confident something will work out. And if Susannah is sure of it too, it will, believe me."

"Who's Susannah?" her mother asked.

Jill realized there was so much she hadn't told her mother for fear of her mother finding fault. But now that she'd finally faced her and spoken out, she was free to do so. In the twenty minutes it took for them to drive to her house, Jill told her mother about Susannah, Melanie, and her summer job. She didn't mention the possibility of owning part of Camp Sunnyside one day. She'd done enough sharing.

When her mother pulled into the driveway of Jill's house, Jill felt a cloud settle over her like a wet, woolen shawl that sent shivers through her. Fighting to free herself of the old defeatism that had plagued her here, Jill got out of the car, grabbed her backpack, and walked toward the house with a commitment to herself to get in, do the job, and leave forever.

With trembling fingers, she unlocked the door and opened it, allowing fresh air to blow into the building. But as she crossed the threshold, nothing could erase the memories of being treated as someone who was so stupid that she could never do anything right, too ugly to be around, too incompetent for anyone to trust her to do the simplest task. Unless others had actually heard Jay speak to her like that, they couldn't understand the daily damage he'd inflicted on her. The insidious part of his behavior was there was no physical proof of it. Her bruises were all on the inside.

Jill stopped and clutched her stomach as pain seared through her. She forced her mind to focus on Florida, her new friends, the little girl who needed her, and the man who thought enough of her to take sailing lessons to impress her.

"Are you all right?" her mother asked, giving her a worried look.

Jill straightened. "I will be. Thanks. Can I borrow your car to go buy boxes and packing supplies?"

"Yes, of course, dear. Why don't you drop me off at my house and then return for dinner? I'll have a hot meal for you."

Jill gave her mother a quick hug. "That would be really nice, Mom. But before you go, is there anything of mine that you want? I'm only taking my clothes, some books, some decorative things, and a few personal items. The personal things I don't want will go to charity, everything else will be left for the new owners."

Jill's mother shook her head. "No, thanks. I'm at the stage in my life when I'm trying to clean out a lot of household items."

"Okay, then, let's go," said Jill, anxious to get this job done.

###

she felt was an entirely new life.

Jill walked through the Tampa International Airport but felt as if she should be skipping. She'd loved seeing the palm trees as the plane swooped down for a landing.

She entered the baggage claim area, searched for the proper baggage belt, and headed down the row of them, coming to a halt when she saw Brody waving at her. He looked like a movie star with his dark, spikey hair, ripped body, and mega-watt smile.

Giddy, she waved back and hurried to greet him.

The smile on his face grew bigger. "Sorry to change plans on you, but Greg couldn't make it."

"N-no!" Jill stammered. "I'm glad you're here!"

Brody wrapped his arms around her and hugged hard. "The three of us missed you."

Unexpected tears stung Jill's eyes. Though she blinked rapidly to try to stem them, one renegade tear slid past her eyelid and down her cheek.

Brody lifted her face. "What's this?"

Jill swallowed to give herself a moment. "I'm just happy to be back. That's all."

His knowing gaze reached inside her. "Same old routine at home?"

"Yeah. It's never going to change. I couldn't wait to leave."

Brody stepped back, put an arm around her shoulder, and gave her a sympathetic squeeze. "Let's get your luggage and get you back to the beach."

Jill thought she'd never heard sweeter words.

CHAPTER SEVENTEEN

As Brody pulled his truck into the driveway of Seashell Cottage, a happy sigh left Jill's mouth in a rush of relief.

Brody turned to her with a grin. "Nice to be back?"

"Oh, yes. Even with the weather so hot, it feels wonderful." She inhaled the salty tang in the air as she climbed out of the truck to help Brody unload her luggage.

As they made their way to the front door, Kacy ran outside to greet them. "You're back!" she cried. "Hurry! Come inside."

Jill gave Brody a quizzical look, but he simply held the door for her and urged her inside.

Puzzled, she stepped across the threshold, set down the suitcase she'd been carrying, and removed her backpack.

Kacy grabbed her hand and tugged her toward the kitchen. "In here, Jill, in here."

Jill allowed herself to be hurried along and came to a quick stop at the entrance to the kitchen.

A white paper banner saying, "Welcome Home, Jill!" hung from the ceiling. A trio of pink helium balloons floated near the banner like bright butterflies.

"Surprise!" cried Kacy, jumping up and down with excitement. "We made this especially for you!"

Jill clapped her hands to her chest. "For me?"

Greg beamed at her. "We're glad to have you back. I've made dinner for tonight, but we can't wait to have you cook for us again."

Jill laughed, and then the tears she'd held back rolled down her face.

Brody put an arm around her shoulder. "Welcome home."

She let out a trembling sigh. "This is the best surprise ever. Thank you all so much."

"It was Kacy's idea," said Greg, nodding his approval at the little girl.

"Thank you." Jill leaned over and drew the girl to her. When Kacy stiffened, Jill held her breath. Then, Kacy's arms crept around Jill's neck and tightened.

Jill looked up to see Brody smiling at them and knew by the tender expression on his face that he was as touched as she to see his little girl's heart beginning to open up.

"Well, this is quite a celebration," said Greg, his eyes suspiciously wet. "Why don't we open a nice bottle of wine and sit for a moment before I put the casserole in the oven."

"I love Uncle Greg's tuna casserole," Kacy announced. "We had it last night."

Jill chuckled. "No wonder you gave me such a warm welcome. I'll make something different tomorrow night."

She gazed at the three people who'd shared this house with her for the last several weeks. In that short time, she, like Kacy, was discovering a new way to open herself to others—without criticism and self-doubt holding her back.

"I love you all," she said simply, though words weren't enough to describe her feelings.

Breaking the silence that followed, Brody said, "Why don't I help you get your luggage to your room."

"Thanks," said Jill, still emotional over her declaration.

At the front entrance of the house, she grabbed a suitcase and her backpack. Brody took the other two suitcases loaded with the clothing she'd decided to keep and followed her to her bedroom.

"There, that should do it," said Brody, setting down the suitcases, straightening, and gazing at her. "Like I said, the three of us missed you, but I might've missed you the most."

Heat burned inside Jill at the intense look he gave her.

He stepped closer.

Her pulse went into overdrive, racing inside her until she could hardly breathe. She knew what was coming next.

He cupped her face in his hands.

When his lips touched hers, she couldn't help the soft sound of pleasure that escaped her. This felt so right. She wrapped her arms around his neck.

When they finally pulled apart, Brody smiled. "I've been wanting to do that for a long time."

Flustered by the desire centered in her, Jill responded, "Thank you. It was ... very nice."

"Very nice? Is that all?" Brody teased.

Heat sprang to her cheeks. "Okay, it was fantastic."

He laughed, and drew her close again. "Let's try for *absolutely* fantastic."

This time, she allowed herself to melt into the kiss he gave her, enjoying sensation after sensation. When they broke apart, they were each breathing heavily.

"Guess that one was better, huh?" Brody winked at her.

"I'd say *absolutely* better. *Fantastic* even," she teased. In truth, she'd never been kissed like that in her life. Brody brought out all kinds of hot feelings in her. She wanted nothing more than to take it to the next level. But this was neither the time nor the place.

As if he'd read her mind, Brody said, "I think we need more privacy."

"Me too," she said, and laughed softly when he winked at her again.

The next afternoon after camp, Jill and Kacy headed home.

"How about spending time on the beach?" Jill said, glancing through the rearview mirror at Kacy sitting in the backseat. "It's a beautiful day and I want to spend some time with a very special girl."

Kacy looked at her and grinned. "Me?"

"Yes, you. Soon, we should have enough shells to start making shell animals, don't you think?"

"Yes! I want to make a puppy out of shells. Maybe Dad will let me have one when he sees it."

"Getting a puppy is a really big decision." Jill felt she had no right to say more. She was saved from getting into a real discussion of it as they reached the cottage. "Get in your bathing suit, and I'll meet you in the kitchen."

Kacy's smile lit her face. "Okay."

As soon as the car rolled to a stop and Jill had turned off the engine, Kacy was out of the car and running to the front of the house.

Jill watched her go, pleased that she and Kacy had taken a giant step forward in their relationship. More than that, Kacy was acting more like a regular kid.

Her feeling of accomplishment continued as she and Kacy hunted for shells together. She listened to Kacy's constant chatter, remembering when Kacy wouldn't talk to her at all.

"Look, Jill! I found a perfect scallop shell," said Kacy, holding it up to her. "It's beautiful! It's for you!"

Touched, Jill accepted the shell and quickly gave Kacy a kiss on the cheek. "Thanks. That's very sweet of you."

Kacy lifted a hand to her cheek and smiled. "Emily says she likes you a lot. I do too."

"And I like you," said Jill. "You're a sweet girl. Pretty too."

A wide smile stretched across Kacy's face as she patted her hair.

Observing her, Jill knew how special this moment was and

drew Kacy into a hug.

A cry startled them both. "Kacy! Kacy! Mommy's here!"

Jill whipped around to see a tall, lean woman with dark hair marching across the sand toward them, followed by Brody.

Kacy glanced at Jill and then began running toward her mother.

Her mother's shriek brought Kacy to a quick stop. "What did you do to your hair? How could you?"

Kacy ran to her father and hid behind his legs.

Jill picked up the bag of shells Kacy had dropped and headed toward the cottage, uncertain whether to meet Kacy's mother or walk away to give them privacy.

Brody called to her. "Hey, Jill! Come meet Allison." There was a tenseness to his voice Jill recognized.

Unwilling to get into a family argument, she paused.

Allison walked toward her, looking like a model in the navy dress she wore. "So, you're Jill? The cook I've heard about?"

"Hello, I'm Jillian Conroy. Yes, I'm in charge of the meals." Jill held out her hand, and Allison shook it. "Welcome! Are you staying for long?"

"I'm here to get my daughter. I've missed her." Allison studied Jill closely. "I suppose you're the one who gave Kacy the idea of having short hair."

Jill shook her head. "Actually, it was Kacy's best friend, Emily, who made her decide to have her hair cut. I love it. It's perfect for the beach and pool."

"Not helpful for the rest of the year," said Allison. "I won't be able to do anything about bows for a while." She tugged Kacy to her and ran her fingers through her curls. "Don't worry. We'll let it grow out."

"Nooo!" cried Kacy in what was once a familiar whine. "I want to look like Emily!"

"Who is this Emily?" Allison asked Brody. "A friend from camp?"

He nodded. "Her best friend. A girl her age from a great family."

"Emily's got the T's and puppies," Kacy said. "I want a puppy. Emily said she'd give me one."

"Oh, sweetie, no puppies for us. Marcus has allergies. Remember?"

"I don't care. I want a puppy," Kacy pouted, glaring at her mother.

Allison fluttered her hands. "Now, let's not get fussy. We'll talk about it later."

"Jill's going to get a puppy," Kacy said.

Allison looked at Jill with surprise. "You are?"

"I'm thinking of it," Jill replied. "First, I have to find a permanent place to live."

"She's moving to Florida and is looking for housing," Brody explained.

Allison studied them both. "Is she why you might be thinking of moving to Florida, Brody?"

"What?" Brody frowned.

"Daddy likes Jill," said Kacy. "Emily and I do too."

"Well, guess I'd better get back to the cottage," Jill said. Allison was frowning at her.

"Don't bother to cook for us," said Allison. "We're going out to dinner. Right, Brody?"

Brody looked at her with surprise and nodded. "Okay. That's what we'll do."

As Jill walked to the cottage, she felt Allison's stare on her.

Greg looked up at her from the rocking chair in which he was sitting. "I see you met Allison."

"Yes. I understand a lot more what both Brody and Kacy have gone through. Excuse me. I'm going to my room. I think it's best to give the family some privacy."

"I understand."

"Where is Allison staying?"

"At a nearby hotel. Brody insisted on calling one for her. I think she thought she'd be staying here, but Brody said no."

Jill left the porch and went into her room. She needed time alone, apart from Brody and his family. She'd told herself not to get too involved with either Kacy or him, but she realized she already had. The precious moment with Kacy on the beach was something she'd never forget. Nor the way her mother had put Kacy down in a matter of moments upon seeing her. And the idea of Brody liking her made her feel ... special.

A few moments later, she heard a knock on her door. She knew who it was and let out a sigh.

She opened the door. "Yes?"

"Can we talk?" Brody said.

"Sure." Jill held the door open, and he walked in, closing the door behind him.

"I'm sorry about Allison." Brody ran his fingers through his hair, a gesture she hadn't noticed before. "She can be nasty in her own way. You see what she does to Kacy."

"Yes, I do. Kacy and I had a special moment on the beach, and in an instant, upon seeing her mother, she changed back into the temperamental child she was. That's the part I'm having trouble with. And, yet, I know it's none of my business."

"You've been very much a part of the healthy changes we've seen in Kacy. I don't want you to step away from her. Allison and Marcus are fighting, and she's thinking of leaving him. I'm trying to talk to her and make her see that it's really a silly squabble, not worth destroying the relationship. Personally, I think she just wants attention."

"She sure doesn't like the idea of anything going on

between the two of us," Jill said. "That's another reason I don't want to get involved."

At the sound of knocking at the door, Brody grimaced. "Bets as to who it is?"

Jill didn't reply. She walked to the door and opened it. "Yes?"

"What's going on here?" Allison demanded. "Why are the two of you in here together?"

"Actually, it's not what you might think it is," Brody said before Jill could respond. "We're discussing Kacy."

Allison gave Jill a vicious stare. "You have no right to discuss my child."

"As a person staying in the house with her, I don't think there's a way to avoid it," Jill said, keeping her voice calm. "I'm a grade-school teacher, so I do feel I'm qualified to offer some guidance when it becomes necessary. But, don't worry, I have no intention of becoming involved with your family. I'm here at the cottage for only the summer."

Allison swept her gaze from the top of Jill's head to her bare feet. "I guess there's no need for me to worry." She turned to Brody. "Darling, we should think about where we're going to eat. I'm sure if we asked Greg, he'd watch Kacy for us if we want to dine alone."

Brody frowned and shook his head. "Dining alone wouldn't be fair to Kacy. She thinks you've come here to see her."

"Well, of course, I did, but I also wanted to talk to you, spend some quality time together. I might have been too hasty ..."

Brody held up his hand. "Don't do this, Allison. You can't always be the center of attention. It's not going to work. But we do need to discuss Kacy. When I drop you off at your hotel this evening, we can talk. Until then, I'm sure your daughter would like some time with you."

"Okay, if you insist." Allison turned to walk away and stopped. "Brody? Are you coming? It isn't wise to let Kacy think something's going on between the two of you."

Jill forced a smile. "See you later. Have a nice family dinner."

Brody left with Allison, allowing Jill to be alone once more. She sat on her bed wrestling with her feelings. She was attracted to Brody, was falling in love with his daughter, and enjoyed being part of the household with them. But her first priority was the move to Florida and getting settled in her new life.

CHAPTER EIGHTEEN

When Jill walked into the kitchen the next morning, she was surprised to find Brody there. "No work today?" she said.

"I'm taking Allison to see the camp. She wants to give her approval before considering having Kacy continue there."

"I thought you had Kacy for the summer and could make your own decisions," Jill said, observing the look of unhappiness on his face.

"I'm trying to convince Allison that not only is it a wise idea for Kacy to stay with me for the summer, but for us both to stay in Florida for the next school year. Greg really wants me here to keep the business going. He's not getting any younger, and I owe him a lot. If he and Annie hadn't taken me in, I don't know where I'd be today. Probably on the streets."

"Do you think Allison would ever agree to that? She claims to miss her daughter."

"Claims is the right word. In truth, she never wanted to be a mother."

"Maybe seeing Kacy so happy will help her decide."

"I think the idea of traveling with her husband might be the key. He has seminars in some pretty cool places. And she told me a lot of her friends are spending time abroad. She's hoping to get Marcus to agree to rent a flat in Paris for a while, using it as a home base while she travels around Europe."

"How would that work with Kacy?"

"That's my point. I think it would be disruptive for her. She's begun to make friends here and do well. I'd hate to see her go back to her old ways under the constant disapproval of her mother."

"Me too. I understand how worried you are."

"Thanks. I'd better get going. I promised to take Allison to breakfast at Gracie's at the Salty Key Inn. She's heard that it's the *only* place in the area to go to for breakfast."

"I'll go ahead and make tuna salad for you guys for lunch before I go to work."

"Thanks. See you later."

Jill poured herself a cup of coffee and took it out to the porch.

"Good morning!" Greg said cheerfully from his place in one of the rocking chairs.

"Hi! What a beautiful day!" she responded, smiling at him. The sun was casting a warm glow on the water, crowning each wave with a soft gold. Flowers bobbed their heads in the soft breeze, drawing attention to their vibrant colors.

"It looks like another hot one. I hope it cools off tonight because I have a date."

"Oh? Is it with the one your friend arranged for you?"

He grinned. "She still won't give me her name, but says it will be a leap of faith for both of us. At my age, I decided I could do it. Not many more leaps left."

Jill gave him a quick hug. "I don't believe that for one minute."

He chuckled. "We'll see."

Jill took a seat beside him. "I didn't realize you were so anxious to bring Brody into the business. He's genuinely concerned about you."

"I'm trying to convince him to come to Florida, away from the rut he's in now. I know of an opening in his field, and, frankly, if he would help me out from time to time, it would be a way for me to keep my business. It's important for me to keep moving. His being here could be a wonderful thing for both of us, and especially for Kacy."

"Wow! It's a lot to think about."

"It didn't take you long to decide to move here," said Greg. "I'm hoping it will be as easy for Brody."

"I don't usually make such quick decisions, but it feels perfect. And the fact that everything is coming together quickly and easily makes me think it was meant to be."

"A way to let out old secrets and move on?" He smiled at her. "I like seeing that happy smile of yours."

"Thanks." She couldn't ever remember feeling so at peace.

When Jill pulled into the parking lot of Camp Sunnyside and saw Brody's truck, her heart sank. She had no desire to run into Allison.

She got out of her car and headed into the office, determined to keep her distance. Susannah met her at the door. "Hurry! Come with me," she said, and rushed Jill into the kitchen.

"What's going on?" Jill asked.

"Stay here." Susannah closed the door to the kitchen and turned to Jill. "I don't want things disrupted."

"What things?" Jill asked.

"Things shaping the future."

In the quiet that followed, Jill could hear the voices of Allison and Brody in the hallway on the other side of the door.

"Nice to meet you, Melanie," said Allison. "I'm sorry to miss meeting Susannah. I understand she's an excellent cook, unlike Brody's cook at the cottage."

"She means Jill," Brody said with a clear tone of annoyance.

"Jill Conroy? She's a doll," said Melanie. "We don't like

hearing unkind things here."

"We'd better be going," said Brody. "Thank you for giving Allison a tour, Melanie. I wanted her to see how happy Kacy is here."

"Yes, she's doing much better. It pleases us when that happens."

"Thanks for helping her to lose some weight," said Allison. "That's very important to me."

"Yes, you've made that clear," Melanie said. "Safe travels home."

As soon as they heard the front door close, Susannah let out a long sigh. "Okay. They're gone."

Melanie knocked on the door and opened it. "What's going on? Why is the door closed? And why did you refuse to meet Kacy's mother?"

"I was given a warning sign," said Susannah. "I just knew I couldn't do it."

"Susannah, sometimes I don't know about you and your feelings," said Melanie shaking her head. "Good morning, Jill. How are you today?"

"Fine. And you?"

"Okay. Just trying to get through the day."

Susannah winked at Jill. "Melanie has a date tonight. A friend of a friend."

"Anyone we know?" asked Jill.

Melanie held out her hands. "I don't know who it is. My friend told me to trust her. I decided to go with it. What the heck? What have I got to lose?"

Jill felt a smile stretch across her face. "I think it sounds like fun. If things go bad, it's only for one evening." *Oh my! Is Greg her date?*

"I think it's wonderful," Susannah said, glancing at Jill and winking.

A shiver ran down Jill's back as a thought hit her. Susannah had already told her that Melanie would be spending more time away from the camp. Was it because of something like this?

"Time for me to do some finishing touches on the lunch," Susannah said, breaking contact between them.

"Jill, why don't you see if Kelly needs help with the swimmers, and then after lunch, you can help me in the office," suggested Melanie.

"All right." The look of satisfaction on Susannah's face was telling.

Amused, Jill headed outside.

Kelly waved, and Jill went right over to her.

"Glad you're here," Kelly said. "There's something I need to talk to you about. Kacy's mother was here, and now I can't get Kacy to join the group. Any suggestions?"

"What happened?" Jill asked, trying not to stare at Kacy's tear-streaked face.

"I overheard her mother tell her that if she lost more weight, she'd buy her a new swimsuit. A pretty blue one." Kelly caught the corner of her lip. "I didn't say anything at the time, didn't feel it was my place to do so, but my heart goes out to Kacy. She's been very proud of her bathing suit. She and Emily have pink ones just alike."

"I'll mention something to Brody about it when I get the chance. In the meantime, let me speak to Kacy."

"Thanks. She responds to you."

Jill made a point of saying hi to the group of girls gathered at the shallow end of the pool before going and sitting down beside Kacy on the lawn.

"Why are you over here?" Jill asked her gently.

"I've got a tummy ache," Kacy said, staring into the distance.

Jill put her arm around her. "Can I get you anything for it?"

"No. My Mom says I need to lose weight."

"Sometimes you should forget what other people say, especially things that hurt your feelings. You're beautiful, Kacy. More than that, you've made great friends here who like you just the way you are. That's what's important. Now, let's go back to those friends."

Jill stood and held out her hand, hoping her words made sense to an eight-year-old.

Kacy let out an exaggerated sigh, took Jill's hand, and together they walked toward the group.

As they approached, Kelly gave them a bright look. "Okay. Now our group is ready for some fun. We're going to play games. Emily, you may be the first to choose a partner."

Emily grinned. "I choose Kacy."

Jill and Kelly exchanged looks of satisfaction. Kacy was smiling.

Later, at lunch, Kelly said to Jill, "I hope you can talk to Kacy's father about what happened. I know what it's like to feel persecuted as a kid, and I hated to see the joy of being part of the group leave Kacy."

"It's a tough situation. I don't want to get overly involved, but I can't stand by and say nothing. I owe that to Kacy. She and I are forming a close relationship."

"I see that. It's nice."

"For me, too." Jill realized how much she meant it. Married to Jay, she'd given up on the idea of a family of her own, but friendship with Kacy was creating other thoughts.

Jill returned to the cottage alone. Brody and Allison had picked up Kacy from camp and were on their way to Orlando to spend a couple of nights so Kacy could go to Disney World.

With Greg about to go out on a date, she was looking forward to an evening by herself.

"Guess you're going to be by yourself for a while," Greg said upon seeing her stroll into the house. "I'm leaving shortly for my big date." He looked adorable in freshly pressed khakis and a madras plaid shirt that set off his blue eyes and gray hair.

"You don't know who it is?" Jill asked, remembering her earlier conversation with Melanie.

He shook his head. "Nope. All I know it's a friend of a friend."

Jill couldn't help the smile that spread across her face. It had to be Melanie. "Well, I'm pretty sure it's all going to work out fine."

"We'll see. I'll never stop missing Annie, but I think I'm finally ready to consider meeting other women." He held up his arm, still in a cast. "This is just a small bump in the road. I've got a lot of living left to do."

She chuckled at the impish grin he sent her. "Of course, you do!

Still smiling, she went into her bedroom to freshen up. She noticed a book she'd recently bought and picked it up. Tonight, she'd make a bowl of popcorn, fix herself some iced lemonade, and read.

She was in the middle of a touching story when her cell phone rang. She hesitated and let it go to voice mail. This was one of those "Me Moments" she really needed. It wasn't until she was dabbing at her eyes with a tissue over the book's happy ending that she remembered the phone call.

She checked her messages mail and was surprised to see one from her sister. Her breath caught. *What now?* Her eyes scanned the words: ... emergency ...coming home ... need to talk ... will call later.

Jill caught her lip between her teeth. She had no desire to talk to her sister. Dealing with Cristal was difficult at best. Still, the idea of an emergency big enough to come home from her European trip was worrisome. She checked the time. Too late to call. She'd wait for Cristal to call her back.

She got up from the couch and headed into the kitchen. It was late, and she was ready for bed. A good cry over the book was exactly what she'd needed to relieve the swirling emotions meeting Allison had caused.

At the sound of someone at the front door, she turned around to greet Greg. "Hi! Have a good time?"

"The best," he said, beaming at her. "You know my date, Melanie Heckinger."

"Really? It was Melanie all along? That's wonderful!!"

"Yeah, she's a very nice woman. She thinks the world of you," said Greg.

"And I think the two of you would be great together," Jill said.

"She's a little younger than I am, but we clicked right away."

"Age shouldn't matter. Like you told me earlier, you have a lot of life left in you."

He chuckled. "We'll see how it goes, but for the first time in a long time, I really enjoyed spending the evening with a woman other than Annie."

"Sweet. I hope it works out for you. I'm turning in. See you in the morning."

Later, as Jill lay in bed, staring up at the ceiling, her thoughts turned to Cristal. An emergency to her might be as trivial as not having the right color lipstick for an outfit. But coming home? Something traumatic must have happened.

Jill pushed troubling thoughts of her sister away, fluffed her pillow, and rolled over, hoping for a good night's sleep.

The sound of her cell phone shattered Jill's dreams. Groggy, she reached out and checked the time. Two AM. She gave a bleary-eyed glance at the caller's name and groaned. *Cristal.*

"What's so important that you had to call me at this time of night?" she muttered into the phone.

"Sorry, I keep forgetting your time is behind not ahead of me," said Cristal. "Something's come up, and I'm returning to the States."

"What's the something?" Jill asked warily.

"I fell and twisted my ankle, but there's something else. I want to come and stay with you at Seashell Cottage. It has three bedrooms, right?"

"Yes, it does. Three bedrooms that are already full. I'm cooking for two men and a little girl, thanks to you."

"Who's the extra guy?"

"Greg's nephew and his little girl."

"I should have told you about Greg," Cristal admitted. "I was afraid you'd back out if you knew about that ahead of time, and I thought it was important for you to get away from Ellenton for a while."

"As it turns out, you're right. It's been wonderful for me."

"See? Once in a while it's wise to believe your big sister. By the way, do NOT tell Mom I'm coming home. As I said, I really need to talk to you alone, without any interference from her."

"She's going to be furious if she finds out," Jill warned her.

"Yeah, well, this is really important. Listen, don't worry about my getting there. I'll see you as soon as I can."

"But ..." Jill began and realized Cristal had already hung

up. Wide awake now, Jill got out of bed and padded into the kitchen. A cup of hot tea would help her get back to sleep. Her mind was spinning all kinds of scenarios in her mind. A lot of them not so great.

CHAPTER NINETEEN

As soon as Melanie saw Jill, she ran over to her, her face alight with excitement. "Jill, I didn't know Greg Campbell was living in the cottage with you! Such a wonderful guy! We had a great evening together."

"I know. He told me. He really enjoyed it."

She giggled. "I know I sound like a love-struck teenager, but I can't help myself."

Jill gave her a quick hug. "I hope it's the beginning of something wonderful for the two of you."

"Susannah has been bugging me to teach you a lot more about the business end of things. How do you feel about that, Jill?" Melanie studied her.

"I'd like that very much," Jill answered honestly.

Melanie grinned. "She's telling me it's all part of a bigger plan. I'm okay with that. Let's get you trained and then we can talk more about the future."

Out of the corner of her eye, Jill saw Susannah give her a thumbs up from her place next to the kitchen door. Chuckling to herself, she turned to Melanie. "Okay. Sounds like a plan."

Instead of helping Kelly with swimming lessons, Jill worked with Melanie in the office.

"Have you come up with a new slogan?" Melanie asked her. "'Sunny Days and Ways ...' is a little tired."

Jill withdrew a sheet of paper from her purse. "I was doodling around with words the other day and came up with two suggestions: 'Camp Sunnyside—A Sunny Experience For All,' and 'Camp Sunnyside—A Warm Welcoming Experience

For Everyone.'"

"Oh, I really like the second one," said Melanie. "Let's use that going forward. I also want to change up the logo a bit, maybe play with the sizing of it."

"As a matter of fact, I was playing around with that too," said Jill. "Here. Let me show you." She handed her a piece of paper on which she'd drawn several designs.

"Very nice. Let's work with our printer and get him to come up with something for us to look at for stationery, business cards, and the new flyer we're working on." Melanie beamed at her. "If things go the way I hope, you'll become a permanent part of the team."

"I hope so, too," said Jill, liking the idea of balancing teaching and camp work. Susannah had already told her it would happen, but Jill kept quiet about that. She didn't want Melanie to feel pushed out. Besides, she still had work to do to get settled in her new living style in Florida. Third-grade teaching was going to take time to get used to. At least there would be no more struggling with kindergarteners' snow boots and coat zippers before recess.

As Melanie showed her more and more about the workings behind the scene, Jill realized it was a bigger business than she'd thought. The safety of the children was paramount. The state and county were careful about the licensing requirements and qualifications needed to oversee an operation like this. The amount of liability insurance the camp carried was eye-popping.

Jill's mind continued to spin with details as she drove back to the cottage. When she pulled into the driveway, she was surprised to see Brody's truck. Concerned, she hurried inside.

Brody was sitting at the kitchen table with Greg.

"Hi! You're home early. What's up?" Jill asked. "Where's Kacy?"

"I dropped her off at Emily's house after taking Allison to the airport."

"Is everything all right?" Brody looked exhausted.

"Allison and I got into a fight last night. The whole time we were going through DisneyWorld, she complained about the heat, the waiting in line, the cost of the food, everything. It ruined the time for Kacy." Brody let out a long sigh. "Allison has agreed to let me have Kacy for the rest of the summer, and she and Marcus are going to talk about Kacy staying with me for the next school year. If they agree, we'll draw up papers and present them to the court for approval."

"Having Kacy with her might interfere with Allison's plans for a fall trip to Paris," said Greg, looking as disgusted as Brody.

"What does Kacy think of all this?" Jill asked.

"She heard us talking last night and told Allison she never wanted to live with her again. I had to explain to Kacy that even if she spent the school year with me, vacations and holidays would be shared."

"What did Allison say?"

"She's thinking things over. I'm hoping she and Kacy can come to some kind of truce, but I don't see that happening any time soon. Kacy understands she has the right to say how she feels. I was really surprised by how well she handled herself."

Jill plunked down in a chair at the table. "Well, this is turning out to be a summer of surprises. My sister called to say she's leaving Europe early and coming to stay with me. I tried to explain the situation here to her, but she hung up before I could. My room has two queen beds, so I guess I'll be sharing my room with her. Hope you guys don't mind."

"Not at all. In a month or so, we'll go back to our normal schedules," said Greg. He shot a glance at Brody. "Or not."

"I'm going to apply for a position here in St. Petersburg,"

Brody said to her. "There's a small group of psychologists who've opened a practice I'm interested in joining. That will help me determine whether I make the move or not. I've already alerted the people in Pennsylvania that I might not come back."

"I hope it works out and you can stay," Jill said, suddenly embarrassed by the eagerness in her voice.

Greg chuckled. "It seems there might be even more surprises. I've called Melanie, and we're going out tomorrow night."

"This morning, she couldn't stop smiling," said Jill. "Guess you two have really hit it off. I'm happy for you both."

Brody patted his uncle on the back. "Me too, Greg. I know how lonely you've been without Annie."

"Yes. Even though Melanie suffered through a divorce, she understands my devotion to Annie and respects that."

"That's sweet." Jill got to her feet. "I'm going to change my clothes then take a walk on the beach before I get dinner ready. I thought we'd grill some chicken and have some fresh broccoli and a fruit salad."

"I'm happy to grill the chicken," said Brody. "After an expensive, tense dinner last night, this sounds perfect."

Jill emerged from her bedroom in denim shorts and a cut-off T-shirt to find Brody waiting for her.

"Mind if I walk with you?"

"Not at all. It would be nice."

They headed out to the beach, hand in hand.

Jill liked the fact that they were becoming more and more comfortable with one another.

He turned and smiled at her.

A flashback caught her breath. Her college boyfriend used

to look at her that way ... until he saw Cristal and dumped her.

Jill pulled her hand away from Brody's and came to a stop.

"What's wrong?" Brody asked.

"I'm just thinking about my sister."

"What is it? You don't look happy."

"Ah, you don't know what it's like when I'm with her. She's beautiful and comfortable meeting others ..."

Brody took hold of Jill's hand. "Stop. I don't know what's going on, but if you're comparing yourself to her or anyone else, you don't understand how beautiful you are inside and out."

"But ..."

"It's that asshole, dead husband of yours that's made you think that way, isn't it?" His eyes narrowed, his gaze boring inside her. "It's guys like that who deserve to be strung up. Greg told me a little about your situation, and I know of other cases similar to it."

Jill stood frozen in her spot as painful memories pierced her like a sharp knife, leaving her bleeding all over again. Not only memories of her marriage, but those of her childhood. Cristal, the pretty one, Cristal, the talented one, Cristal, the one all the boys and girls liked best. It had left Jill with just scraps of praise now and then, none of them exciting. And then Jay had taken even those tiny pieces of recognition and torn them like tissue paper, making sure she thought she was ugly, clumsy, and unlovable while pretending to others to be her devoted husband.

Jill lowered herself onto the sand, feeling so nauseous she didn't dare move.

Brody knelt beside her and wrapped an arm around her. "Listen to me," he said quietly in her ear. "Tell me what's bothering you. It's safe. There isn't anything you can say that I haven't heard."

"You'll think I'm silly, or stupid, or worse," said Jill. If he knew how frightened she was to tell him her worst fears, he'd run, not walk away from the relationship that was building between them.

"You can tell me..." Brody's voice was soft, full of understanding.

She turned to him. "For most of my childhood, my mother made sure Cristal and I and everyone else knew Cristal was the favored one. And Cristal? She grew up knowing it, loving it."

"Was there a lot of sibling rivalry going on?" asked Brody.

Jill shrugged. "Not really. There was no point, really. We knew our places."

"And what was your place?" Brody gently asked.

"I was the one who studied hard and deserved to do well in school because I couldn't dance or sing like Cristal. And looks? I was the one with the Davis nose while my mother told everyone Cristal was the fairy princess who took after her."

"Is it true that they look alike?"

Jill shook her head. "A little bit, but not too much. Cristal's a natural blonde, blue-eyed beauty. My mom's hair isn't naturally that way."

Brody took hold of her elbow. "Get up."

Jill got to her feet, feeling wobbly, as if she was recovering from a long illness.

"Look at me," Brody said.

She stared into his green eyes full of concern. "What?"

"I'm not going to give you a lot of platitudes, but I will say that it might be time for you to think about all you're doing on your own here in Florida because you are smart and capable. Your beauty is not to be questioned, but to be set aside. Appearance is changeable, but a person's innate character isn't. You have one of the kindest hearts I've known. You're courageous and able to make a new future for yourself. You've proved that, so why go back to old thinking?"

"You know, more than most, that childhoods shape adults," she said, not ready to let go of all that had hurt her.

"Indeed, and baggage can get very heavy. If your sister is coming here, it might be time to unpack all those feelings." He wrapped his arm around her, and they stared out at the waves rolling into shore in a continuous pattern.

The movement of the water, as timeless as the sunrises and sunsets over it, soothed her. She drew in and let out several deep breaths. Maybe, she thought, he was right. Maybe it was time she and Cristal talked openly and honestly.

After the walk on the beach with Brody, Jill made an effort to push aside her worries about spending time with Cristal. They hadn't been close growing up, but maybe they could forge a better relationship going forward now that Jill had left their hometown and was away from her mother's influence. She'd give it a try. She went into her room to change clothes pleased by her new resolution.

In the kitchen, Jill went about preparing broccoli and cutting up oranges and grapefruit for a fresh fruit salad. After being resentful at being given the task of cooking, she realized she enjoyed it, especially when her meals were enthusiastically devoured.

Greg handed her a glass of wine. "For the cook."

"Thanks." She smiled at him. "As I said earlier, I'm pleased you and Melanie got along so well."

His gaze rested on her. "Thanks. I see how well you and Brody are getting along and, believe me, I'm happy to see it. He's one of the good guys. You can count on it."

Jill nodded but didn't say anything. He certainly seemed

like it, but they were still getting to know one another.

"Any idea when your sister is going to get here?" Greg asked.

"Nope. That's how she likes it. I left a message for her, but she hasn't responded."

"Well, I guess it doesn't matter. She'll show up when she does."

"And when you least expect it," Jill couldn't help adding.

CHAPTER TWENTY

The next morning, Jill checked her calendar. School was due to start in mid-August and she had yet to see her classroom. And she still hadn't heard from Kay Branson at Palm Rentals and Realty regarding the condo she wanted to rent come September. She couldn't move before then because of her commitment to stay at Seashell Cottage for the summer. Besides, Brody, Greg, and Kacy needed her.

Realizing how fast the days were going by, she lifted the phone to call Kay.

"Hi, Jill! I'm sorry I haven't gotten back to you. Right after you and I talked, the property came under contract with a friend of the family. Until now, I wasn't sure if it was actually going through. There was a problem with the inspection. But it turned out to be nothing."

Disappointment coursed through Jill. "So, it's not available?"

"No. The issue is now resolved, and the property is off the rental market. But don't worry, there are plenty of other properties available to rent for the fall. However, if you're in the market to buy, it's a good time. Let's plan to meet and we'll discuss it."

"In the meantime, you know what I'm looking for. I'll call you." Jill hung up the phone wishing things could be a little easier. She needed to sit down and draw up a realistic budget for herself. She had a sizable down payment to make on a house, but she wouldn't be able to afford a big mortgage. Not on a teacher's salary.

Before she left for work at camp, she made arrangements to visit her classroom. She'd been told the teacher who'd had the classroom before her had left a lot of education materials and instructional items behind and had no further use for them. Another third-grade teacher, Leigh McKinnon, agreed to meet her later that afternoon. Jill knew from experience how important it was to set up the classroom to her own liking. Having a roomful of active children did not give a teacher time to search out needed materials or to decide if the space arrangement would work for her.

Jill arranged with Brody for him to pick up Kacy that afternoon and then drove to the camp wondering how she was going to make everything work. She had yet to find a place to live and to get settled. On top of that, she was trying to learn about running the camp and take on more work there so future summer months off from teaching would produce income for her.

From the moment she walked into the camp until she left at four o'clock to meet Leigh, Jill worked in the office, where she was inundated with information about setting up mailing and advertising campaigns for the next holiday and summer camps.

"It's like anything else in retail, so to speak, you've got to keep one season ahead so that you can keep camp slots filled. It makes a huge difference in profitability, which is not all that much after expenses," said Melanie.

Jill took notes, amused by Melanie's sudden urgency for her to learn all she could. That, no doubt, came from meeting Greg and Susannah's prediction that all this would happen quickly.

Jill was on her way to her school when her cell phone rang.

"Hi, Jilly! Cristal here. I'm in Miami and should arrive at the cottage tomorrow. I know you won't mind seeing that a few of my favorite food items are there, so I'm texting you a list of all the things I need. Thanks. See you tomorrow."

"Wait!" But the silence in her ear indicated Cristal had already disconnected the call.

Jill gritted her teeth. Her earlier resolution about making things work with Cristal disappeared in a wave of frustration. Dammit! Would things never change between them?

She pulled up to the school and forced herself to soothe her ruffled emotions. This was her future—a new beginning that had nothing to do with her sister, her deceased husband, or her mother. This was about her.

She got out of the car and walked briskly toward the front of the dark-brick building of the Palm Creek Elementary School. She loved seeing the open-air, roofed walkways around the school, an indication of the warmer weather and students spending more time outside.

She walked to the front door and opened it. A small woman was hurrying toward her. Jill stepped inside and was immediately assailed by an odor she would always associate with schools—a mixture of cleaning supplies, art supplies, kids' clothes, and what she called optimism.

"Hi! You must be Jill. I'm Leigh." The tiny woman, not much over five feet Jill guessed, held out a hand. Her smile brightened a pretty face and brought out the blue-green color of her eyes. Dark hair was pulled back from her face and tied in a ponytail. She looked about ten.

Jill shook it. "Nice to meet you."

"Me too. You and I will work closely together during the coming school year. Our rooms are right next to one another, so we can help each other out. Bathroom breaks and all."

Jill laughed. "Glad to hear it. That's always a problem."

"We'll work on that together. Carole, who had the classroom last year, and I got along great. I think we will too. I love teaching third grade and have a lot of instructional materials I can share with you."

"I'm used to kindergarten, so I need to know more about the standards and what supplemental teaching aids are available," said Jill, following Leigh down a hallway.

"Not a problem. I've already been creating a list of things for you. It will make my job much easier if you're well prepared. It's an important year for reading, vocabulary, learning about the past, present, and future, work on the solar system. So much good information."

Leigh led her to a classroom and flipped on the lights. Chairs were carefully placed upside down on a number of circular tables. Green tweed carpeting covered the floor. A white board covered one wall.

"This is your room," Leigh said. "Mine's next door. Let's take a look at some of the things I've done to it, things you might want to consider for your own room."

When Jill walked into Leigh's room, she smiled. The addition of book covers, pictures of different planets, and other colorful posters made the room come alive. She also noted the bookcase loaded with books and decided to buy more books for her classroom. She'd always loved to read and still used it as an escape.

As Jill continued to study the room, Leigh handed her a small notebook. "You can make notes here. Inside, I've listed all the places you can find items discounted for teachers. One of the stores around here usually has notebooks like these on sale for nineteen cents each before school starts. There are other places that offer teacher discounts. I understand you're new to Florida."

Touched to the core, Jill turned to her. "How can I ever

thank you for giving me all this information and being so nice to me? I was starting to get worried about being able to handle third grade. I'm not so concerned now, though I'm sure I'll need your advice and guidance."

"I continue to need all of that, and I've been here for six years. The principal, Dennis Magee, is the best. He's really nice, supportive, and lowkey. He's willing to help in any way and is open to suggestions." She looked up. "Oh, here he is now."

Jill whirled around to face a large man who looked like a former football player. His smile stretched like a crescent moon across his dark-skinned face. But it was his sparkling, dark-brown eyes that captured Jill with their open friendliness. She returned his smile, liking him immediately. No wonder Leigh had spoken so highly of him. If he was as great as Leigh had said, Jill knew she'd have no trouble adjusting.

"Hello, Jill. After our phone interview, I read through your history once more and am delighted you've joined our team here at Palm Creek. I like to keep things pretty open, so if you have anything you need to discuss with me, feel free to do so. How do you think you're going to like third grade?"

"I think I'm going to love it. After being in kindergarten for a number of years, I'm ready for a change."

"You come highly recommended. Sorry I was out of town during your initial interview, but I'm glad we found you to fill in for us. Leigh, here, is right on top of things, so you can rely on her for help."

Leigh's cheeks turned a pretty pink. "Thank you, Dennis."

Dennis held out his hand, and Jill shook it. "Thank you for stopping by. As it gets closer to August, I'll be here every day." He reached into his pocket and handed her a key. "Here's a key to your classroom in case you want to come in and do some work on your room."

"Thanks. I'm going to be working on a number of projects," said Jill. "And I want to make sure my room is decorated."

"I've already given her a list of places where she can find educational things cheap," Leigh said.

Dennis gave them a salute and left the room.

"Wow! He's so different from my principal back in New York. She can sometimes be difficult and unwilling to deal with what she thinks are petty details from teachers."

"Dennis is true to what he says. Teachers, parents, and students adore him. The kids call him 'Big D', as in 'Be careful, Big D is watching.'" She laughed. "It's all too cute."

Still smiling, Jill left the school, feeling as if she could dance across the parking lot. She'd been so stuck in her rut back home she'd accepted a comparatively difficult work environment without thinking of leaving. God! What a mess she'd been.

She checked the time and called Brody to tell him dinner would be a little late.

"No problem. Why don't we order in pizza when you get home? Greg and I have started to prepare the exterior for painting, and I can hardly move. Besides, it'll be a treat for Kacy."

"Perfect. I met with another teacher and the principal at the school where I'll be teaching, and I want to stop at one of the stores they suggested to see what might be available for my classroom."

After the call ended, Jill sat in her car in a daze.

Dennis came out of the building and waved to her before getting into a low-slung sports car. She almost laughed at the thought of him squeezing behind the steering wheel. But then, what guy didn't like a car like that, including "Big D?"

She left the school parking lot and drove around a few of

the nearby neighborhoods to get a sense of the surrounding community before heading to one of the stores on the list.

By the time she returned to Seashell Cottage, she was more excited than ever about starting the school year. She wanted to get Kacy's reaction to all the things she'd bought for the classroom. At eight, Kacy would be going into the third grade herself.

When she pulled into the driveway, she was surprised to see a strange car parked there. She studied the silver Audi and wondered whose it was.

She parked, gathered her packages, and walked inside.

"Surprise!" cried Cristal, smiling at her from the couch where she was sitting with Brody. "I decided not to wait until tomorrow, after all."

CHAPTER TWENTY-ONE

Struggling to retain a grip on her packages, Jill gaped at her sister. "Cristal! You're here? Why the change in plans?"

Cristal gave her a smug smile. "Like I said, I decided not to wait. The thought of lying in the sun on the beach was too irresistible. Besides, we haven't seen each other for a couple of years. I thought it was time we did." She turned to Brody with a bright smile. "If I'd known who was fixing up the cottage, I might have come sooner."

Brody stood. "Can I help you with your packages?"

"Sure," Jill said, handing him a couple. "I've got a few more in the car. Where's Kacy? I want to show them to her."

"She's staying with Emily. They're working on something for a talent show." He followed her into the bedroom.

Two suitcases were piled on the bed Jill had been using. The closet door was open and clothing was half hanging out, crammed together, pushing Jill's things out of the way.

She set down her packages in the corner and attempted to lift one of the suitcases.

"Here. Let me do that," Brody said. "I wasn't sure which bed was yours."

They moved the suitcases to the other bed and faced one another.

"How did your meeting at school go?"

"It was great. I love the teacher I'll be working with, and the principal is a real gem." She knew she sounded stiff, but couldn't help the insecurity that had overcome her when she'd seen Cristal sitting so close to Brody on the couch.

"Hey! Come here," Brody said. He held out his arms.

Jill hesitated, and then went into them, needing his reassurance. "I know I'm being foolish ..." she began.

Brody's lips on hers stopped her.

"Well! Sorry I didn't knock. I didn't know things were like *that* between you."

Jill jumped away from Brody and turned to face her sister. "After dinner, we'll get things sorted in here. You'll be sleeping on that bed."

"I brought a lot of things with me, but I don't know how long I'm staying. I've moved out of the condo I was sharing with Hope. We've had a big fight. I decided she's not the friend I thought she was."

"She's still in Europe?"

"Yes, she and Jacques, who was my boyfriend, are traveling together now."

"You said you sprained your ankle." Jill stared down at Cristal's feet whose nails were painted a pretty pink. She saw no signs of any injury.

"Yes, but that was more or less an excuse to come here. It turned out to be nothing big. That's not why I'm really here. Did you get the groceries and other items I asked you to buy for me?"

"No. You told me you were coming tomorrow."

"Oh, well, tomorrow you and I can go shopping."

"No," Jill said calmly. "I work tomorrow from eleven to four. Before and after that, I'll be preparing for my teaching job. I'm moving here and will be teaching third grade."

"Well, I'll be damned. That's a big change for you."

"I'm going to let the two of you talk in private," said Brody, shifting restlessly from foot to foot. "Greg and I were about to sit down outside when Cristal came. We can order the pizza anytime."

"Pizza? Is that what you call cooking?" Cristal said. "Heck! I could've done the job myself."

Jill and Brody exchanged meaningful glances before he turned to go.

Cristal watched him leave and turned to Jill. "Wow! He's hot! Better watch out! He won't be free for long."

Jill placed her hands on her hips. "What? Are you going to try to take him away from me, like you did with Rob Swope in college?"

"Are you still stinging from that? Why? He was never good enough for you."

"We were doing well together until you ruined it for me," Jill said, feeling as if the years were peeling back, exposing her for the loser she'd always thought she was.

Cristal held up her hand. "Okay. Let's stop this. I'm sorry, but that was a long time ago."

"Okay, truce," Jill readily agreed. "It's in the past."

Greg knocked on the door. "How about a glass of wine before we order in?"

"Sounds perfect," said Jill. It would take more than wine to settle her nerves, but it was a beginning. What she really needed was to see both herself and her sister in a new light so she could continue to move forward. Besides there was something off about her sister—a sadness to her eyes and a stillness that was new.

On the porch, Jill took a seat next to Brody in the swing. Cristal settled in a rocking chair next to Greg.

"Here's to a bright future for all of us," Greg said. "Melanie told me you worked in the office most of the day at the camp. How'd your meeting at school go, Jill?"

"Fine. I think it's going to be a good school year for me."

"Whoa! Camp and school? What are you doing, Jill? Working two jobs?" said Cristal. "I thought this was going to be a relaxing summer for you."

"I need to work," Jill reminded her. "And with my unexpected move to Florida, I have to get things settled in a hurry."

"Guess you didn't even consider moving to South Beach with me," said Cristal.

Surprised, Jill said, "I can't imagine you'd want me to."

"Not in the past maybe, but now it would be kinda nice." Her voice sounded wistful.

Jill locked gazes with Cristal. This wasn't the sister she knew.

"How'd the painting go today? It's got to be hot working in the sun," Jill said to Brody.

"Yeah, it is. We'll try to work outside in the morning and then do different projects inside. The owner has decided she wants all the cabinet doors in the kitchen re-stained."

Jill took a sip of wine and turned to Greg. "So, you talked to Melanie today. I'm surprised you two aren't going out to dinner."

"Tomorrow," Greg said, beaming. "I didn't want to rush her."

Jill laughed. The two of them were acting like teenagers in love, exactly as Melanie had stated.

"How was Europe?" Brody asked Cristal.

"It was really great. We started in Spain. We saw the usual places including Madrid, Barcelona, and Toledo. In Paris, we met Jacques. That was the beginning of what went wrong between Hope and me. She decided she wanted to be with Jacques, not me. They went off to Provence without me, leaving me to pay the hotel bill."

"And now you're here," said Brody.

"Yes," said Cristal. "For as long as I can be. I, too, need to make arrangements."

Jill waited for her to say more, but she remained quiet. Jill studied her. Yes, something was definitely wrong. Her sister was never this reticent.

Brody stood. "Before I have any wine, I need to pick up Kacy. Care to ride over to Emily's house with me, Jill?"

"Sure." She jumped to her feet, happy for the chance to be alone with him. She was curious to know how his talks with Allison were going. And he was waiting on word from the medical group in St. Petersburg, the one he'd been talking to about joining them.

He held the door for her as she climbed into his truck, and then went around to the driver's side and climbed in.

"Glad we have a chance to talk privately. I've been offered a partnership with the medical group in St. Petersburg."

Jill flung her arms around Brody's neck. "That's fantastic! You were very impressed with them. I'm glad they feel the same way about you!"

"It'll take a while for me to move my business there, but the process has already started. And that's not the only exciting news I got. Allison called. She and Marcus have agreed to let Kacy stay here in Florida with me for the next school year. We'll coordinate visitation and holidays when they get back from Europe." A huge smile spread across his handsome face. "I've called my real estate agent in Pennsylvania and I've already put my condo up for sale. I'm going to look for a house here. If I find one big enough, Greg might move in with me. We're talking about it."

"That sounds superb. My rental plans fell through. My real estate agent here is pushing me to buy, but I'm going to rent until I know the area better."

His eyes twinkled. "Why don't you move in with me?"

She laughed. "Move in? So I can cook for you?"

"That too," he said, chuckling. "But that's not the first thing

I had in mind." The smile left his face. "By the way, I have no idea why you feel intimidated by your sister. She's beautiful, but so are you."

"There is no comparison," Jill began.

"That's true," he said. "And you're the winner."

He leaned over and brushed a curl away from her face. Then his lips met hers.

The warmth of his kiss felt delicious. She wound her arms around his neck.

When they finally pulled apart, Jill gazed at him in a dreamy haze and sighed.

He grinned. "Now, let's go pick up my little girl so you can show her some of the loot you brought home."

"Sounds like a plan," she said as Brody took off.

CHAPTER TWENTY-TWO

They were greeted at Emily's house with cries of laughter as four fluffy white puppies chased two girls around the front lawn. Emily's grandmother oversaw them with a smile on her face.

Jill got out of Brody's truck and stood a moment to observe the activity. Kids and dogs just seemed to go together.

"Hi, Carolyn! Where's Niki?" Jill asked walking over to Emily's grandmother.

"Inside with the T's," Carolyn responded. "She's giving me a break."

"You're such a fantastic grandmother." Jill couldn't imagine her mother doing any of the things Carolyn seemed to enjoy.

While Brody talked to Kacy, Jill ducked inside to say hello to her best friend.

Niki was feeding the triplets, moving smoothly from one highchair to another to refresh food on their trays.

"Hey, girlfriend!" said Niki. "Long time no see."

Jill gave her a quick hug. "I know. I'm sorry. Life has gotten in the way. And now my sister is here. Heaven knows what she wants. She says she needs to talk to me about something. Last time I talked to her I ended up here in Florida, taking care of Greg, Brody, and Kacy."

Niki arched an eyebrow at her. "And look how well that's turned out for you. Even though I haven't given up on something working out between you and Charlie, I'm delighted that you've found Brody. A decent guy to help you get rid of those bad memories of yours."

"Memories that not even my sister knows about," said Jill.

"It might be time to let everything out," said Niki, wiping the mouth of either Luke or Mark, Jill wasn't sure. "Let's plan to get together soon. I've missed our talks."

"Definitely," said Jill. "I've got to go. I'm asking Kacy to check over some of the materials I bought for my third-grade class."

"How are things coming?"

"My grade-level teaching partner is someone I really like, and the principal of the school is great! I'm hoping for a good school year."

"How about housing?"

"Brody is suggesting I stay at any house he might buy until I know for sure where I want to live. I was going to rent, but my real estate agent is suggesting it's a good time to buy."

"Aha!" said Niki with a gleam in her eye. "The plot thickens."

Jill laughed. "We'll see. First, I have to deal with my sister."

Amid the noise of toddlers trying to squirm out of their highchairs, Jill gave Niki another hug and left the kitchen. Even though she now knew she hoped to have children someday, she wanted them one at a time. Niki was a miracle worker.

Outside, Kacy ran up to her. "Hi, Jill! Daddy says I might be able to have a puppy! We have to see if we get a house."

"Oh, wouldn't that be wonderful," said Jill, beaming at Kacy and then looking up at Brody.

He gave her a sheepish look and shrugged. "They're awfully cute."

She laughed. Brody had such a soft heart.

On the way to the cottage, Jill explained to Kacy that her sister would be staying with them for a while.

"Is she nice?" Kacy asked.

"I think so," Jill responded. "Pretty, too. Now, I have something special to ask you. I've picked out some things for my third-grade classroom, and because you're going into the third grade, I want to show them to you so I know if they'll like them. Will you help me?"

"Really? Me?" Kacy's face lit with pleasure.

Jill nodded solemnly. "Yes, I want your honest opinion."

"Okay," said Kacy, smiling. "I'll tell you if it's cool or not."

Jill and Brody exchanged amused glances.

When they returned to the cottage, Cristal was sitting on the porch with Greg sipping a glass of wine. "We decided not to wait for you," she said lifting her wine glass and smiling at Brody before turning to Jill. "Guess it's a safe thing you're ordering in. There's not much in the refrigerator."

Kacy stood beside Jill staring at Cristal. "Are you Jill's real sister?"

Cristal smiled. "Yes. I realize we don't look alike, but we are sisters."

"Are you going to be nice?" Kacy asked, frowning as she continued to study Cristal.

Cristal drew her lips together. "I'll try."

"Okay," said Kacy. "You can stay." She opened the sliding door and went inside.

"Really?" Cristal said. "You let a kid talk to me like that?"

Jill shook her head. "She's just testing boundaries. Excuse me, but I have some things in the living room that I need to show her."

Inside, Kacy was sitting next to the pile of paper bags Jill had brought home. She peered inside one of them. "Is this what you want me to see?"

"Yes, said Jill, kneeling beside her. "I need to choose things for the walls of the classroom—pictures and learning tools." She lifted out a folder with several photographs of planets, stars, and the solar system. "How about these?"

"Yes! They're cool. Dad bought me a book about this."

"You think the kids in my class will like them?" Jill asked. From the delight she saw on Kacy's face, she knew it was unnecessary to ask, but she wanted Kacy to enjoy the feeling of helping out.

"Yes. They're gonna *love* them!"

"Okay, thank you. How about these?" Jill held up a series of letters and words, accented with colorful paintings of objects.

Kacy shrugged. "All the teachers have them."

"Okay, now these," said Jill. She handed Kacy a packet of photos of kids in different parts of the world showcasing different parts of speech used in sentences that stressed kindness.

Kacy nodded. "I like these best."

Jill and Kacy smiled at one another. It was another special moment between them, Jill thought, remembering how whiny and difficult Kacy had been when they first met.

Cristal walked into the house, shattering the quiet. "Hey! What's going on? Aren't we about ready to order the pizza? I'm still on French time, and I'm starving."

Kacy's smile morphed into a frown that wrinkled her brow. She stared up at Cristal. "Miss Melanie says it's rude to interrupt."

Surprised, Jill hid a smile. "Kacy and I are done here. Let me check with Brody and Greg and we'll see about dinner."

Kacy got to her feet. "Did I help, Jill?"

Still kneeling, Jill pulled Kacy into a hug. "You helped a lot. Thanks."

After Kacy ran off, Jill finished tucking her items into bags.

"You should have scolded her for talking to me that way," said Cristal. "And who is Miss Melanie?"

Jill stood and faced her sister. "First of all, Kacy was right. It was rude to interrupt. Miss Melanie is one of the owners of Camp Sunnyside where I work and where Kacy goes to summer camp."

Cristal let out a sigh. "I never was good with kids. Remember how we used to babysit together? You were the one the kids wanted to be with."

"I was the one who took care of them," Jill countered. "You were the one who used to fix all the girls' hair."

A wistful look came to Cristal's face. "Growing up, I wanted to be a hairdresser, but Mother thought I should be an actress or a model."

A rush of sympathy filled Jill. She wasn't the only one who'd been programmed by their mother. She took Cristal's elbow. "C'mon! Let's go to the kitchen. I'll fix a salad to go with the pizza. You can sneak in a few bites before the pizza arrives."

The next morning, as soon as she heard movement in the bed next to hers, Jill rolled over and studied her sister, asleep on her back. In the early morning light, Cristal looked more like the thirty-five-year-old she was than the fresh, dewy teenager Jill always remembered. The circles under her eyes were appalling.

Cristal's eyes fluttered open. She turned toward Jill. "What? I can feel you staring at me. Stop it."

"Sorry. I was just checking to see if you were awake. I've been worried about you all night. What's going on?"

Cristal sat up in bed and clutched her knees to her chest.

"I've got breast cancer."

"Whaaat? When did you find out?" Jill tried to keep her voice down so she wouldn't wake the others in the house, but her voice was high with shock.

"I got word while I was in Paris. I'd had a biopsy done in Miami before we left for Europe, but I was told it probably was nothing because of all the cysts I usually get. But when I got to Paris, I received a message from the clinic saying they'd sent a report to me and were waiting to hear from me."

"Is that why you and Hope fought?" Jill asked, distressed by the idea.

"Partly. When I started talking about going home, Hope got mad. We argued and Hope ended up leaving Paris with Jacques. That's when I decided to come home, and instead of having any medical issues taken care of in Miami, I made arrangements with the Moffit Cancer Center in Tampa to have surgery. That way, I'd be close to you."

Jill clasped her cheeks trying to absorb all the information. "Breast cancer? How bad is it?"

"I'm not sure yet. In any case, they found it in the early stages. It may turn out not to be a big deal." Her beautiful blue eyes filled. "Or worse. It might be the beginning of the end."

"Oh, hon! I'm so sorry." Jill rose, padded over to her sister's bed, and sat down. "In today's world, breast cancer doesn't necessarily mean death. With drugs, surgery, and radiation treatment, it isn't the same disease it once was." She gave Cristal a hug. "No matter what, I'll be here for you."

Tears spilled from Cristal's eyes onto her cheeks. "You're always so sweet. That's what I was counting on to make things right between us. I've been thinking about a lot of things. Sort of like they tell you to do when you're facing mortality. You know?"

Jill's mind spun, trying to make sense of it all. "You told me not to mention your visit to Mom. Does she know about the cancer?"

"No, and that's the way I want to keep it until I know more. She always turns things around so it's all about her. I don't think I can cope with that right now."

"All right. I won't say a word to her about it. Mom and I don't talk that much anymore. She knows I'm busy trying to get settled in my new life here. And she certainly told me off when she learned about my selling my house in Ellenton and moving to Florida without first getting her 'approval.'"

Cristal lifted the edge of the T-shirt she was wearing and dabbed at her eyes. "Sounds like a plan for as long as we can get away with it."

"When's your appointment in Tampa?" Jill asked.

"The day after tomorrow."

"I'll let Melanie know I can't be at camp that day, and I'll get my classroom posters and other items posted this morning before I'm due at camp."

"What about the grocery store?" Cristal said.

"We'll do that right now. Get dressed. They're open 24/7."

Cristal shook her head. "I've always envied you, Jill. You make everything seem so easy. Even your life with Jay seemed idyllic."

Jill caught her breath and let it out slowly. "We need to talk."

CHAPTER TWENTY-THREE

Jill tapped her foot, telling herself to be calm, but Cristal was taking forever to get ready to go out. She'd quickly dressed but wanted time to put on makeup before leaving the house. When she finally emerged from the bathroom, she looked ... well ... gorgeous.

As Jill was pouring a cup of coffee for Cristal in the kitchen, Brody walked into the room wearing a pair of cut-off jeans and nothing else. Jill couldn't help staring. He looked ... yummy.

Brody smiled at her and turned his gaze on Cristal. "You're all dressed up. What's up?"

"Jill's taking me grocery shopping," said Cristal, beaming at him. She stood with one leg forward and her arms pulled back to show off her body. It was an artful pose Cristal had perfected from the time she wasn't much older than a child.

Brody turned to Jill. "Do you need me to take Kacy to camp? You mentioned going to your school this morning."

"It would be great if you dropped her off. I'll bring her home with me."

Cristal was quiet during this interchange. But when she climbed into Jill's car she said, "You and Brody sound like an old married couple. What's up with that?"

"Nothing. Let's get your groceries and then I have to be on my way."

"But I thought we were going to have some time to talk," said Cristal.

"Yes. First, I want to know more about what they said about your cancer. Do you have the report they were trying to send to you? If you don't mind, I want to do some research on my own, so I have a better understanding of what you're going to go through."

"I can't remember everything they said, and I don't have the report with me. I find it confusing. I can't deal with medical issues, especially when they're mine." Cristal's lips quivered. "I'm not ready to die."

"We're going to do everything we can to ensure that doesn't happen," said Jill, patting Cristal on the back. "Now, let's get you some groceries."

Cristal smiled and nodded. "You really don't mind that I'm staying with you?"

Jill took a moment, fighting honesty. "I'm glad we have this time together to sort things out." After saying the words, she realized how true they were. Thinking of her sister dying had made her realize how wrong it was they were always at one another when they were together. This time, they both wanted it to be different.

"You've changed, Jill. I like you this way. In charge."

"Thanks. I've been working on it. Being away from home has helped a lot."

"I can't believe you sold your house. You loved that place."

"Yes, I did ... before my marriage. After? Not so much." Jill's lips thinned at the memories of Jay's treatment of her.

Cristal gave her a puzzled look. "Why not? It was perfect for you and Jay."

Jill turned to her for a moment as they approached the grocery store. "That's just it, Cristal. My handsome husband who was adored by all was really a monster when we were alone. And I was too afraid to call him on it."

"Wait a minute! Are you saying you were abused? Jay always treated you like a queen. He worshipped you. You never showed any signs of any abuse whenever I saw you."

Jill swerved the car into a parking spot at the grocery store, slammed on the brakes, and faced her sister once again. "Listen to yourself! You and everyone else can't imagine he wasn't what he pretended to be. He was never a gentleman when he was alone with me." She slammed a fist on the steering wheel. "The few times I tried to talk to others about it, no one believed me. And why not? His behavior to me in front of others was worthy of an Academy Award."

"Oh, my God! Didn't anyone ever see the bruises?"

Jill's bitter laugh came out as a snort. "Some bruises are inside only. I'm talking about emotional abuse. When I think of how I worked so hard to please him so he wouldn't find fault and tell me how useless and pitiful I was, how no one else would put up with me, or call me vile names, I feel sick to my stomach."

"Why didn't you ever tell me?" Cristal said.

"That's a laugh. You and I never got along. I was the unfortunate one who had the Davis nose and other boring features while you were the one who looked like Mom and her family." She sat back in her seat and stared out the front window of the car. Even now, it hurt to say the words.

"Wow!" uttered Cristal. "Guess you never knew how much I hated being compared to Mom and her family."

"What? No! You loved it. You used to prance around as if you were the princess Mom always talked about."

"No, Jill. I envied you with your excellent grades and plans for the future. Dad always preferred you. He once called me a flibbertigibbet. I had to look up the word, of course, but I always knew he preferred you. Mom knew it too."

They glared at one another for a few moments and then Cristal started laughing.

"What's so funny?" Jill demanded.

"I just realized what Mom did to us. It's no wonder we've

By the time she was scheduled to take Kacy back home, Jill's mind was spinning with facts and figures. She liked the idea that, though it was a small operation by anyone's standards, Melanie and Susannah were being very specific about what joining them as a part owner would mean in commitments of both time and money.

Back at the house, she discovered Cristal lying on a chaise lounge by the pool wearing a skimpy black bikini that left very little to imagination.

"Hello," chirped Cristal. "Back so soon?" She sat up and checked her phone. "Four fifteen already? Where did the time go?"

"Better be careful. The sun's hot," said Jill, noting the red tone to Cristal's skin.

"Why in hell should I care?" said Cristal. "I already have cancer. What's a little afternoon sun?"

Jill sat in a chair next to her. "Look, I know you're upset, and I understand how frightening it is to hear the word 'cancer.' But I'm optimistic you're going to be okay. You said you caught it early. That means a lot. It's better for you to concentrate on the upside. How about walking down to the beach with me? We can talk privately there."

"Okay," said Cristal. "I can use the exercise."

"I'll get changed and meet you by the front door."

Jill walked into her bedroom and sighed. Cristal's things were spread all over. She told herself not to be annoyed, but couldn't help it. This was her private space and though she had to share it with Cristal, she needed a sense of peace away from the others.

She took off her clothes and reached for the pink, one-piece suit that had become her standard wear. Staring at her naked body in the mirror, she re-assessed herself. Not bad unless you were with someone like Cristal. Then the comparison hurt. Cristal looked like a bathing-suit model.

Jill pulled up her swimsuit, smoothed it over her stomach and hips and grimaced. Sighing at what she couldn't change, she walked out of her bedroom and came face to face with Brody.

"Going for a swim?" he asked, letting his gaze drift over her, sending heat soaring through her.

"Cristal and I are taking a short walk on the beach."

He frowned at her. "What's going on? Cristal told me she didn't need sunscreen, that she already had cancer."

Jill motioned for him to come into her bedroom and closed the door after him as she filled him in on the situation. "I'll accompany Cristal to her appointment, of course. In the meantime, I'm trying to keep her from believing she's about to die."

"Good thing she has someone to go with her. Allison found a lump once and totally freaked out. It turned out to be benign, but it was pretty upsetting."

"Yes, it would be. But I'm hoping to make it a bonding time for the two of us. You know, the old silver lining to a cloud sort of thing."

Brody stared into her eyes. "Cristal quizzed me about you and our relationship."

"Really?"

"Yeah. I wasn't sure where she was going with that, so I didn't say much. Figured it wasn't her business." He lifted her chin and gazed at her. "Besides, I wasn't sure what exactly to tell her. Can you help me here? What's does our relationship mean to you?"

Willing to play along, Jill returned his smile. "Well, we're friends. And I like your daughter."

"And ...?"

"And I like you a lot too."

He grinned at her. "It's a beginning. Anything to add?"

"Maybe in time," she said.

He laughed. "Okay, we'll take it from here." Brody pulled her into his embrace. "In the meantime, how about letting me know exactly how much you ... like ... me?"

"Okay." Jill placed her arms around his neck and smiled up at him.

"That much?" he teased.

She fit her body up against his, nestling close enough to know he was aroused.

His lips came down on hers, sure and warm.

She was floating in a sea of happiness when she heard tapping at the door. She reluctantly stepped away from him.

"Daddy? Are you in there?" came a voice from outside the door.

"Hold on, Kacy. What's up?"

"It's Mommy. She's on your phone."

CHAPTER TWENTY-FOUR

Brody opened the door and accepted the phone from Kacy. Jill started to leave the room, but he signaled for her to stay and for Kacy to go. As he talked, she caught bits and pieces of the conversation.

"Paris? Now? Okay. Yes. I'll pick up Kacy's things. What? My cook? Do you mean Jill? Yes, I suppose she can help with Kacy's school clothes. I'll ask. Did you tell Kacy about that? Okay. I understand. Have a safe trip. Goodbye."

"What was that all about?" Jill asked.

He gave her a sheepish look. "Allison and Marcus are leaving for Paris at the end of the week, a few days ahead of their schedule. While they're gone, she needs me to come and pick up Kacy's things for the move to Florida, and she wants you to assist me with clothes that Kacy will need for school."

"I see."

"Will you help me get all the things she'll need? I can handle school supplies, but I'm not sure about the clothing issues."

"Yes, as your *cook*, I will be glad to help you," she teased.

"You heard that?" He shook his head. "Allison has delusions of grandeur. Sorry about that."

"No problem. Just let me know what I can do."

"I'm going to book a flight for Kacy and me to go to Pennsylvania to pick up things for her and arrange to ship some other things."

"This is a big move for her. I'm glad you're taking her with you so she'll understand," said Jill. "I'm happy also that she'll get to spend the majority of time with you for the next year or so. She's a happier child than when she first arrived at Seashell Cottage."

"While you and Cristal are walking on the beach, I'll spend time with Kacy and explain everything to her. We can also put together a list of things she wants brought here."

"When I get back from my walk, I'm going to call my real estate agent to see if she's found any rental for me."

"Hmmm. Sure you don't want to bunk in with me? My real estate agent called. I'm looking at a house to buy in Niki and Jed's neighborhood. It's been empty for a while, and I can get it for a good price. There'd be plenty of room for you. Greg, too."

Jill chuckled at his teasing smile. "Thanks, but no." She was falling in love with Brody, but she wasn't ready to move in with him.

On the beach, Jill remained silent as she walked with Cristal. Now that they were alone, she realized how unaccustomed it was for her to share meaningful moments with her sister. They'd spent so much time apart.

Regret filled her. What if the cancer was much worse than she suspected? She'd been annoyed when Cristal had announced her visit, but now that she'd reached out to her at her most vulnerable point in life, Jill vowed to stay by her side for as long as Cristal wished.

"I'm glad you're going to be with me tomorrow," Cristal said. "Hope was willing to go to appointments with me, but not until she was ready to leave Europe. I told her she was selfish. She got mad, and then she and Jacques left me."

"You're right. Hope wasn't a good friend at all. And Jacques? Not one of the good guys. This is a situation you need to address right away."

Cristal stopped and studied her. "You honestly think I'm going to be all right?"

Jill thought of Susannah's words about healing and nodded. "Yes."

Cristal let out a puff of air. "Whew! Just believing that helps me a lot." She slung an arm around Jill's shoulder. "Tell me more about Jay. I want to hear all of it. I should've been paying attention."

"Realistically, you couldn't. You were living in Florida and seldom came home. And when you were around, Jay was on his best behavior. That was always the frustrating part of it."

"You tried to talk to Mom about him?" Cristal asked.

"Yes, but she told me I was too sensitive—the same kind of crap Jay used to say to me. He warned me over and over again that if I told anyone else about our private lives, he would punish me. I had no reason not to believe him."

"It wasn't always that way between the two of you, was it?"

"No. When he was courting me, he was sweet, and so supportive. We'd been married about six months when it started. He was passed over for a promotion at work for a job he was convinced was his. In fact, he'd already bought that little red sports car of his to celebrate."

"Why didn't you tell me?" Cristal said, then held up a hand to stop her. "Don't say it! I probably wouldn't have listened anyway. I was too busy trying to be everything Mom wanted me to be. After he died, were you able to talk to someone about his behavior?"

"Yes," Jill said. "A psychologist at school recommended a friend in the business. She turned out to be a great help to me. But it's only since I've been here that I've been able to let go of a lot of my anger and frustration. And Brody has helped. Did you know he's a psychologist?"

"How great is that?" Cristal tugged Jill to a stop and studied her. "I know I've been here only a couple of days, but I think he loves you, Jill, truly loves you. You should see the way his face lights up when he talks about you. Don't make the mistake of letting him get away because of your past experience with Jay."

"Is this more 'big sister' advice?" Jill said, arching an eyebrow at her. "First, I have to come to Florida, and, now, I have to be with the man you think is perfect for me?"

Cristal's face split into a wide smile. "I probably don't deserve any credit for all the changes, but yes."

"I'm falling for Brody, for sure. Being with him is both exciting and comforting. That probably doesn't make sense, but there it is."

"But?"

"I'm not going to rush into anything. I have my freedom. I don't want to give that up for anyone. Once you've had everything you do criticized by someone who's supposed to love you, it takes a lot to give another man your trust."

Cristal gave her a quick hug. "I'm sorry you were so badly hurt."

"Thank God, it's over. Moving forward, Mom will have to understand that Jay wasn't the man she always thought he was."

"I'll make sure she does," said Cristal with a firmness to her voice that Jill appreciated. Having her big sister look out for her was something new.

"What are we going to do about Mom?" Jill said, changing the subject.

"I still don't want her to learn I'm here in Florida with you and undergoing surgery. Once I know my status and the prognosis, I'll tell her. Besides, I want some alone time with you. This whole idea of maybe dying has made me want to do things differently. Know what I mean?"

Jill nodded. "Like you said, maybe it's time for us to be real sisters. Mom's still mad at me for moving away, which is one reason we haven't been talking very much."

"See what I mean? It's all about her," said Cristal.

"Not always, but in this case, her pouting isn't going to work," said Jill. She didn't like the idea of ganging up on her mother, but she needed to be open with Cristal.

They walked on in silence.

Jill lifted her face, enjoying the salty breeze that cooled her cheeks. She walked to the water's edge and observed little holes bubble in the surface of the packed sand as the water drew away. She thought how like her existence this scene was. Her new experiences, similar to the water pulling back, were exposing the holes in her previous life. She knew too, like the movement of the water rolling in, there would be more challenges ahead. The thought of Brody and the fresh relationship taking root with her sister made her feel as if she was ready to begin anew.

Cristal came up beside her. "It feels very peaceful to stand and gaze out at the water."

"I agree. I realized soon after I came here that this is where I wanted to live. The thought of going back home didn't hold any appeal. That's why I've moved so quickly to make all the changes." She turned to Cristal. "What are you going to do after your surgery?"

"Believe it or not, I'm thinking of going to a beauty school and opening my own hairdressing shop like I've always wanted."

"Wow! I'm surprised. Would it be someplace in Florida?"

"I'm not sure." Cristal kicked her foot in the sand. "Do you think I'd be any good at it?"

"Are you kidding? You'd be perfect doing this. And working

with others on makeup and all the other beauty tricks too."

Cristal gave her a hug. "Thanks. I needed to hear that. I know Mom always had other plans for me, but I've grown to hate the 'make-believe' life I've been living, and thirty-five is ancient for the world I've been in for the last ten or twelve years. There has to be a change."

Jill stood back and smiled at her sister. "You know what? I like the new you."

"You think?" Cristal asked in a small voice.

Jill hugged her. "I know I do."

When they returned to the house, Greg was sitting on the front porch dressed in tan slacks and a bright golf shirt.

"Ready for your date with Melanie?" Jill asked. "Aren't you a little early?"

Greg's smile was sheepish. "Thought I'd get ready anyhow. We're going to drive up to Clearwater to a seafood restaurant Melanie suggested."

"Have fun!" Cristal said and went into the house.

Jill stayed behind and lowered herself into a rocking chair next to Greg. "I have something to ask you, and I need you to give me an honest answer."

"Sure. Shoot."

"Melanie and her business partner, Susannah, have offered to have me buy into their camp to help run the business end of it. Melanie wants more personal time to travel and have more of a life away from the camp. I'm excited about doing this, but it means I'll have to spend some of the money I've set aside for a down payment on a house. I'm not ready to buy in any case. Not until I'm comfortable about where I want to live."

Greg nodded thoughtfully. "Melanie told me about the

camp. It sounds like it could be a valuable new opportunity for you."

"Thanks. I needed to hear that from someone who knows the area and the people involved. What are you going to do after you're through here? You mentioned renting a condo."

"I'm not sure. Brody has talked to me about moving in with him. I might consider it. Melanie and I have already talked about traveling together someday. I've recently been looking for a traveling companion because taking long trips was something Annie didn't like to do. There are a lot of places in the world I'd like to see. Melanie feels the same way. So far, we're talking about just traveling together, but I think something more permanent may come of it. We'll have to see how it goes."

Jill clapped her hands together, delighted by the idea of something romantic happening between Greg and Melanie. "Oh, Greg, that would be so wonderful for the two of you."

"One day at a time, my dear," said Greg, but the twinkle in his eye told her he was rooting for them to be together.

Jill went into the house and into her bedroom to change into a different bathing suit. The idea of taking a swim in the pool was very satisfying on this hot summer day. As she was removing her clothes, her cell rang. She checked caller ID and smiled. *Niki's brother, Charlie Beachum.*

"Hi, Charlie! Niki and I were recently talking about you," said Jill, pleased to get a call from him. He was such a nice guy.

"I'm coming to Florida the day after tomorrow and would like to take you to dinner. I enjoyed being with you last time."

"I did too. And dinner sounds great."

They made arrangements, and then Jill hung up relieved for a chance to tone down her relationship with Brody. She needed time and perspective.

CHAPTER TWENTY-FIVE

The next morning as Jill drove Cristal to Tampa, her hands felt stiff on the steering wheel. She'd looked up the directions and other information regarding the Richard M. Schulze Family Foundation Breast Cancer Center, which was part of the H. Lee Moffit Cancer Center & Research Institute. The long names seemed so formal, so cold, but she knew from her research what a wonderful establishment the center was. Founded in 1981 by the Florida Legislature, it opened on the University of South Florida campus in 1986.

"What if they tell me I'm dying?" Cristal asked, her cheeks pale.

Jill reached out and squeezed her sister's hand.

They tried to make small talk, but the tension in the car grew as they pulled into the McKinley Campus, and she searched for a parking spot at the center.

She parked the car and they headed inside. Two gray concrete globes marked the main entrance. Inside, Cristal spoke to the woman behind the information desk and was directed to Dr. William Noble's office.

There, her sister was handed more forms to fill out and the person behind the desk informed them they had received all the materials they needed from her physician in Miami. While Cristal filled out information, Jill found a seat by a window and checked her phone.

A text message from Melanie wished them both luck. Another text, from Leigh McKinnon at school, told her she loved the way Jill had decorated her classroom.

Jill sighed with satisfaction. Her life, so abruptly changed, seemed to be working out.

Cristal sat down beside her. "I hope I don't have to wait too long. Seeing all these other women here is making me nervous. Some of them look as worried as I feel."

Jill patted her sister's hand. "The staff will do the best they can to see everyone as quickly as possible. Including you."

"Do you think we should have told Mom?" Cristal asked, knotting her fingers together.

"I think we need to call her right after this visit," Jill said. She didn't want to get her mother riled up, but felt her mother had a right to know.

When Cristal's name was called, Jill stood with her. They followed a nurse down a hallway and entered an office whose walls were painted a pleasant, soft cream. A tall, rangy man with gray hair hurried inside and introduced himself. William Noble had light brown eyes that radiated kindness and interest—something Jill immediately liked as she shook hands with him.

After pleasantries were exchanged and two chairs in front of a desk were offered to them, Dr. Noble sat behind the desk and took a moment to look through paperwork and a set of images.

He leaned forward. "I'm sure you're anxious to know more about your condition and to come up with a plan of treatment. What do you understand about your status so far?"

"Not much," admitted Cristal. "I was traveling when I got the news, and I've been so nervous about it I left the letter from my doctor behind."

"Well, let's calm a few of those nerves," said Dr. Noble, kindly. "You have Stage 1A cancer in your left breast. The biopsy, 3-D imaging, and reports indicate the tumor measures less than 2 centimeters and has not spread outside the breast.

That, and the fact there is no history of breast cancer in your family is very good news."

"What does that mean for treatment?" Jill asked as Cristal fought tears.

"I'd suggest doing what we call a lumpectomy. We would go in to make sure we remove all the tumor and a small area of healthy tissue around the tumor, called a margin. Even though we see no signs of it on the materials given to us, we'd also check the lymph nodes in that area. My feeling is this procedure will take care of the problem. But if further treatment is necessary, we'll apprise you of that. Does that make sense?"

Cristal nodded. "The surgery would be just a little more complex than what I've gone through before. Right?"

"Yes," Dr. Noble said. "Your incision probably won't be much larger." He smiled at her. "You're the kind of patient we prefer. I predict a good outcome for you."

"When can I have this done? I don't want to wait. I want to get it over with," said Cristal.

Dr. Noble nodded. "That's understandable. We can schedule you for outpatient surgery on Friday, four days from now."

Cristal turned to Jill. "You'll be free to come with me?"

"Yes. School doesn't start for me until the following week."

"Okay, let's do it," said Cristal. She gave Dr. Noble a wobbly smile. "Thank you so much!"

"You're welcome." After they talked about pre-op procedures, Dr. Noble rose. "I'll see you on Friday, Cristal."

They all shook hands, and then Jill led her sister out of the office, feeling as if she could fly. Cristal was going to be all right.

As they walked through the waiting area on the way out of the building, Jill couldn't help studying the women sitting there, hoping they'd have as good a prognosis.

When they got back to her car, Cristal said, "Let's go to lunch. I want to celebrate."

"That sounds great. But if you don't mind, let's head down to the Seashell Cottage and find something closer to home with less traffic."

"Still not much of a city girl, huh?" Cristal said.

"You got it," Jill replied. She suspected traffic in the area around the cottage would get worse in the winter, but it would still be easier for her than driving in the city.

\#\#\#

They chose the Key Hole at the Salty Key Inn for lunch. Close to the cottage, it offered just the kind of thing Jill was looking for—a crispy chicken Caesar salad and a private booth in a corner of the bar.

After they placed their orders, Cristal pulled out her cell phone. "I'm calling Mom now, so she can't complain we kept her out of the loop."

"You're not going to get off that easy." Jill chuckled when Cristal rolled her eyes at her before she punched in a number on her cell and waited.

"Hi, Mom! It's Cristal. I'm going to put you on speaker phone. I'm with Jilly. We're having lunch."

Jill leaned closer to hear.

"Jilly? She's in Europe?"

"No, Mom. She's in Florida with me. I came back early from Europe to take care of a medical problem."

"Medical problem? What's the matter? Do you need me to come there? Jill's too busy to help."

"Actually, I'm here because I wanted to spend some time with my sister. She's helping me." Cristal took a deep breath. "I have stage 1A breast cancer. The surgeon is going to do what they call a lumpectomy to remove all traces of it."

"And you didn't call me first?" wailed their mother. "What kind of daughter are you? Any mother deserves to know things like this. Jill, did you put her up to this?"

Jill spoke into the phone with a quiet determination not to let the situation escalate. "No, Mom. I was as surprised as you are about all of it. But I'm very glad Cristal chose to come to the Moffit Cancer Center here in Florida. It's one of the best. Better yet, we've had the opportunity to spend some time together."

"Well, I can see that I'm not needed," huffed their mother.

"Actually, we thought you might want to come here," said Cristal, surprising Jill.

"Where would I stay? With you two at the cottage?" asked her mother.

Cristal turned to Jill with a questioning look.

"I might be able to work something out to free up a bedroom. Greg and Brody are just about through with their work, and Brody may be about to buy a house. They're both anxious to move out."

"I'm booking a flight to Tampa this afternoon," their mother said. "I'll let you know when I'm arriving."

"Why don't you book it for tomorrow? That'll give me time to make sleeping arrangements for you," said Jill.

"Okay, but you'll have to fill me in on everything you've done. You've managed to hurt my feelings."

"This is about Cristal and her surgery, Mom," said Jill.

"You aren't going to be disfigured by this surgery, are you, Cristal?"

"No, Mom, I don't think so. Here's our food now. Gotta go." Cristal clicked off the call and turned to Jill. "That wasn't so bad."

Jill shrugged. "It won't be easy, but we can do it."

Cristal studied her. "I'm sorry I didn't ask you first about having room at the cottage."

"Me, too. But we'll work around it. Right?"

Cristal nodded, giving her a penetrating look.

When Jill returned to the cottage, she walked inside to find things a mess. Clothing and toys were piled on the couch and the floor nearby.

Brody looked up from a cardboard box he was filling with Kacy's toys. "Hi! This morning while you were gone, I made an offer on the house and it was accepted. Until all the paperwork goes through, I'm renting the property. Kacy's thrilled with the idea of living close to Emily, so we're moving out of the cottage today. Hope you don't mind the last-minute decision. But moving into the house will give me a chance to see how the space will work. Greg has agreed to move in with us, at least temporarily." He winked at her. "Do you mind if we have dinner here?"

Jill worked hard to keep a smile on her face. With them gone, Seashell Cottage wouldn't be the same.

"As it turns out," said Cristal, standing beside her, "we can use the room. My mother is arriving tomorrow and will be staying for several days."

Brody glanced at Jill. "Guess it works out well that I'm leaving."

"I didn't want it to happen quite this way," said Jill, disappointed to lose them. "Where's Greg?"

Brody grinned. "Seeing a certain someone about a trip he wants to take to Ireland. He's moving out too. He's already moved a bunch of his belongings to the house. He'll pick up the rest tonight."

"Guess I'll go lie down by the pool," Cristal said, starting to leave the room.

"No, Cristal," said Jill firmly. "First, you're going to help me strip the beds in Greg's room and clean the bathroom."

"But ..."

"I need your help. You know how Mom is. She'll want everything perfect."

"Okay," sighed Cristal with a whine in her voice.

This was the sister Jill was used to.

Jill decided to turn dinner into a special party to help with Kacy's transition from the cottage to her new home. She brought out a red-checkered tablecloth she'd found earlier in one of the kitchen drawers and made a quick trip to the grocery store for supplies.

Later, she stood in the kitchen admiring her work. Colorful helium balloons were tied to the backs of the chairs around the kitchen table, the table was set to look like a picnic, and a frosted cake sat on the counter with the words, "Happy Moving Day!"

"All this fuss for Kacy?" Cristal said, walking into the kitchen.

"Yes," said Jill. "I want her to remember her time here at Seashell Cottage as a pleasant one. But I also want her to know that no matter where she lives, I will treasure our special times together."

"You really love kids, don't you? Teaching kindergarten all those years and now third grade proves it. But then, you've always wanted to be a teacher." Cristal sighed. "Even as a kid you were so sure about what you wanted."

"Well, I knew I could never be a model or an actress," Jill said, and stopped herself from saying more. That was an old pattern that needed to be broken. "Sorry. I don't want to go there."

"Me, either," said Cristal. "Can I help you with dinner?"

Jill hid her surprise. Cristal had always said she was no help to anyone in the kitchen. "Thanks. It would be nice if you'd take care of the salad. I'm fixing Kacy's favorite spaghetti sauce."

"Okay. I make great salads. It's mostly what Hope and I fix for dinner."

"You're actually ready to move away from South Beach and open your own business? I can see how happy you'd make your customers, but it's a ton of work to own a small business."

"What? You think I can't do it?" snapped Cristal.

"Wait a minute. That's not what I meant," said Jill, understanding why Cristal might react that way—she was the girl with the beauty, not the brains. "It's a huge time commitment day after day, and unless you had someone helping you, it might be difficult to have any free time for yourself. I've heard other people talk about how hard that is."

"Oh, I see what you mean. You're right. I'd have to have either an assistant or a partner." Cristal looked contrite before a rueful smile crossed her face. "I wonder if Linsey Logan is still living in town. Remember her? She and I were going to open our own hairdressing salon way back when."

"Last I heard, she was living in the South. Atlanta, I think."

Cristal shook her head. "It doesn't really matter. I'll find someone at beauty school. There are several schools in Florida. Maybe I'll stay in this area. It's a lot quieter than what I'm used to, but I might like the change." She shrugged. "Or maybe I'll spend a few years in Ellenton. It might be pleasant to experience real winters again."

"Wherever you land, I'm sure you'll do well. You've always done a beautiful job with hair."

Cristal studied her. "I like your hair short, but may I make a suggestion?"

Jill laughed. "Okay. Tell me."

Cristal brushed hair away from Jill's face. "I think you should cut it about two inches shorter so that it shows your neck. It would open up your face and give you a different, more sophisticated look."

"Okay. I'll do it. Come with me sometime and meet Frederick, my hairdresser. Who knows? Maybe you'll end up working with him one day."

Cristal laughed. "I don't know about that, but I'd like to meet him and talk to him about schools and all."

Jill nodded, wondering what Susannah with her intuition might have to say about Cristal's future.

CHAPTER TWENTY-SIX

Jill waited with her sister inside the baggage claim area of the Tampa International Airport desperately wanting to chew her fingernails, a habit she'd given up long ago. Their mother's visit was going to be difficult for both of them. They were going to confront past issues in an effort to move forward in a new way. Jill realized she should've done this a long time ago, but years of being the daughter who worked to keep things peaceful had prevented her from doing it. Maybe, she now thought with surprise, that was why she'd been such an easy target for a man like Jay. But then, no woman should be a target for any man's cruelty.

"Are you all right?" Cristal asked, giving her a worried look.

Jill shook off her morbid thoughts. "I am." She felt it, too. Seashell Cottage had provided a kind of balm to her battered mind.

Cristal grinned. "Here comes Mom now."

Valerie Davis was a stylish woman in her late fifties with a body she kept trim and hair she kept blonde. Seeing them, she walked toward them with a quiet assurance as she lifted her hand and waved.

Jill and Cristal moved together to greet her.

"Hello, girls! I'm so glad to finally be here," Valerie said. "The trip was awful. I was so worried about you, Cristal. To think my own daughters kept such news from me. As I told the man sitting in the seat next to me, it was such a disappointment."

Jill and Crystal exchanged meaningful glances.

onversation, carefully
pt light and easy.
f the Seashell Cottage,
! Cristal, it was so nice
mer vacation here."
passenger seat.
mitted. "But I'm pretty

Brody, Kacy, and all the

orida would turn into
said. "My friends have
me as having a daughter

id, "Come take a look at
ed."
er suitcase and carry-on
of the car and studied the

r mother to the front door.
stood aside. "Welcome to

oment, gazing around. "It
n just left, you said?"
he house to ourselves," Jill

need to get settled."
n next to mine," Cristal said,
nd her.
n Greg had used. Freshened
om scrubbed well, it was all

" her mother said. "When is

lunch being served? I refuse to pay for what amounts to junk food on the airlines, and I'm hungry."

Jill and Cristal exchanged glances.

"I thought we'd have a fresh salad for lunch. Later this week, we're taking you out to dinner," said Jill.

"It's going to be my treat. I finally got paid for a bit of modeling I did at one of the hotels," said Cristal.

Valerie smiled. "How lovely, dear. Will you be able to continue modeling after the surgery?"

"Mom, why are you so worried about that?" Cristal frowned at her. "For your information, I've left South Beach. It's become harder and harder for me to live and work there. I decided it was time for a change."

"Oh? I didn't realize. Maybe it's time to head for a bigger city. New York City, perhaps. You'd be much closer to me there."

"I'm going to start lunch," said Jill. "I'll be in the kitchen." She knew if she stayed any longer she might say something she'd regret.

"I'll let mother get unpacked and join you," said Cristal. "We can talk about this later, Mom."

Their mother frowned. "What are you two up to? You're acting so different, so secretive."

"It's nothing. Hurry and get unpacked," said Cristal. "This afternoon we can walk on the beach or go swimming in the pool." She left the room and followed Jill into the kitchen.

"We don't have to dump everything on her all at once," Jill said quietly.

"You're right. Let's enjoy the time together as much as possible. I want to relax before Friday's surgery."

Jill pulled out a package of fresh greens and arranged the leaves on three separate plates, adding cooked shrimp and slices of hardboiled egg atop them. She'd whipped up a King

l asked, diverting her

raid, but I didn't know

ve to check in with the to go," said Cristal. ough by then?" Valerie cry.

Right, Jill?"

ut this is a fairly routine isn't sure any further

She's met the doctor and 's meant so much to me." you. I'm your mother!"

while you're here, Jill and f things," said Cristal. She mother a tentative smile. mother said, studying Jill

where we'll have privacy to moved out, so we have the lidn't want any scenes in the

onversation. Traveling today st," said Valerie. "There's my

istal.

ore surprised, her mother or ht in her throat. Yes, a lot of y taking place in the family

Louis dressing earlier and drizzled that over the salad.

Cristal heated fresh French bread slices, placed them in a basket lined with a crisp napkin, put the basket in the center of the table, and poured iced tea into three glasses.

As Jill set the salad plates on the table, their mother entered the kitchen.

"This looks wonderful. I can't remember the last time I had the chance to have lunch with my two girls." Beaming at them, she took a seat at the kitchen table between them.

"The last time was just before Jill's wedding," said Cristal. "I remember it well. You were fussing about my dress for the rehearsal dinner."

"The one that was so short?" their mother said. "Well, yes, I didn't want you to take too much attention away from Jill."

"Ugh, I remember," said Jill. Her mother had ruined the evening for her by declaring to anyone who'd listen that it was a time for "poor Jill" to get some attention, not Cristal. Her mother might have thought she was being fair, but the way she'd said it had made it seem very unkind.

"Well, enough of that. It's all so sad. The marriage turned out to be such a tragedy with Jay's early death."

Jill felt heat build inside her. She set down the fork and glared at her mother. "In the privacy of our home Jay turned into a monster, berating me, calling me names, demanding perfection from me. It's something you've never accepted about him, but it's the truth."

"Oh, Jill," her mother sighed. "He loved you. When I asked him if everything was all right, he told me he adored you. He even cried telling me how much you meant to him. He was a steward in our church, a beloved member of the community. Remember all the work he did with the young men's baseball league?"

Tears stung Jill's eyes. "What do any of those things have

to do with the abuse I suffered daily? It's taken me a couple of years of therapy to deal with the damage he did. Now, I refuse to listen to your ... your bullshit response to my very real life. I don't care about the fact that he was a steward in the church, or a beloved member of the community, or about the work he did with the baseball league. I care about the hell he put me through."

"Why don't you believe her?" Cristal asked. "You of all people should have seen something was wrong. We all should have."

Their mother straightened in her chair and stared at Cristal, her lips thinning. "How dare you blame me!" She turned to Jill. "And don't you ever talk that way to me again."

"You should've believed your own daughter when she told you what was going on, even if you didn't want to hear it," said Cristal. "Why didn't you ever mention the situation to me?"

"Enough," said their mother, holding up a hand to stop conversation.

"I'll stop," said Cristal. "But it's not over."

Their mother dabbed at her eyes. "You girls are being mean to me. This, after all I've done for you."

"Cristal and I have begun to talk," said Jill. "It's time we were all honest with one another, whether you like hearing things or not."

"Do you want me to go back home?" their mother asked defiantly. "I will, if you're going to treat me this way."

Cristal placed a hand on her mother's arm. "We're just trying to work out a few things, get a better understanding of all of us. Having cancer has made me realize we're lucky to have this time together. We're all going to be better people because of it."

"Cristal's right," said Jill. "It'll be healthy for all of us."

Their mother let out a long, noisy sigh. "I'm here to help

Cristal through this crisis. So, I'll stay."

"You're here because Jill was nice enough to make room for you here at Seashell Cottage," Cristal reminded her.

"Yes, of course. That, too," their mother said, giving Jill a forced smile.

Jill sat at the table waiting for the moment when she could leave. She needed time alone. Memories of Jay acting the role of perfect community leader had taken her appetite away. When her cell rang, Jill jumped up from her chair and hurried to answer it, grateful for the interruption.

She smiled when she saw the name. *Brody.*

"Hi! What's up?" she said, her voice a little shaky from the emotions that still whirled inside her.

"Okay if I bring Kacy by the cottage after I pick her up at Sunnyside? She left a shirt behind that she wants to wear to camp tomorrow."

"Sure. No problem. Where is it? I'll try to have it ready for her."

"In one of the drawers in our room. Probably the bottom one." He hesitated. "Everything all right? You sound upset."

"I'll tell you later. I'm in the kitchen with my mother and Cristal."

"Okay. I'm ready to listen anytime."

"Thanks," said Jill, feeling better already. It was so easy to slip back into familiar roles in a family, but she refused to let go of all she'd learned about herself living here in Florida.

"Who was that, dear?" her mother asked when Jill returned to the table.

"Brody. His daughter left a shirt here. They'll stop by later this afternoon."

"He's someone you'll want to meet," said Cristal, giving Jill a sly smile. "A hottie if I ever saw one."

Her mother's eyebrows shot up. "Oh? What's going on?"

Jill smiled. "We're friends. Very good friends." She didn't want to say more. She was falling in love with Brody, but she was meeting Charlie for dinner.

Jill studied herself in the mirror, wondering if Cristal was right about her hair. A little shorter might be just right. The brown in her hair had bleached to a golden hue that was attractive. She put on makeup, accenting her eyes with a green eye shadow that brought out the different colors in her hazel eyes, especially with the green sundress she'd recently splurged on.

When she walked out of the bedroom, Cristal and her mother looked up at her and smiled.

"You look great, sis," said Cristal.

"Yes, that's very attractive on you," their mother added. "I had no idea you were dating, but then, we haven't talked much lately. I used to know everything you were doing."

"Not everything," Jill said.

The sound of someone at the door caught their attention.

"I'll get it," said Cristal. "You don't want to seem too anxious. Right?"

Chuckling nervously, Jill nodded.

Cristal returned with Charlie in tow. Smiling, Jill walked toward him. She'd forgotten how attractive he was.

"This is my sister, Cristal, and my mother, Valerie Davis," Jill said.

Charlie tipped his head. "Happy to meet you both." After a bit of pleasant small talk with them, he turned to Jill. "Ready to go? I thought we'd go to the Key Pelican tonight. Gavin's was booked with a couple of private parties."

Outside on the porch, Charlie smiled at her. "You look nice."

"Thanks," Jill said, telling herself to relax. She stilled as Brody's truck pulled into the driveway. She observed Kacy open the door of the truck and run over to her on spindly legs that were a lot longer than when she'd first come to Florida.

"Hey, Jill! We're back," cried Kacy. "Dad says you have my shirt."

"Yes, it's folded and on the kitchen counter all ready for you."

Kacy stopped and stared up at Charlie, her face wrinkling with disapproval. "Who are you?"

"A friend of Jill's, and Emily's uncle," Charlie answered pleasantly.

"Oh." Kacy glanced at Jill and hurried inside.

Brody approached, giving Charlie an appraising look as he held out a hand. "Hi, I'm Brody Campbell."

"Charlie Beachum."

Cristal stepped out onto the porch. "Hi, Brody! Come inside and meet my mother."

"Nice to meet you," Brody said to Charlie before facing her. "You look nice, Jill."

"Thanks," she replied, and waited as he went inside.

"Who's that?" Charlie asked as they continued on the way to his car.

"A friend," said Jill, wondering if she was being fair to Brody. Even though she'd decided she needed her freedom, he was someone very special to her.

CHAPTER TWENTY-SEVEN

The next morning, Jill awoke and lay in bed, staring up at the stripes of sunlight on the wall. Though she really liked Charlie, it was Brody who made her feel as if she was the best thing that had ever happened to him. She loved the way he kissed her, made her laugh, and how carefully he listened to her.

She got out of bed and padded to the window. The sun was glistening on the water's rhythmic movement, crowning each wave in gold. At the sight, she sighed with pleasure. She loved waking up to the scene around her.

When she went into the kitchen, her mother was seated at the table, sipping coffee.

"Hi!" Jill said cheerfully.

"Good morning. I've been sitting here thinking. I'm worried about you. I noticed that it bothered Brody no end to see you dating someone else. You might want to be careful about hurting his feelings."

Jill opened her mouth to reply and closed it. When she spoke, she couldn't contain her frustration. "Mother, pleasing other people without taking care of myself has already proved devastating."

"I mean well, Jill ..." her mother began.

"Even so, I've learned I need to take care of myself," said Jill, her earlier mood ruined. "I'm going to grab a cup of coffee and then I'm going to get dressed. Charlie is taking me out for breakfast."

Her mother shook her head. "You always were so stubborn.

It's another Davis trait."

Jill stopped herself from shouting and spoke with quiet determination. "I don't want to hear any more about the Davis traits."

"My goodness, you're acting cross with me," her mother said. "If I weren't here to help Cristal, I'd pack my bags and leave."

"I'm sorry you feel that way, Mom. It's past time I set boundaries with you. I'm not going back to old behavior. I can't."

"I'm trying to understand all the changes in you," her mother said, getting to her feet. "Guess I'll go walk on the beach. I need some fresh air."

Sighing, Jill watched her leave. She knew she'd sounded snappish, but she had to let her mother know the acceptable way to treat her or she'd be in trouble.

While she was putting lipstick on, Jill heard a truck enter the driveway and stared into the mirror with widened eyes. *Brody?*

Jill went outside to greet him. "You're up early."

He grinned. "Thought I'd take you to breakfast."

"Sorry, but I already have plans. Charlie is due to pick me up any moment. We're going to breakfast."

"What's up? I thought you and I had something going on between us. Are you walking away from what has been building between us?" He kicked at the driveway with his sneaker and then studied her.

"I'm not walking away; I'm merely having breakfast with him on this, his last day here."

Charlie's car pulled into the driveway.

"I'd better go," said Brody. "See you later." He quickly

walked to his truck, got in, and drove away.

"Did I interrupt anything?" Charlie asked, approaching her with a worried look.

"Not really. Thought we'd go to Gracie's at the Salty Key Inn. They have the best breakfast around."

Charlie grinned. "A great way to start the day."

She walked with him to his car and climbed in, still rattled by her conversation with Brody. Now, more than ever, she needed to concentrate on her emotional well-being. And that meant no commitment to anyone else until she was settled into her new life.

Gracie's was as busy as Charlie had warned her it would be. But Jill liked the convivial atmosphere, crowded tables, and noisy talk as they were led to a table for two in an out-of-the-way corner.

Their waitress, a woman named Lynn, smiled and handed them menus. "Welcome to Gracie's. We're happy to have you here. May I bring you some coffee or other hot drink?"

"I'll have a black coffee," said Jill. "What is that delicious smell? Cinnamon?"

"Bertha's cinnamon rolls. They're delicious," said Lynn. "If you want, I'll save a roll for you now. We run out of them pretty quickly."

Jill looked at Charlie and grinned. "Do you want one?"

He nodded. "Make that two cinnamon rolls to set aside, Lynn. Thank you. I'll also take a coffee."

"Coming right up." She poured each of them a glass of water and a cup of coffee, handed out menus, and hurried away.

Jill glanced around the room. Nautical items were hung on the walls, matching the carved and painted wooden sailor standing sentinel beside the front entrance. "Nice touches."

Charlie nodded. "No wonder this place is so busy. I've been checking out the food going to other customers. Everything looks delicious."

"Smells delicious too," said Jill, beginning to relax after the confrontation with Brody.

"I don't know what you have planned today, but I wonder if you're free to do a little sightseeing with me. I thought I'd drive down to Sarasota and look around."

Jill smiled and shook her head. "Thanks, but I have to work at the camp today. I've taken off way too much time. Next week school starts for the teachers, and I'll be able to work only late afternoon hours at the camp."

"Niki says you're really good with kids. As I told you, my ex-wife and I didn't have any children, but someday I hope to have some of my own." He chuckled. "No triplets, though."

Jill returned his smile. "Believe me, I understand. I don't know how Niki handles the three of them all at once."

"My Mom loves being with the kids, and that's a big help."

"Is your family still trying to get you to move here?" The thought was appealing.

He nodded. "Yeah, I might consider it. Especially if I could have a boat of my own here. But I'm pretty happy where I am." He studied her. "Who is this guy, Brody? Are you dating?"

Jill hesitated, wanting to be careful. "Not really. We've become good friends through staying at Seashell Cottage together. I'm enjoying a new freedom here in Florida and don't want to be tied down to anyone while I'm getting settled."

"I like you, Jill."

"Thanks," she said, still thinking of her meeting with Brody earlier.

Lynn took their orders and returned shortly with a plate of

pancakes for Charlie and a vegetable omelet for Jill. "Enjoy!" Lynn said, refilling their coffee cups before leaving them to help other customers.

"That looks delicious. What kind of pancakes did you order?" Jill asked.

He grinned. "Pineapple Pecan."

Jill watched him take a bite and release a sigh of satisfaction. He was such a down-to-earth guy. She pushed all thoughts of romance with Charlie or Brody away. She had to find a place to live, get settled in her new job, and resolve the issue of buying into the camp.

Later, when Charlie dropped her off at the cottage, she was happy she already had plans for the day. Being interested in two different guys at the same time was definitely not her style.

She hurried into the house to see what she could do about housing now that her stay at the cottage was drawing to a close. She called Kay Branson at Palm Rentals and Realty and waited impatiently for her to pick up the call. She was about to give up when Kay came on the line.

"Hi, Jill. I've been thinking about you," Kay said. "You know the condo you first looked at?"

"The one that was being sold?"

"Yes, the furnished one you really liked. The sale went through all right, but one of the owners has become very ill and they won't be moving in for some time. It just came on the rental market. Is it anything you'd be interested in? I still like the idea of your buying rather than renting, but this would give you time to find exactly what you're looking for."

"It would be perfect," gushed Jill. "Is it in my price range?"

"Yes. I've been given some flexibility on the rental fee depending on who I rent it to. No children or pets, right?"

"Right," said Jill, swallowing hard, thinking of one of the

puppies Niki had offered her.

"That makes it easy," said Kay. "Stop by my office this morning and we'll work out the details."

Jill checked her watch. "I'll come right now. I have just enough time before I have to go to work."

Jill walked into the real estate office feeling as if fate was playing a part in her life, backing up her plan to step away from any serious relationship. She'd loved the condo when she'd seen pictures of it and couldn't wait to make it her temporary home.

Kay greeted her warmly. "Nice to see you, Jill."

"I can't believe this is all happening," Jill responded. "It's so perfect for me right now."

"In this business, timing is everything. It's working out for both you and the owner, which is very nice." Kay waved her over to the desk. "I've got the paperwork ready for you. It's our standard lease which will begin for you on September 1st. I've circled the wording about the time required for either of you to give notice, though you must agree to stay at least ninety days. Is that okay with you?"

"Yes," Jill said. "In that time, I hope to decide whether I'll continue to rent or buy. December isn't the greatest time to be looking, but by then, I should know this area pretty well."

While Jill looked over the paperwork, Kay took a phone call. Overhearing the conversation, Jill realized how lucky she was to have found a lovely place to rent on a golf course in a development close to the water.

After signing the lease, she headed to camp. The accountant had worked out numbers for her and she was eager to see them.

CHAPTER TWENTY-EIGHT

The moment Jill walked into the camp office, Melanie hurried over to her. "I can't wait for you to see our accountant's report. And the lawyer has made a couple of changes to the agreement for you to accept."

Jill smiled at her eagerness. "Okay, okay. Give me a minute to set down my purse and we can look at them."

Melanie clasped her hands. "Greg showed me pictures of Ireland and suggested a travel group we might want to join. I'm so excited! It's difficult traveling alone. Now, we can do it together."

"I'm so pleased for you both! You two should have a lot of fun together."

Susannah walked into the room. "Ready to sign away your life?" she teased.

"This is the day to do it. I've signed a lease for a condo to rent this morning and I'm ready to buy into the camp if everything looks right."

Susannah smiled and nodded. "It's all good."

The three of them sat down and went over the contract and the figures the accountant had drawn up. Feeling confident about all of it, Jill signed the papers. "You don't mind that I'm starting off as a partner unable to do much work for a few weeks?"

Susannah and Melanie exchanged glances. "Not at all," Susannah said. "We understand how important it is for you to get settled in your teaching job. Things here at the camp taper off considerably when kids return to school. That's when we'll start our weekend programs."

"And tomorrow you go with your sister while she has the surgery. Right?" said Melanie.

"Yes. She has to be at the clinic by nine AM. The doctor is saying that she should be ready to go home mid-afternoon."

"We're wishing her all the best," said Melanie.

"Of course," Susannah said. "It's a trying time for any woman to go through. I'm a breast cancer survivor myself."

Jill turned to her with surprise. "I didn't know."

Susannah waved away her concern. "I usually don't mention it."

Melanie wrapped an arm around Susannah. "She's a survivor for many reasons and in many ways."

"Yeah, nobody's about to get rid of me anytime soon," Susannah remarked.

Jill joined in the laughter that followed. She couldn't imagine anyone wanting to hurt Susannah in any way. She was such a sweet, gentle soul.

After working out a revised schedule for the last two weeks of summer camp, Jill went to help Kelly with her swim class. She loved seeing the progress all the girls had made. She was especially proud of Kacy's ability to be comfortable and strong in the water. Living in Florida, where swimming pools were the norm, it was wise for all kids to learn to swim well.

As she approached the class sitting on the grass next to the pool, Kacy noticed her and waved. Jill waved back, enjoying the special bond between them.

"Hi, you're just in time," said Kelly. "We're going to work on a water ballet program as part of the camp's talent show we put on for parents."

"Wonderful. How's it coming?"

"Better than I thought," said Kelly quietly. "This is a great group of girls. Stand by and help me see where we need improvement. I'll get in the water with them."

The girls followed instructions to jump into the pool and gathered at the shallow end of the pool. Following Kelly's instructions, they formed a circle in the middle of the pool, turned onto their backs, and held hands. A fountain effect emerged as they kicked their feet, splashing water in a circle around them.

"Bravo!" Jill cried. "Great job, girls."

Kelly blew her whistle. Together, the eight girls did backward somersaults, disappearing in the water behind them and popping to the pool's surface together. Their smiling faces were a joy to see.

Jill clapped a hand to her chest. This was not the same group of girls she'd worked with at the start of camp. They'd come such a long way. She couldn't wait to see Brody's response to Kacy's performance when the show took place next week.

At the end of the camp day, Kacy climbed into the car with Jill. "Are you going to take me to the cottage?"

"Yes, I told your father you can come back to Seashell Cottage with me and stay until he can pick you up. He's meeting with his partners in St. Petersburg."

"The other doctors?"

"Yes. Isn't it wonderful that he's found a job here?"

Kacy nodded. "I like living in Florida. Marcus Dear has a job too. But he's never home. Dad told me he'll be home every night."

"That's going to be wonderful."

"Are you coming to live with us like Uncle Greg?" Kacy said.

"I've rented a condo at a golf community nearby."

Kacy's worried gaze met hers in the rearview mirror. "But

I want you to be with us."

"Oh, sweetheart, the condo is a better place for me right now. But you can visit me anytime. How about that?"

Kacy was still quiet when Jill entered the driveway of Seashell Cottage. Jill decided to let it go.

As Jill pulled the car to a stop, Cristal emerged from the house and came over to her.

"What's up?" Jill asked, noting the slump to Cristal's shoulders.

"Mom's driving me crazy. She's got it in her head that I need to move to Ellenton and open up a hair salon there. She told me Chance Nelson has moved back to town and has opened a law practice. He's divorced and single."

"Wow! The same Chance Nelson you mooned over in high school?"

"Yeah, in all the years I've been away from home, I've never met anyone quite like him. But that's no reason for me to move back home." She stared into the distance and then settled her gaze on Jill. "Would I be crazy to move back? I think it would be a good opportunity for me to open my own business because a lot of people in town would still remember me, and Mom has connections that could be helpful."

"Before you decide, why don't you visit Mom for a while and see if that's what you really want to do. But be warned. She can be pretty demanding. On the other hand, everyone there is friendly and supportive. You might like small-town living."

Cristal gave her a quick hug. "Some very sweet 'little-sister' advice. I think that's what I'll do."

Jill looked around. "Where did Kacy go?"

"Inside," said Cristal. "Mom and I made some popcorn. I bet Kacy is having a bowl of it now."

"Let's go see. I've got some news to share."

They found Kacy sitting at the kitchen table with their mother, munching popcorn and talking about her day at camp. Observing them, Jill wondered if this is how her mother would be with her own grandchildren. The thought made her smile. Especially now that she'd begun to wonder what it might be like to have children of her own one day.

Her mother looked up at her. "How did your day go? Cristal and I had a good chat catching up. I was telling her about Chance Nelson being back in town ..."

"She knows all about it, Mother," Cristal said, interrupting her. "I said I'd think about your proposal to move back and I will, if you don't mention it again."

"Oh, but ..."

"I have news to share," said Jill, hoping to stop the bickering. "I signed a lease for a condo this morning, and I also signed all the papers needed to buy into the camp. I'm now a proud part-owner of Camp Sunnyside."

"It's your camp now?" Kacy said, her eyes wide.

"Miss Melanie, Miss Susannah, and I now own the camp together," said Jill, thrilled to be able to say the words. After seeing the changes in the girl's swim team and the way the group had come together, she was excited to be part of such a positive organization.

"How interesting," her mother said. "Where's the condo?"

"At the Pelican Place development nearby."

"She's supposed to come stay with Daddy and me," said Kacy, her lips turned down.

Jill glanced at Kacy and back to her mother. "We'll talk later."

"Can we go on the beach?" Kacy said, scooping the last of the popcorn into her hand. "I want to look for shells. We're making crafts at camp. It's a surprise."

"Sure. Maybe Cristal or my mother would like to join us."

Jill's mother shook her head. "Thanks, but it's too hot for me."

"I'll come," said Cristal.

As they stepped out onto the porch, Brody drove up to the cottage.

They waited while Brody climbed out of the truck and walked toward them with long purposeful strides.

"You go ahead. I'll stay here," said Cristal. She turned and went back inside, leaving Jill alone on the porch.

"Hi, Dad!" Kacy cried, running up to him.

Brody kissed Kacy and swung her around, grinning as she giggled. *Such a good man, a wonderful father*, Jill thought.

Brody set Kacy down and looked up. "Hi, Jill. Can we talk?"

"Sure." The serious tone to his voice sent worry weaving through her.

"Let's take a walk on the beach," said Brody.

Kacy ran ahead of them as they stepped onto the sand.

A safe distance away, Brody stopped and turned to her. "What's up with us? Should I back off? I don't want to push you into anything."

"I'm stepping away until I get more settled. I need space. This morning, I signed a lease for the condo I tried to rent earlier. It became available. I'll be moving there when I leave Seashell Cottage. That'll make it easier on everyone."

Observing the way Brody grew still and the disappointment that shone in his eyes, regret filled Jill. She hadn't wanted to hurt him. She'd thought of a future with him many times.

Brody let out a long breath. "I understand why you need the time. I really do, but I'm feeling a little bit like a yoyo."

"This decision to move into the condo isn't about us; it's about me getting my life in order. That's all."

He nodded. "I get it. but I can't go through wondering if what we share is real for you. It's not fair to me or Kacy. We'd better go." He turned and walked away from her.

Tears blurred Jill's vision as she watched him leave and felt the ache that seeped into her heart.

CHAPTER TWENTY-NINE

The next morning when the alarm went off, Jill's eyes flew open. She'd spent a restless night thinking of Brody and worrying about Cristal's surgery. Holding back a groan, she climbed out of bed. Today was about her sister, not her.

Before popping into the shower, she raced into the kitchen and started the coffee maker, well aware of how much she'd need caffeine to keep her going. Last night, her mother had broken down and sobbed at the idea of Cristal fighting cancer and disfiguring her body. Cristal had cried too. Jill kept reminding them of what the doctor had said about a good recovery, but after drinking a couple of glasses of wine, neither her mother nor Crystal was about to listen.

Her mother strolled into the kitchen. "Wonderful. You're taking care of coffee."

"Good morning! Let's keep it light this morning as we drive to Tampa. Okay?"

Her mother nodded. "It's a scary time, but I'll do my best. Just wait until you have children. You'll understand how upset I am."

Jill let the remark go. She was still hurting from her conversation with Brody. "I'm going to take a shower. See you later."

She poured herself a cup of coffee and carried it into her bedroom. In the silence of the room, she sat looking out the window at the water. A peace settled over her as she watched the waves move in and out, and she suddenly knew everything would work out well. Maybe not in the way she'd imagined, but the way things were meant to be.

Feeling better about her decisions and the time ahead, Jill prepared for the day. She liked being able to support her sister. In the short time Cristal had been at the cottage, they'd made excellent progress on becoming closer.

At the clinic, Jill sat with her mother in the waiting room trying not to let her mother's anxiety penetrate the mental curtain of healthy thoughts Jill worked to hold onto. She knew so many other women faced a much worse diagnosis than Cristal's, but the word "cancer" was frightening at any level.

Dr. Noble came into the waiting room, introduced himself to her mother and greeted Jill. "As I mentioned earlier, we expect a good outcome. If for any reason, we receive any unexpected findings with the surgery, I'll report back to you. We feel it's important for both the patient and her family members to be apprised of any unexpected results."

"Thank you, Dr. Noble," Jill said. "We appreciate it."

He smiled. "It's nice to see such devoted sisters."

After he left, Jill's mother turned to her. "It surprises me to see you and Cristal so close. What happened to change things?"

Jill paused, searching for the right words. "We decided to get to know one another for ourselves, not through the filter of you and others back home."

"You're blaming me for not getting along in the past?" Her mother's nostrils flared.

Jill patted her mother's hand, willing herself to be generous. "Family dynamics enter into every sibling's relationship. It's easy to assign roles. Cristal's role was the pretty daughter; mine was the smart one. It hurt both of us, but we're beginning to see that we don't need to be those people any longer."

"A mother sees each child a little differently," her mother said. "You were always so focused—something your father adored in you. I had to boost Cristal's self-image. Until you came along, she got all the attention."

"That was then. We've decided to think of ourselves differently now, become the people we want to be. Did you realize Cristal was serious about becoming a hairdresser? It might not be as glamorous a job as you always wanted for her, but she's going to be terrific at it."

"She's very artistic," Jill's mother conceded. "I think she'll do well in Ellenton. And with her looks she might attract Chance Nelson."

Jill shook her head. "Mom, listen to yourself. I would hope if Chance is attracted to her, it isn't just because of her appearance, but because of who she is."

Her mother remained quiet and then spoke softly. "I've never told either of you girls, but I was married to someone else before I met your father."

Jill's jaw dropped. "Whaaat?"

"It's true. It was for only a short time. His family had the marriage annulled. I wasn't good enough for them. That's when I decided if I didn't have the proper social credentials, I'd make sure I at least looked the part." Her eyes glistened with unshed tears.

Jill gave her mother an impulsive hug. "Oh, Mom. That's so sad. I'm sorry."

"It was a long time ago. I was fortunate to meet your father. He was one of the kindest people I ever knew. You're a lot like him, Jill."

"Even if I have the Davis nose?" Jill asked, desperately trying to bring some levity to the confession.

Tears spilled onto her mother's cheeks even as she laughed

softly. "Such a dumb thing for me to keep saying, huh? Look at you! You're lovely."

Jill smiled. They were words. Silly ones at that. As she'd told her mother about Cristal, she didn't want anyone judging her by her appearance. With his interest in finding out more about her and his willingness to talk about anything, Brody had proved to her that he was truly interested in her as a person.

"Would you like me to get you a cold bottle of water or a soda?" she asked her mother. The need to get up to move was too strong to resist.

"I'd love a fresh bottle of water. I know it hasn't been long, but it feels like hours, not minutes have gone by."

Jill left her mother, still shocked over the news of her mother's annulled marriage. The summer had been full of one surprise after another.

At the café, she bought bottled water for each of them, grateful for the opportunity to gather her thoughts. It now made sense how her mother had come to think of one's appearance as being so important. Cristal had been as caught up in it as her mother for understandable reasons.

Jill returned to the waiting area and handed her mother a water, seeing her in a new light.

"I'm glad you told me about your first marriage. It gives me a whole different perspective on you."

"I guess I should've told you, but I put it in the past. Frankly, I haven't thought of it in some time."

Dr. Noble entered the room.

They turned to him.

"Cristal came through the surgery perfectly. She's resting while the anesthesia wears off, but she should be ready to go home in another couple of hours. A nurse will come and get you when they're ready for you to see her."

"What did you find, Dr.?" asked Jill.

"As we initially thought, there were no signs of the cancer spreading to the lymph nodes. The tumor was self-contained. To be safe, we took out a bit of the healthy tissue surrounding it, but I'm pretty confident we got it all."

In a rush of gratitude, Jill and her mother hugged one another.

"I'm so relieved," her mother said, echoing Jill's thoughts.

"Thank you, Doctor." Jill rose and shook his hand.

He smiled. "You're welcome."

After he left, Jill sat down beside her mother and turned to her with a smile. "Such happy news. I'm glad you're here with me."

"Me, too," responded her mother, giving Jill's hand a squeeze.

When she saw Cristal dozing in the bed assigned to her in the recovery area, tears stung Jill's eyes. She looked so young, so vulnerable, so beautiful.

"Hi, sis," she said softly, leaning over to touch Cristal's hand.

Cristal's eyes fluttered open.

"Everything went well. You're going to be fine."

Cristal smiled and nodded. "I know. Glad you were with me. Where's Mom?"

"I'm right here, honey," said their mother, moving to stand next to Jill. She lifted one of Cristal's hands and kissed her fingers.

"I can't wait to leave," Cristal said. "They said I could go home soon."

"We're staying with you until you're ready to leave," Jill assured her.

"I'll get up in a minute." Cristal closed her eyes.

As they waited for the anesthesia to wear off, Jill sat with her mother, who was abnormally quiet. *Funny how people shape one another with a word or a deed, causing them to live life in unexpected ways.* She glanced at her mother out of the corner of her eye. Valerie Davis was a lovely woman. She didn't need makeup or beautiful clothes to make her appear that way. How awful it must have been for her to be rejected by her first husband's family. It had been traumatic enough to her that she'd chosen to live her whole life worrying about how she looked. Maybe having the Davis nose had been a blessing in disguise.

Later, back at the cottage, the three of them sat out on the porch together. It was a cloudy day filled with the soothing sound of the water and the cries of the birds circling above it, searching for food. A perfect day for reflection.

"I told Jill a secret this morning," her mother said to Cristal. "You need to hear it too."

Listening to her mother talk about her previous marriage, Jill's heart constricted with sympathy all over again. Rejection was such a hurtful thing. In her own way, her mother had rejected a part of each of her children. Jill vowed she would not do that to any child she might have. She thought of Kacy and how spending the summer apart from her mother had done wonders for Kacy. She seemed an entirely different child from the temperamental little girl who'd first arrived at Seashell Cottage.

She tuned back into the conversation her mother and Cristal were having.

"Okay," said Cristal, "Jill and I talked about it. I'm coming to Ellenton for a couple of weeks to see if that's where I eventually want to live and set up my own business. And, Mother, this decision isn't about me and Chance Nelson, but about me doing what I want with my life. I've had time to think over a lot of things. I want to find a man one day, but like Jill, I need to get my life in order before I become serious about anyone."

Hearing her sister say the words, it sounded so right.

With her mother and sister napping, Jill hurried to the camp. She and Melanie were going over payroll procedures. Even though it was a simple operation, government requirements made it seem more complicated than that.

Melanie was on a conference call with a parent when she arrived.

Jill walked out onto the beach to check the activity.

Jed Carter, Emily's father, as the camp counselor in charge of the volleyball game taking place on the beach, waved at her and jogged over. "Hey! I'm glad I saw you. Charlie wanted me to tell you that he hopes next time he's in Florida you two can get together. Niki hopes so, too."

"Thanks, that's sweet," Jill said.

Jed studied her. "Look, it's none of my business, and Niki would kill me for saying anything, but I think you should know that it'll be a long time before Charlie decides whether he's moving to Florida or not. He's a decent guy who wants to please his family, but I don't think he really wants to leave Beantown."

Jill nodded. "I understand. I've got my own life to work out. But thanks for telling me."

"I shouldn't say anything about this either, but Kacy and Emily have taken to dressing up like brides and playing wedding." His gaze penetrated her. "Your wedding to Brody."

Jill felt the blood leave her face. "Oh, no! Can you stop them? Brody is a wonderful guy, but I'm not ready to take that step, and I don't want anyone to get hurt."

"I've spoken to them about it. We'll see. Kacy loves you, Jill."

"And I love her," she responded truthfully. "I hope she understands that no matter what might happen between Brody and me, I'll always love her."

Melanie stepped out onto the beach.

Jed indicated her with a tip of his head. "You'd better go. 'Boss Woman' is calling." Giving Jill a crooked grin, he added, "Guess you're 'Boss Woman' too. Congratulations! I think it's great!"

"Thanks!" Jill trotted toward Melanie, but her mind was full of thoughts of the girls.

A sense of peace pervaded the atmosphere in Seashell Cottage as Jill ate dinner with her mother and sister. It was as if by sharing their feelings about the past, they'd opened new doors to the acceptance of the people they now were.

"Mom and I are going to drive up to New York with a lot of my things next week," said Cristal.

"We'll take our time, perhaps stop in Washington DC to look around," Jill's mother said. "There are quite a few things I've yet to see."

Jill set down her fork as an idea popped into her head. "Mom, how would you like to do some traveling with friends of mine? Melanie, one of the owners of the camp, and Greg Campbell, Brody's uncle, are starting to draw up plans for traveling with a group. They're talking about a trip to Ireland. I'm sure they'd love to include you."

"Seriously?" Color flooded her mother's cheeks. "I've

always wanted to go to Ireland. My single friends either can't afford to travel or don't want to."

"I'll introduce you to both of them, and you can take it from there," said Jill, pleased to be able to do this for her mother.

"Great idea," said Cristal. "Someday I'd like to go back to Europe. There was so much to see."

"By the way, when is Hope coming home? Have you heard from her?" Jill asked. "I can move into the condo September 1st, but I promised I'd stay at Seashell Cottage until Labor Day."

"She finally texted me to say she was sorry. I promised I'd let her know how things went with my health issues," said Cristal. "I'll ask her about your schedule. I still have some of my things at the apartment we shared and will have to make arrangements to get them."

"So, she understands you're not coming back?"

"Yes. I'm off the hook there. She knows of someone who'd be happy to take my place."

Jill's mother clasped her hands. "All these plans. It's so exciting to see everything come together."

Jill acknowledged her words with a smile, but she thought of Brody and Kacy and knew that, for her, nothing was settled.

CHAPTER THIRTY

Early on the following Friday morning, Jill stood in the driveway of the cottage and watched her mother and sister drive off, feeling both a sense of sadness and relief to see them go.

Their visit had been wonderful in many ways, but she needed time alone to continue getting comfortable in her new teaching job and to take on more responsibility at the camp with the upcoming weekend camping program. And always, at the back of her mind, thoughts of Brody lingered. She hadn't seen or talked to him since their conversation on the beach. She had, however, met the nanny he'd hired to pick up Kacy at camp—a beautiful, pleasant young woman from Sweden named Inga Swenson.

Jill gave a last wave to the car disappearing down the road and turned back to the cottage. She'd promised Hope she would stay until Labor Day, and though she'd move many of her things into the condo when September 1st arrived, she was happy to stay at Seashell Cottage alone for the following week.

Jill started a load of laundry and prepared to head out. It was teacher's week at school, and she didn't want to miss out on anything. The fellow teachers she'd met were full of enthusiasm for another year under the leadership of Dennis. "Big D" was an all-around great guy who made routines seem like fun. Jill wasn't the only one enamored of him as an administrator. He was a person she truly liked.

At school, she sat next to Leigh and a fourth-grade teacher who reminded her of Britney Spears. Together, they listened to a talk on how to handle a troubled student. Jill had heard similar discussions like this before, but each time she found it useful. Teaching grew harder every year with more and more rules set in place that took control out of a teacher's hands.

Jill received a list of students assigned to her class and studied it. The ratio of boys to girls was pretty even, and the number of students with English as a second language was low enough to be workable. Still, seeing the names, Jill couldn't help wondering about each child. Teaching kindergarten, she'd mentally "adopted" many of her students, showering them with love in subtle ways. Teaching third grade would be more of a mental challenge with harder course work.

Because it was Friday in the last week before school would begin, they were dismissed early. Jill headed over to Camp Sunnyside, happy for the opportunity to spend some time there.

When she walked out to the pool to check on the swim team, Kacy ran up to her. "Hi, Jill! Can you come sit by me and Emily?"

"Sure," Jill said, pleased.

Kacy took hold of her hand. "Dad says you need to have a space all by yourself, but it can be next to me, right?"

"Of course," Jill said, hiding her amusement. She was pleased Brody had been talking about her. Even though she'd made clear to Brody she needed time to proceed with a relationship, she missed him like crazy.

"How's Inga?" Jill asked, chiding herself for pumping Kacy for information.

"Dad likes her a lot. She's nice to me too."

Jill stumbled and caught her balance. The thought of losing Brody was like a stab to her heart.

"Hi, Jill!" said Kelly. "Glad you're here. The girls are resting between practices for the talent show tonight."

"Can't wait to see them perform," said Jill. She knew from all the planning that had been put into place parents would be encouraged to go from one demonstration to another, allowing them to observe the many opportunities the camp gave each camper to succeed.

Jill stayed with the swim team until lunch time and then went into the office to check on things there.

"Your mother sent me a sweet note," Melanie said, holding up an envelope in her hands. "I was glad to meet her. She wants to travel with our group."

Jill grinned. "It's going to be great for her. She enjoyed both you and Greg and is willing to take a chance on getting to know new people."

"Wonderful. I'm hoping she and I can room together," said Melanie. "Now, let's get to work on the talent show for tonight. Jed is heading a crew to set up chairs around the pool and in other spots. The maps we've been working on need to be finalized and printed. We'll hand them out as we greet people upon arrival."

"I'll take care of the maps now," Jill said, excited about showing off the camp. A special discount was being offered to those who signed children up for the Weekend Program, and a list started for those interested in next summer's camp.

Later, the smell of cookies baking drew Jill into the kitchen. Susannah looked up at her and smiled. "Can't let our guests go hungry," she said, stacking cookies on cooling racks.

"How about me?" Jill said. "Can I have one?"

Susannah chuckled. "Yes, you and every other member of the staff. Does my heart good to see how we've all come together this summer. Jed informed me he'll work a number of weekends when he's not coaching his baseball team."

"That's great. The kids love him." Jill picked up a warm cookie and bit into a taste of chocolate that filled her mouth with a sweet sensation. "Mmm, delish," she managed to say before taking another bite.

"How's it going with that young man of yours?" Susannah asked.

"My young man? Do you mean Brody?"

Susannah nodded. "His nanny is picking up Kacy now. Like you used to do."

Jill wiped crumbs from her mouth with the back of her hand. "What are you trying to tell me?"

Susannah wiped her hands on her apron and stepped away from the table. Looking into her eyes, she spoke softly. "I've observed you all summer, watched as you flourished socially. The glow that used to be around you is gone, replaced by something I'd call fear. You've told me all about your painful marriage, so I understand why you're hesitating. Taking a chance on love is a huge leap of faith. Without the courage to take the risk, where would we be?"

Jill's heart sank. The thought of losing Brody stung. She lowered her eyebrows and stared at Susannah. "What does the future hold for me and Brody?"

Susannah shook her head. "There are no easy answers, Jill. Just be aware of the choices offered to you. That's all I'm saying."

Troubled by the thoughts that were whirling inside her, Jill left the kitchen and told herself she'd think of her relationship with Brody later. For now, she had to get ready for a big night at the camp.

After a quick meal and a shower, Jill returned to the camp dressed in the camp uniform of a bright yellow T-shirt and navy shorts. When she arrived at the festivities, she was pleased to see all the other staff members dressed similarly.

Melanie wore a yellow sundress. Susannah had put on a fresh T-shirt with a pair of jeans, over which she wore an apron with the Camp Sunnyside logo splashed across the front. They were ready.

The onslaught of parents and kids happened all at once. From the moment the cars lined the drop-off lane in front of the house until all were safely inside the camp took less than a half-hour.

With each new arrival, Jill exchanged greetings and handed out a map and instructions for the party. She felt, rather than saw, Brody walking toward her with Kacy and Inga.

"Welcome to Camp Sunnyside," she said automatically, concentrating on the words. She'd forgotten how her pulse raced when she was around him.

"Good evening." Brody's gaze turned to Inga. "You've met Inga. She's helping out at my house."

"Hello, Inga. Glad you could make it."

Inga smiled at Brody. "Me too. I'm here with him," she said, making it seem as if they were on a date.

Flustered by the conversation, Jill turned to welcome a set of parents, helpless to say more to Brody as he and Inga moved forward into the house.

Susannah's words came back to her, like bullets to her brain. *Taking a chance on love is a huge leap of faith. Without taking the risk, where would we be?* Only, in this case, she might be too late.

Jill forced herself to think of other things as she interacted with parents and kids, hoping to sign up as many kids for the fall and next summer programs as possible.

When it was announced it was time for the water ballet show, Jill hurried over to the pool and stood beside Niki. Across the pool from them, Brody was talking to Inga.

"Here they come!" said Niki, indicating the line of eight and nine-year-olds marching to the deck of the pool, led by Kelly.

After they lined up along the edge of the pool, Kelly accepted the microphone Melanie handed her and began to speak. "One of the aims of Camp Sunnyside is to have the campers learn how important it is to become a team member by respecting one another as they work together on a project. I've never been prouder to present this year's 'Mermaids.' Each girl in this group has earned her right to call herself one."

Emily and Kacy gave a little wave to Niki and her. Then they followed the others diving into the pool.

Niki turned to Jill with moist eyes. "Emily looks so grown up I can hardly believe it. Kacy too."

"Yes, they're so darn cute together," Jill commented.

Jill watched as Kelly put the girls through their routines. Seeing how they'd all become friends gave her a warm glow. Girls could be mean, but she and Kelly had worked with them on not allowing that to happen.

After they got out of the water, the team lined up and took a bow together. Then, shrieking gleefully at another round of applause, they scattered to go to their families.

Emily and Kacy ran over to Niki and Jill.

"Did you see me underwater?" Emily asked her mother.

"We did our best," said Kacy to Jill, "just like you taught us."

Brody walked up to them. "Hey, Kacy! Great job!"

"Thanks," she said and turned back to Jill. "Dad said he'd take Emily and me out for ice cream after the show. Want to come?"

Jill glanced at Brody, but he remained quiet. "Maybe next time, Kacy."

"But I want you to come with us, Jill," cried Kacy, grabbing hold of her hand.

"You can join Brody, me, and the girls," said Inga. "We would love to have you. Right, Brody?"

"Sure," said Brody without much enthusiasm.

"I'll come too," said Niki, winking at Jill.

Jill sat in a booth beside Niki, facing Brody and Inga while the girls stood in front of the ice cream coolers talking about which kind they wanted. Scoops was a popular place on a Friday night, and the buzz of conversation around them was cheerful. Still, Jill felt awkward, observing the easy communication between Brody and Inga.

A young man behind the counter called her name with her order.

"Stay there. I'll get it," said Brody. "Niki's is just about ready too."

He rose and came back with small cups of ice cream—butter pecan for Niki and coffee for her.

"Thanks," Jill said, startled by the electricity that passed between them when his hand touched hers. His eyes showed his surprise, but he turned away to pick up ice cream for Inga and himself.

Giggling, Kacy and Emily joined them, each holding a cone that had been dipped in chocolate.

"Eat it quickly or it'll drip over everything," Niki said to them. She turned to Jill. "I don't know why I'm worried about that. I do at least one load of laundry every day."

Jill chuckled. "I don't know how you manage everything."

"One day at a time," Niki said. She smiled at Inga. "Interested in taking on more work while Kacy is at school?"

Inga glanced at Brody.

"Go ahead. You'll have time when school starts."

"Okay. I can give you a few hours each week." Inga's smile

lit her blue eyes.

"Great. We'll set up a schedule and then, Brody, you and I can talk about sharing her."

"Okay," Brody said. "As long as she's at my house when Kacy comes home from school."

"Yes, I'll be there. But I still won't cook." Color filled her cheeks. "Greg and Brody do the cooking. Not me."

Brody glanced at Jill. "Not like you used to do, but we get by."

"I want Jill to come and live with us," said Kacy. "You promised me she would."

Brody shook his head. "No, Kacy. I said I hoped she would, but Jill changed her mind."

Kacy studied her. "Why can't you live with us?"

"Kacy, you know what I told you," said Brody. "Enough said. Understand?"

Kacy's eyes filled. She nodded.

Jill squeezed her hand. "It's going to be all right."

Kacy looked down at her lap where drops of vanilla ice cream were gathering.

"I'd better go," said Niki. "The babysitter needs to get home early."

"Me, too," said Jill, inching along the red-plastic-covered seat of the booth to let Niki out. *Talk about awkward.*

"Thank you again for the ice cream," Jill said to Brody before enveloping Kacy in a hug. "I am very proud of you. You and Emily did a wonderful job with the water ballet show."

Kacy kept her face toward the ground.

Jill rubbed Kacy's back a stroke or two and left the store feeling as if the world she'd wanted to create was lying at her feet like the puddle of ice cream Kacy had spilled on the floor.

CHAPTER THIRTY-ONE

With the arrival of the children at school in mid-August, Jill's life went into overdrive. Leigh McKinnon was a welcome source of information and encouragement. She was a natural with the kids and also spoke fluent Spanish, something Jill vowed to learn as soon as possible.

From school, she drove to the camp each day to help Melanie in the office as they began the process of ending the summer camp and setting up the fall weekend schedule. By the time she returned to Seashell Cottage in the evening, all she wanted to do was crawl into bed and recover from her grueling day.

One evening as she sat on the porch of the cottage, enjoying the cooler air, she got a call from Cristal.

"How's it going in Ellenton? Have you made a decision about living there?" Jill asked her.

"I'm going to do it," Cristal replied with a new confidence Jill admired. "And this has nothing to do with Chance Nelson, although I must say he's about the dreamiest guy I've gone out with in years."

"Dreamiest? God! You sound like you're fifteen again," Jill commented, amused.

Cristal chuckled. "I think I'm returning to those years, living here with Mom and in this town."

"I'm so glad it's working out for you, and I'm sure Mom is happy to have you there."

"Yeah, well I'm moving out as soon as I can. Gotta go. She's calling for me."

Jill chuckled. "Talk to you later." She knew very well how demanding her mother could be, though she'd changed, become softer somehow since they'd all been together at Seashell Cottage. It was surprising that the three of them hadn't made an effort to understand one another better before now. But families were complicated, no matter their size.

As the days flew by and September approached, Jill concentrated on her move to the condo, creating lists of things she'd need to purchase, including such basic items as spices and utensils for the kitchen.

Kay Branson called from Palm Rentals to tell her that the owners of the condo had agreed to let Jill move in a few days early so she could make the move over a weekend. Eager to go ahead with her plans to be on her own, Jill hurried to the office after school to pick up the keys to the condo.

At her condo building, she parked, got out, and taking a deep breath of satisfaction, opened the door to her apartment and stepped inside. A sigh of pleasure escaped her. It was just as she remembered it—open, spacious, and nicely decorated.

She walked into each room to evaluate what she might need and made careful notes. She was willing to buy a lot of staples she could move with her in the future, but wanted to avoid spending money on anything she didn't need. With the cost of buying into the camp, she was determined not to use any more of the money she had set aside for a down payment on her own place.

She was just finishing up her inspection when she received a call. *Niki.*

"Hey, girlfriend, how are you?" Jill said.

"Ready for a break. Are you at the cottage?"

"No, I'm at the condo I'm renting. The owners have allowed

me to move in early. Come see it." Jill gave Niki directions, pleased she would be her first visitor.

Niki arrived with a bottle of white wine, cheese, crackers, and fresh, cold green grapes. "Thought this was cause for a celebration," she announced, smiling as she set her gifts down on the kitchen counter. She gazed around. "Wow! This is great!"

"Let me show you around," Jill said, moving easily through the well-laid-out space.

"It's lovely," Niki said after they returned to the kitchen. "But, Jill, is this what you truly want? You and Brody seemed so happy together. I thought you'd move in with him."

Jill sighed and searched for the right words. "I was falling in love with Brody, but the thought of turning my life over to another man scared me to death. It was moving too fast. Brody and I might have lived in the same house but we hadn't even gone out on a date. I made one mistake. I need to be sure. Especially because it isn't all about Brody and me. It's about Kacy too."

Niki's eyes rounded. "What do you mean turning your life over to another man? Are you serious? Because you marry someone, it doesn't mean you give up being you or losing what you want out of life. True love is sharing and growing together, each becoming better because of the other, not allowing someone to make you less than you could be."

"I know but ..."

Niki shook her head. "That ex-husband of yours was a real bastard. You know Brody well enough to know he'd never treat you that way."

Jill's eyes stung with tears. "It might be too late to do anything about it."

"Hold on!" A wicked gleam came to Niki's eyes. "I shouldn't even admit what I did, but I decided to find out exactly what was going on with Inga. So, I quizzed Kacy." She held up her hand. "I know, I know. Kind of low of me to prod a child like that, but I couldn't help it."

"What did she say?" Jill asked, unable to hold back the question.

"Apparently, Brody and Inga had an argument of some kind. Inga threatened to leave, then decided to stay, though she knows Brody is not going to be her boyfriend."

"You got all that information out of Kacy?" Jill couldn't hide her smile.

"Kacy didn't put it in those words, but that was the essence of what she said." Niki nudged Jill with her shoulder. "So, I say you still have a chance, if you choose it."

"We'll see. I've got a lot going on. In the last few months, I've quit my job, sold my house, make peace with my sister, set boundaries with my over-bearing mother, moved to Florida, got a teaching job at a different grade level, rented a condo, and bought into a day camp. I'm not ready to take on a serious relationship just yet."

Niki's jaw dropped. "Wow! When you put it like that, I totally get it."

"I've taken control of my life. Now, let's open that bottle of wine and sit for a while. How are the T's?" Jill said, relieved Niki understood what she'd been facing.

While Niki launched into a story of the latest escapades with the triplets, Jill got the wine and cheese tray ready, making a mental note to buy a cheese knife.

They sat outside at the high-top table on the patio, enjoying the view. The golf course was quiet except for the occasional sound of a club hitting a ball at the hole to the far right of them.

"So peaceful," said Niki emitting a sigh of contentment. She frowned as her cell rang. She picked it up. "It's Brody. I wonder what he wants?"

Curious, Jill listened to Niki's end of the conversation. "No, I haven't seen her today. Right now, I'm at Jill's condo. Did you ask Jed?" Niki was quiet for a moment. "And what did the people at school say?" Pause. "Okay, Jill and I will start at the school and trace Kacy's route home to look for her in case she got off the bus before her stop. We're on our way."

Niki turned to Jill with a troubled look. "Kacy never came home from school. Inga thought she was playing with Emily, and I'd picked her up. But I knew nothing about such plans, and she didn't come to our house. The school said she left on the bus."

"Oh, my God! What if something bad has happened to her?" Jill's stomach lurched. She gripped the edge of the table when she noticed the time. "It's been a couple of hours. Anything could've happened."

Niki's face turned white. "The thought makes me sick. Brody is beside himself. I promised we'd look for her. C'mon! Let's go!"

They left everything on the table and hurried inside.

"I'll start at the school," Niki said, grabbing her purse and taking off.

"I'll meet you there," said Jill. She locked the door behind her and ran to her car just as Niki pulled out of the parking lot.

Her minding spinning, Jill climbed into her car. Her cell rang. *Brody.*

Jill immediately clicked on the call. "Hi, I heard what happened to Kacy. I'm going to look for her. Any idea of where she might be?"

"None. She's been unhappy at home. Apparently, she

doesn't like Inga. I've been too busy to find a replacement, but when I know Kacy is safe, Inga will be gone. She should've been more careful about Kacy's schedule."

"I'm so sorry. Where are you now?"

"At Niki's house," Brody responded. "I'm going to drive around the neighborhood. Inga is driving around the downtown area. Niki's at the school."

"Okay, I'll meet up with you. But first, I want to check something out. I'll call you as soon as I know anything. Good luck!" Her voice broke. "I love that girl."

"Yeah, I know. Me too." Brody's words shook with emotion.

She knew how close to tears he was as she clicked off the call. Taking a deep breath, she bowed her head, gathering her thoughts. Then she threw her car in gear and took off.

CHAPTER THIRTY-TWO

Jill drove into the driveway of Seashell Cottage, praying she wasn't wrong. Kacy was a strong girl—bright and determined.

Jill parked, cut the engine, and ran to the front porch. Her heart fell when she saw it was empty. As sharp disappointment cut through her, Jill clutched her body in pain. It was the one positive thought she'd had about Kacy's possible whereabouts.

With the key she still had, she unlocked the front door and entered the cottage, calling for Kacy as she checked all the rooms. Outside, she dashed around the perimeter of the cottage and peered into the screened-in swimming pool area, but found no trace of her. Fighting tears, she headed out to the sand to search.

The beach was all but empty. In the distance she saw two boys playing frisbee and a couple of women sunbathing. But no Kacy. She trotted back to the cottage, each step a beat of defeat.

Hating to admit defeat, she called Brody. "Any news?"

"Nothing," said Brody.

"I'm at Seashell Cottage. I thought Kacy might have come here, but there's no trace of her. Any suggestions?"

"Niki is still searching around the school. I'm going back to the neighborhood. The school authorities have talked to the bus driver. She said she thought Kacy got off at her stop with the other kids. I thought I'd talk to the parents of the kids in the neighborhood to see if they know anything."

"I'll come help you. Kacy might have said something to one of them." Jill clicked off the call, her hands so cold the phone slipped through her fingers and fell to the sand. She bent over to pick it up and stopped when she noticed a figure running toward her. She blinked away the tears blurring her vision and took another look.

"Kacy? Oh, my God! Kacy!" Jill ran to meet her. Sweeping the child she'd come to love into her arms, she said, "Baby girl! Are you all right? Everyone's been looking for you! We've all been so worried!"

Kacy stood before her, breathing hard, her hair and T-shirt soaked with sweat. "I ran as fast as I could."

"Oh, my darling," said Jill, kneeling in front of her, brushing Kacy's damp curls away from her face and kissing her sweaty, hot cheek. "You scared us."

"I ran away. I want to live here with you, Jill." Kacy threw her arms around her and lay her head on Jill's pounding chest. "I love you."

Jill's fresh tears of relief mixed with growing concern. She rubbed Kacy's back, never wanting to let her go. "Kacy, I love you too, but living here with me isn't possible. It's complicated. If I could, I'd make it happen."

"But I need you," Kacy said, her big blue eyes glistening with tears. "Dad does too. I just know it."

"We have to call him right now." Jill got up, pulled her cell out of her pocket and punched in his number. "Brody? I've got Kacy. She's here with me at Seashell Cottage. Yes, she's all right. Okay. Here, you can talk to her." She handed the phone to Kacy.

"Hi, Daddy." She looked up at Jill with a stricken expression. "I'm sorry. I didn't mean to scare you. I ran away from home. I want to stay with Jill at Seashell Cottage."

Jill clutched her body as waves of adrenaline left her body, making her legs feel like butter. If anything had happened to Kacy she didn't know how she could bear it.

Kacy handed her the phone. "Dad's on his way."

Jill took the phone, punched in Niki's number, and explained that Kacy had run to Seashell Cottage. "Yes, Yes, thank God, she's safe. Talk to you later." She held out a hand to Kacy. "C'mon, sweetheart, we'd better get you some water and go sit on the porch to cool off. Dad will find us there."

A short while later, Jill heard the roar of Brody's truck and braced herself.

Brody ran toward them. "Kacy! Kacy!"

"Daddy!" responded Kacy, allowing herself to be swept up in her father's arms.

Observing them, fresh tears blurred Jill's vision. At Kacy's disappearance, they'd all thought the worst. Seeing the way Brody was hugging Kacy to him tore at her heart.

Brody set Kacy down and faced Jill. "I don't know how to thank you enough. Each minute Kacy was missing felt like a year taken off my life." His eyes swam with tears. "I don't know what I would've done if anything had happened ..."

Jill enveloped him in a hug. "Sssh! I know. I know. Everything's going to be all right."

They clung to each other, and then turned to Kacy, drawing her to them.

"Are we going to live here together like I want?" Kacy said, staring up at them with a hopeful expression.

Brody looked at Jill and then down at his daughter. "No. But I need to speak to Jill in private. Okay?"

Kacy's lower lip jutted out, but she nodded and headed out to the sand, giving them the privacy that they needed.

Jill waited for Brody to speak, afraid to say anything in her emotional state.

He clasped her face in his strong hands. "You see how

you've affected not only Kacy, but me. We love you, Jill. You made us a family. Is there any way we can start over? I don't want you to walk away again." His earnest expression cut through her fear.

"Yes, let's start over," she said simply, honestly. The thought that she might have lost him was devastating.

Brody drew Jill into his embrace. She nestled against his chest, hearing his heartbeat, realizing now that what they shared was special not only because of what the two of them felt for one another, but because of the love they both shared for a child who loved them.

When they finally pulled apart, Brody smiled at her. "Jill Conroy, let's begin with this. Will you go out with me?"

"Yes!!" Jill said, laughing even as tears of joy blurred her vision.

The next Saturday night, Jill waited at the cottage for Brody to pick her up for their first date. She'd made an appointment to have her hair cut and lightened, then decided to have a fresh mani/pedi, feeling more like a teen on her first big date than the tired schoolteacher she was. After living in the same house with Brody for weeks at the cottage, she was surprised by how nervous she felt about going out on an actual date with him.

She heard the sound of Brody's truck pulling into the driveway and drew a deep breath. Jay had dazzled her when they'd first started dating. She didn't want to get pulled once again into something that wasn't healthy or real.

When Jill saw Brody at the door wearing creased tan slacks and a new golf shirt that showed off his trim figure, she smiled. He'd fussed with his appearance too.

"Hi!" Brody beamed at her as he handed her a bouquet of

bright-colored blossoms. "Kacy told me I was supposed to bring you flowers. She said she and Emily talked to her mother about it and they all decided it was the right thing to do."

Jill chuckled. "They're beautiful. Thank you. I'll put them in water and then I'll be ready to go."

"Thought for this first date, we'd do something casual, maybe go to the Purple Pig. Their food is good and we can even dance on their outside deck, if we want."

Jill's eyebrows shot up. "You dance?"

He shrugged. "Not usually, but Kacy and Emily wanted me to do that too."

"Well, then, that's what we'll do," Jill responded, hiding her amusement at Brody's willingness to make this date what Kacy wanted.

"So where is this social director of yours tonight?" she teased as she carried the flowers into the kitchen. "Staying with Greg?"

Brody shook his head. "Greg and Melanie are away for the weekend. Kacy's staying over at Emily's house." He grinned and winked. "We have all night if we want."

Jill laughed. "This is our first date. Remember?"

"I do." He sobered. "We're not going to rush into anything. I don't think either one of us wants that."

"I agree. One step at a time." She placed the flowers in a vase and turned to him. "This evening will be a wonderful start."

Later, when Jill lay in bed hugging her pillow, she relived the time with Brody. He was fun to be with, easy to talk to, and a wonderful kisser. Even now, there was a part of her that wished she'd thrown caution to the wind and invited him inside. But as attracted as they were to one another, neither wanted to begin their romantic relationship that way.

CHAPTER THIRTY-THREE

The days that followed were times of discovery for Jill. She and Brody moved from dating to quickly being exclusive. She loved being with him.

Two months after seriously dating, talking about everything they could think of, and sharing the ups and downs of moving into new places and new jobs, Jill realized she was ready to take their relationship to the next step. She knew now that Brody was a very different man from her ex.

Their lovemaking was every bit as wonderful as Jill had hoped. Brody was a patient, tender lover who knew how to please her in ways Jill hadn't experienced. He was equally satisfied. Jill often thought of that first time of making love with Brody as the moment her life divided in two—before Brody and after. She knew it might seem silly to others, but she felt as if her life as it was meant to be began that evening. Even weeks later, the memory of the way their two souls had come together remained with her.

"I must say," Niki said one night when she was having wine with Jill at her condo, "You and Brody together could light a dark room with the glow of happiness on your faces."

Jill smiled at her best friend. "He's something special."

"And so are you," said Niki. "I can't believe the changes in Kacy since you and Brody have gotten together. She's a joy to be around."

"She knows how much I love her just the way she is," said Jill. "I understand exactly how important that is to her."

Niki smiled her agreement. "Just so you know, she told me

that Brody is going to marry you."

"I hope so. He's the one I should've married all along."

One Saturday morning on a fine April day, Brody and Kacy picked her up in his truck. To celebrate her spring break from teaching, they'd decided to have a picnic on the beach near Seashell Cottage.

"Dad's going to help me build a sandcastle," said Kacy. "Do you want to help?"

"Sure," said Jill. She'd always thought sandcastles were special. "First, I'll get things ready for our picnic."

After Brody parked his truck, they headed out to the sand. While Brody and Kacy lugged pails and shovels to the water's edge, Jill set out beach towels, a beach umbrella, and organized the cooler of food and drinks. She'd needed a lazy day like this.

Waving to Brody, she signaled that she was going to take a walk along the beach. She'd been busy with school and camp activities and wanted to stretch her legs. As she walked, Jill lifted her face to the sun, delighting in the sweet caress of its warm rays. A soft, cool, onshore breeze fingered her hair playfully. She watched birds scatter at the water's edge with tiny sure steps. The fast pace of their feet along the hard-packed sand left tiny prints behind like happy memories. After living most of her life up north, she loved observing life at the shore.

After a time, she turned to walk back to Brody and Kacy building a sandcastle together. How she loved them!

As if her thoughts had drifted to him in the soft breeze, Brody looked up at her and smiled, his teeth white against his skin darkened by the sun. Behind his handsome exterior was one of the kindest people she'd ever met. It was he who'd helped her through this past summer of surprises, dealing with one after another, and through the following months of learning to be accepted for the person she was.

Kacy came running up to Jill. "Come look at the sandcastle Dad and I built. We've made a special room for you."

"Okay." Jill grinned, recalling the first sandcastle they'd made together. Jill's room had been purposely placed outside the castle.

Kacy raced ahead while Jill crossed the sand to Brody. He stood and waited for her, watching her closely. Jill's pulse raced as his gaze swept over her, almost as if his eyes were doing what his hands ... those marvelous hands ... had done to her body recently.

"Did Kacy tell you about your special room?" Brody asked, beaming at her.

Jill nodded. "This time, I made it inside the castle."

His amused expression changed, became serious, then filled with tenderness. "Jill, I don't want to rush you, but I can't imagine not having you at my side every day and every night. I love you so much."

"I love you too," she said, her heart filling with gratitude for all they'd shared.

"Kacy and I will give you all the time you want to decide, but we need you." His cheeks flushed with emotion. "You complete us."

"We have a question to ask you," prompted Kacy, bumping up against her father.

"Right," said Brody, smiling at Kacy before kneeling on the sand.

"Jill Conroy, will you marry us?"

Jill clutched her hands and gaped at Brody as he drew a small, black velvet box from the pants of his shorts and opened it.

A large solitaire diamond sparkled up at her from a band of smaller diamonds.

"You're supposed to say yes," said Kacy, throwing her arms around Jill's waist.

"Yes, oh yes! I will marry the two of you!" Jill said, laughing and crying at the same time.

Brody got to his feet and the three of them hugged one another, filling Jill with a joy she'd never known, a joy she knew would last forever.

EPILOGUE

"Hurry Kacy! We're going to be late!" Jill cried, juggling her two-year-old daughter, Missy, on her hip. At twelve, going on thirteen, and as a special maid-of-honor for her aunt's wedding, Kacy was determined to look her best. Jill understood, but she wanted nothing to detract from Cristal's special day. It had been an up and down journey for them, but Cristal and Chance Nelson had finally decided they couldn't live without one another.

Jill was thrilled for Cristal. Chance was a very nice guy who adored her sister. They were evenly matched in the success of their businesses. He practiced family law, and she produced beauty and self-confidence in the spa she owned and managed with a little help from their mother. It was surprising, really, how all of their lives had changed in the last four years.

Kacy emerged from her bedroom.

"Oh, you look lovely!" Jill gushed. "The dress is perfect."

"Thanks. Weddings are so exciting. I remember how Emily and I used to play 'brides' when we were younger. The wedding was always for you and Dad."

"Yes, I remember too. But it could never match our real wedding. The three of us and the minister on the beach."

"And Emily and her family, and Susannah," Kacy reminded her, "with both me and Emily as bridesmaids."

"Right," Jill said, though in her mind, it had been just the three of them promising to love and honor one another. Her mother, Melanie, and Greg had been traveling together, and Cristal had just opened her spa and couldn't make the trip, making it the perfect time to have the small, private wedding she'd wanted. Any hurt feelings by those who'd missed the wedding had long since been pushed aside by observing the joy Jill and Brody couldn't contain whenever they were together.

"Where's Matt?" Kacy asked, glancing around.

"With your father," Jill answered.

"Down" cried Missy, struggling to get out of her mother's arms.

Jill chuckled. "No way, little one. You're the flower girl. I can't let you go." She motioned for Kacy to follow her, and they headed outside to the van.

As they approached, Brody looked up at her and smiled. "Are all three ladies ready to leave?

"I think so." Jill hadn't had time to fuss with a fancy hairdo, but she didn't care. Life with twins wasn't easy. She didn't know how Niki did it with triplets. If Niki hadn't taught her a few tricks about handling more than one baby at a time, she didn't know how she would've survived those early months caring for the twins. And now, with them walking and taking off in different directions, it wasn't any easier.

When Brody drove into the driveway of Seashell Cottage. Jill's lips curved. It was such a lovely place, filled with happy memories for her. It was there, at the cottage, that she'd learned to let go of the past and become a woman who learned her value and, more importantly, to have the freedom to be herself.

As if he'd read her mind, Brody turned to her. "I knew from the moment I first saw you here that you were the woman I've always dreamed of. I'm so glad you're my wife." He leaned over and planted his lips on hers, telling her in his own way how much he loved her.

"Oh no! Are you guys going to get all kissy again?" said Kacy from the backseat.

Laughing, Jill pulled away from Brody. "One day you'll understand."

"When I'm a bride?"

"Let's not talk about your being a bride just yet, Kacy," said Brody. "I won't be ready for that for a long, long time."

Jill hid a chuckle. Brody adored all his children, and the idea of Kacy leaving them wasn't anything either Brody or she wanted to think about.

"When it's time," said Kacy, "I want to be married right here at Seashell Cottage."

"Perfect," said Jill and Brody at the same time, in sync as usual.

"Jinx!" cried Kacy. "You two always do this."

Laughing, Jill hoped Kacy would find a love as special as the one she shared with Brody.

"Out! Want out!" cried Matt, from his car seat.

"Out!" echoed Missy before raising a chorus of "Out! Out! Out!"

"Okay, guys! Here we go!"

Ready for another special wedding to take place, Jill climbed out of the car, already feeling the magic of Seashell Cottage.

Thank you for reading *A Summer of Surprises*.. If you enjoyed this book, please help other readers discover it by leaving a review on Amazon, Goodreads, BookBub, or your favorite site. It's such a nice thing to do.

Enjoy an excerpt from my book, *A Road Trip to Remember*,– a Seashell Cottage Book.

CHAPTER ONE

AGGIE

G ran! You can't be serious! I can't do that!"

"Yes, my darling, you can, and you will. I need your help." Agatha "Aggie" Robard put as much pleading into her voice as possible without breaking down and crying. She had a plan for a road trip, and by damn, she was going to do it! At seventy-two and just through recovering from pneumonia, she couldn't make the drive alone, and there was no way she was going to let down the man she'd promised to visit. He was, in some respects, the one who got away. Not that Arnold, God rest his soul, would mind. He'd always known she'd loved Donovan Bailey too.

"Just think about it," Aggie urged. "A road trip to remember."

It would be good for her granddaughter, Blythe, to get out of town, get over her boyfriend, and find a decent young man who'd adore her for being the loveable young woman she was. Two women on an adventure. That's what they'd be. Aggie grinned with anticipation. What could be better on this March morning when the rest of their family was about to leave for a fourteen-day vacation in Hawaii?

Aggie listened to Blythe go on about the need to stay in Ithaca to wrap up her college courses at Cornell before graduation. Aggie knew her beloved granddaughter had used that excuse to escape going home for Spring Break, gotten into an argument with her stepmother, Constance, about it, and was left out of the trip to Hawaii in the process.

"A Spring Break trip to Florida in early April will do you good," Aggie said, dangling this last piece of information in front of Blythe like a piece of her favorite toffee candy.

Blythe let out a breathy, "Oh? *That's* where you want me to take you?"

"Yes. I've rented a place on the Gulf Coast of Florida, the Seashell Cottage, for a week, starting at the end of March. That will give us time to get there, enjoy a week in the sun, and get back home again before anyone suspects a thing."

Suddenly, Blythe began to laugh. Her musical trills filled Aggie's ears and brought a smile to her face. "Gran! You're outrageous!" She paused. "Do you think we can pull off something like this? Constance will be furious if she ever finds out."

The smile disappeared from Aggie's face as if it had been ripped off with tape, leaving stinging skin behind. Constance Robard, her only child's second wife and Blythe's stepmother, was a pain in the behind, always trying to tell her what she could or could not do. Aggie fought to find the right words.

"Constance doesn't need to know everything little thing I'm doing. Just because she manipulated me into selling my house and moving into the New Life Assisted Living Community, it doesn't mean I can't have a life of my own. There's a dance or two in this old lady yet." No one was going to take away the power to live her life her way. Not even if it meant ruffling a few feathers.

"Gran, you're not that old," Blythe protested.

Aggie made her final plea. "So, will you do it?"

"You bet!" said Blythe, a new eagerness in her voice. "Florida sounds fantastic right now. I swear I haven't seen the sun in Ithaca for a week or more. I'll bring some work with me and do it there."

"Good," said Aggie. "Pick me up Tuesday morning at eight o'clock, and I'll take care of the rest. And pack suntan lotion. We'll take the convertible."

"I love you, Gran. Don't worry. I'll come home over the weekend and see you Tuesday morning. This road trip is going to be fun!"

"Don't I know it," Aggie said, feeling as if she was about to be handed a get-out-of-jail-free card.

Still smiling, Aggie clicked off the call. Blythe was a serious young woman in the final semester of her senior year at Cornell. She'd spent years doing what others had dictated and was just beginning to understand that life should be fun too. Aggie hoped if she left Blythe with anything to remember her by, it would be this.

Aggie's one suitcase sat beside the front entrance of the main building of the assisted-living complex she now called home. It wasn't a bad place to be. It had every convenience possible, good food, and lovely surroundings both in and outside the buildings. Best of all, she'd made some good friends here. Two of them, Edith Greenbaum and Rose Ragazzi, had suggested the Seashell Cottage as a place for her getaway. They'd once made that suggestion to Noelle North, the former head of the health program at New Life, and she'd ended up married to some hotel mogul. You never know what could happen. Aggie had sworn these friends to secrecy but felt it was only right for someone to know her true location should anything untoward happen. She owed that to her son, Brad, and daughter-in-law, Constance.

"So, you're going on vacation with your family," commented one of the staff. "How nice for you."

Aggie glanced at Edith and Rose, who'd come to say goodbye, and nodded. She didn't like lying in any form and was relieved she actually was going on a family vacation, even if the only other family member was Blythe.

Her eye caught sight of something. She looked through the glass-paneled front door to see her white Mercedes convertible pull up to the front of the building with Blythe at the wheel. This car represented so much to Aggie. Her purchase of it had sent Constance into a rage, claiming Aggie was losing her mind to buy something like this at her age. It was the beginning of Constance's campaign to get her to move out of her big, old house in Dedham outside of Boston and into New Life.

Aggie had finally given in to Brad's pleas to put his mind at ease about her safety and had made the move. But she'd refused to get rid of the car. She kept the shiny new beauty in a storage facility nearby and gave Blythe the extra key fob to it. After she died, Blythe would have her car for her own use. For now, Aggie needed to know she had "wheels."

"Here's your ride," said Edith, hugging her. "Safe trip! And good luck with Donovan!"

Rose grinned at her and wrapped her arms around Aggie. "We'll be with you in spirit. Remember every little detail so you can tell us all about it."

Aggie held in a laugh. There was nothing Rose liked better than a good, romantic story.

Blythe hurried over to them and grabbed hold of Aggie's suitcase. "Hi, everyone." Green-eyed, black-haired Blythe reminded Aggie of a beautiful young woman who was just coming into her own. Long-legged, thin, and with a wild taste in clothes that drove her stepmother crazy, Blythe was the perfect person to take this trip with her. By the time they got back, Aggie hoped Blythe would have a better appreciation of herself.

After chatting politely, Blythe took hold of Aggie's arm. "C'mon, Gran. Time to hit the road."

Aggie marched to the car alongside Blythe, feeling like she was sprouting wings with each step, loving this new sense of freedom. After she buckled herself into the passenger seat, she turned to the small crowd gathered at the doorway and waved.

"Okay, pedal to the metal, girl," Aggie said, sitting back in her seat, eager to begin the journey ahead.

About the Author

Judith Keim enjoyed her childhood and young-adult years in Elmira, New York, and now makes her home in Boise, Idaho, with her husband and their two dachshunds, Winston and Wally, and other members of her family.

While growing up, she was drawn to the idea of writing stories from a young age. Books were always present, being read, ready to go back to the library, or about to be discovered. All in her family shared information from the books in general conversation, giving them a wealth of knowledge and vivid imaginations.

A hybrid author who both has a publisher and self-publishes, Ms. Keim writes heart-warming novels about women who face unexpected challenges, meet them with strength, and find love and happiness along the way. Her best-selling books are based, in part, on many of the places she's lived or visited and on the interesting people she's met, creating believable characters and realistic settings her many loyal readers love. Ms. Keim loves to hear from her readers and appreciates their enthusiasm for her stories.

"I hope you've enjoyed this book. If you have, please help other readers discover it by leaving a review on Amazon, Goodreads, or the site of your choice. And please check out my other books:

The Hartwell Women Series
The Beach House Hotel Series
The Fat Fridays Group
The Salty Key Inn Series
Seashell Cottage Books
Chandler Hill Inn Series
Desert Sage Inn Series

ALL THE BOOKS ARE NOW AVAILABLE IN AUDIO on Audible and iTunes! So fun to have these characters come alive!"

Ms. Keim can be reached at **www.judithkeim.com**

And to like her author page on Facebook and keep up with the news, go to: **https://bit.ly/3acs5Qc**

To receive notices about new books, follow her on Book Bub - **http://bit.ly/2pZBDXq**

And here's a link to where you can sign up for her periodic newsletter! http**://bit.ly/2OQsb7s**

She is also on Twitter @judithkeim, LinkedIn, and Goodreads. Come say hello!

Acknowledgements

As always, I am eternally grateful to my team of editors, Peter Keim and Lynn Mapp, my book cover designer, Lou Harper, and my narrator for Audible and iTunes, Angela Dawe. They are the people who take what I've written and help turn it into the book I proudly present to you, my readers! I also wish to thank my coffee group of writers who listen and encourage me to keep on going. Thank you, Peggy, Lynn, Cate, Nikki Jean, and Megan. Love you!

Made in the USA
Middletown, DE
08 September 2023